D1247692

A DEATH LEFT HAN

A DEATH LEFT HANGING

A Chief Inspector Woodend Mystery

Sally Spencer

This first world edition published in Great Britain 2003 by
SEVERN HOUSE PUBLISHERS LTD of
9–15 High Street, Sutton, Surrey SM1 1DF.
This first world edition published in the USA 2003 by
SEVERN HOUSE PUBLISHERS INC of
595 Madison Avenue, New York, N.Y. 10022.

British Library Cataloguing in Publication Data

Spencer, Sally, 1949-
   A death left hanging
  1.   Judicial error - England - Fiction
  2.   Woodend, Chief Inspector Charlie (Fictitious character) - Fiction
  2.   Police - England - Fiction
  3.   Detective and mystery stories
  I.   Title
  823.9'14 [F]

ISBN 0-7278-5930-7

Typeset by Palimpsest Book Production Ltd.,
Polmont, Stirlingshire, Scotland.
Printed and bound in Great Britain by
MPG Books Ltd., Bodmin, Cornwall.

For Sharon Payne

Prologue – June 1934

T he woman in the condemned cell was unaware of any of the technical intricacies involved in her imminent execution. She had, however, been assured by the prison authorities that her death – when it came – would be quick and painless. And she believed those assurances, because she had learned to trust the governor and his wardresses, and had come to accept that they genuinely wished to make things as easy for her as they possibly could.

Even though the mechanics of the actual execution itself were kept from her, there were other matters on which she had already been briefed.

'Because it's better for you that you know the procedures in advance, Margaret, my dear,' the governor said in a kindly tone. 'That way, we can be sure they won't come as a shock to you.'

'What kind of procedures are we talking about?' she wondered aloud.

Well, for a start, the governor said, she would be wearing a white hood when she died.

Why *white*? she asked. Why not black – the symbol of death?

Even as she put the question, she knew it was a trifling and irrelevant thing to ask. And yet she somehow derived comfort from the fact that it *was* so mundane – that it avoided, or at least postponed, grappling with the bigger issues.

Why was the hood white? the governor had repeated, as

if he was as grateful as she herself to turn this macabre conversation into some kind of game or puzzle. Well, to be honest with her, nobody really knew the answer to that. It was simply tradition – for centuries the hood had been white, and no one had ever come up with a good reason for changing it.

She pictured the hood as rather like a flour sack, and found that a new and terrible thought had come into her mind.

'Will I have to wear it for long?' she had asked in a sudden panic, as she pictured spending her last few minutes – perhaps even her last few *hours* – in total darkness. 'Will they put the hood on while I'm still in this cell. I don't think I could bear that. I . . . don't . . . think . . . I could bear it!'

'I know that, Margaret,' the governor said soothingly. 'I know just how you feel.'

'How *can* you know?' she demanded, her fear being replaced by a sudden anger. 'Are *you* going to be hanged, Governor?'

'No, of course I'm not. But . . .'

'Because if you're not – if you can't already feel that rope around your neck – then you can't *possibly* read my mind.'

The governor smiled sadly. 'You see this situation as something unique to yourself, Margaret,' he said softly. 'That's perfectly understandable, but it simply isn't the case. Others have trodden the same path you are soon to tread, and they have felt the same concerns as trouble you now. We have watched them, and we have learned from them. We understand your fears, and we sympathize with them. You do not wish to go to your death blinded, and nor will you. The hood will not be put over your head until you reach the chamber.'

'And where is the chamber? Is it far from here?'

The governor shook his head. 'No, not far,' he said vaguely. 'Not far at all.'

*   *   *

2

It was an hour since she had last seen the governor. She was lying down on her bed. Her eyes were closed and her body was still, but her mind was roving far and wide. She was thinking, at that moment, of the parsonage in which she had been brought up. It had been a big, rambling place. The rooms inside it had been large, yet filled as they were with the heavy ugly furniture that previous generations of departed vicars had left behind them, they somehow managed to appear cluttered. Her room in this prison was a complete contrast, containing only a table, a bed and a wardrobe, all of them made of a lighter – more cheerful – wood than the sombre mahogany she had grown up surrounded by.

Next to her cell was her bathroom, and beyond that a third room in which she could see her visitors. See – but not touch. Because though her ex-sister-in-law, whom she loved dearly, had been only inches away from her, the glass partition between them had been as effective as any high stone wall in keeping them apart.

'Don't you worry about Jane,' Helen Hartley had told her. 'If the worst comes to the worst, I'll bring her up as if she was my own.'

'I know you will,' Margaret said gratefully.

'But it doesn't have to come to the worst, you know. I've been talking to a lawyer. A good one. He says your barrister made a real hash of your defence. He says there are strong grounds for a mis-trial.'

'We've been over this so many times before,' Margaret said wearily.

'I know. But this is your last chance. If you'll only—'

'Put your palm against the glass!' Margaret said, so fiercely that there was no doubt it was an order.

'Margaret—'

'Put it against the glass!'

Helen had done as she'd been told, and Margaret raised her own hand to cover it.

3

'We must leave things as they are!' Margaret urged. 'If you say so much as a word I don't want you to, I'll never forgive you. I'll save my dying breath to curse you with. *Do you understand?!*'

'Yes,' Helen had replied, defeated. 'Yes, I understand.'

There were two female wardresses permanently in her cell, and though they were willing enough to talk when that was what she wished, they seemed equally content to remain silent when she wanted to let her mind roam as it was doing now.

She was thinking about her two marriages, the first one to Robert and the second one to Fred. If only Robert hadn't died and she hadn't met Fred, then she might have lived another thirty years. But it had not been meant to be. Instead, Fate had decided that she should meet her death.

No, not Fate! she told herself angrily. Not Fate at all. Her destiny had been in her own hands – was still in her own hands if only she chose to . . .

She was straying towards dangerous ground, she realized. Better not to let that happen. Better, as with the white hood, to concentrate on the mundane.

She did not open her eyes again, but instead strived to visualize her cell. The wardrobe – on the mundane level she was seeking – bothered her. It was so large. Why did she need such a big wardrobe, when the only thing hanging in it was the dress she would wear when they led her down that final walk to oblivion?

Her thoughts were becoming fuzzy, and she realized that she must be falling asleep. She wondered briefly how many more nights' sleep she would have before the end came. And then the drowsiness overtook her and she was thinking of nothing at all.

The condemned prisoner was never informed of the date of execution until the actual day arrived. But those out in the wider world suffered from no such limitations, and as dawn broke the following morning, a small crowd had already begun to gather outside Strangeways Prison.

Those who had chosen to come had done so for a mixture of motives. One group was made up of well-meaning Christians and humanists. They burned candles and held up placards, which announced, 'Capital Punishment is a Sin', and 'Only God can take a life'.

A second group, keeping themselves well apart from the first, took exactly the opposite view. They knew their Bible. They recognized a godly command when they heard one. And they were there to witness that an eye was paid for an eye and a tooth for a tooth.

It was the third group gathered in front of the prison that was the largest, the most amorphous and – probably – the least able to explain its reasons for being there.

They're like iron filings close to a magnet, thought the big young man who was standing at the edge of the crowd. 'They can feel the pull, but they've no idea what's causin' it.'

They certainly didn't expect to see anything, he mused. Executions had ceased to be public nearly seventy years earlier, and the brick walls they were gazing up at would look exactly the same at one minute past eight as they had at one minute to. Yet perhaps it was enough for them to know that the lever would be pulled as the clock struck the hour – and that in this confused and disorganized world there was at least one life which was being ending according to plan.

For a tackler's son from Whitebridge, you're doin' a lot of philosophizin', Charlie, the big young man told himself.

Though her wardresses normally let her sleep as long as she wished, that was not the case this morning, and in her first conscious moment she became aware that she was being gently shaken.

So this was to be the day! she thought.

'What time is it?' she asked aloud.

'Don't go worrying about that,' said the senior wardress,

a plump woman with a tight blonde perm. 'There's no rush yet.' She helped Margaret out of bed, though the prisoner needed no such assistance. 'Would you like to have a bit of a wash?'

'Yes, I think I would,' Margaret replied.

The other wardress – a tall, angular woman – opened the wardrobe and took out the dress. 'And would you like to put this on while you're in the bathroom?' she asked, as if it were no more than a suggestion.

Margaret nodded. This particular dress had not been her first choice to die in. The one she had originally selected had been newer and shorter, but the plump wardress had told her that she should think again.

'I thought I could wear what I liked,' she'd protested.

'You can, but . . .'

'But what?'

The wardress had hesitated before speaking again. 'It's just that if you wear that dress, they'll have to use an extra strap. Around your lower thighs. You don't want that, do you?'

It had taken Margaret a second to realize what the wardress meant, and when she did understand, she laughed out loud.

'They'll have to use an extra strap because they'll be worried that my skirt will blow up above my waist when the trapdoor opens!' she said.

'That's right,' the wardress agreed neutrally.

'Do they really think that what I'll be most worried about at that moment is showing them my knickers?' Margaret asked, her laugh now slightly tinged with hysteria.

'They want you to die with dignity,' the wardress had explained.

And seeing the sense in that, she had chosen the long dress she was now holding in her hands.

'What would you like for your breakfast?' the plump wardress asked.

'What do they normally have?' Margaret wondered.

'You shouldn't go thinking about things like that,' the wardress admonished her. 'You can have anything you like, you know. A fry-up, a steak – whatever happens to take your fancy.'

What! And throw it up on the way to the gallows! Now that *would* be a loss of dignity.

'I'll just have a cup of tea,' Margaret said.

'You're sure?'

'And perhaps a round of dry toast.'

The wardress nodded. 'Don't worry, love,' she said. 'You won't let yourself down.'

It was nearly five to eight. A slight drizzle had begun to fall, but it had done nothing to dampen down the tension within the crowd outside the prison. Far from it – the excitement was growing perceptibly with every second that passed.

Charlie Woodend, still at the edge of the group, felt like a complete outsider – almost a voyeur on other people's voyeurism. He had never planned to be there – would never even have *considered* being there, if his dad's boss hadn't asked him to do it as a favour.

'But I don't see the point, Mr Earnshaw,' he'd protested.

'Neither do I, exactly,' the mill manager had confessed, looking both sad and distressed. 'I just want to know what it feels like. I want to know if you get any sense of what it's like to be inside.'

'Then why don't you go yourself?' Woodend had asked.

'I can't,' the manager had said, in the irritated offhand tone of a man not used to being questioned by people who lived in terraced houses on the wrong side of the canal.

'I can trust you, Charlie,' he'd continued, much less brusquely, much more persuasively. 'You're not like most of the young lads in this town.'

'Aren't I?'

'No, you're not. They're good people round here, Charlie.

7

The salt of the earth. But they're *down* to earth as well. If they can't see it or touch it, it doesn't exist. You're more sensitive. More subtle. I saw that right from the start – even back in the days when you were a nipper in short trousers, following your dad around the mill during the school holidays. That's why, if I can't be there myself, having you there is the next best thing.'

Earnshaw had still not explained why he *couldn't* be there, Charlie Woodend had thought, but you didn't argue with bosses – even if they were your dad's and not your own – which was why he had risen early that morning, caught the first train out of Whitebridge, and now found himself standing in front of the stark, imposing prison walls.

'I don't think they should ever hang women,' said one of the two men just in front of him. 'It's not right.'

'Not right?' his friend repeated. 'After what she's done? She didn't just *kill* her husband, you know. She kept at him with that hammer long after he was dead. They say she crushed his skull to a pulp. They say it looked like she'd spilt detergent all over the floor by the time she'd finished.'

'Maybe she'd been mistreated herself,' the first man suggested.

'An' that makes it acceptable, does it?'

'No, not acceptable, exactly. But two wrongs don't make a right, an' anyway, nobody's got any business hangin' a woman.'

Hadn't they? The question echoed around young Charlie Woodend's head. He'd been wondering for some time whether or not he should apply to the police force, and the question of capital punishment had been one of his biggest stumbling blocks.

The plain truth was that he was still unsure whether it was *ever* right for the state to take a life. And until he *was* certain, how could he even contemplate putting himself in a position in which he might find himself investigating a murder? Because it simply wouldn't be possible to make a proper job of an investigation when he disapproved of the inevitable end it was leading to.

Woodend laughed, more in self-mockery than amusement.

It's a long step from joinin' the police to bein' involved in murder investigations, Charlie, he told himself. Chances are that even if you do become a bobby, the closest you'll ever get to huntin' down killers is chasin' chicken thieves.

He looked up at the clock again. Three minutes to eight. It would soon all be over.

The three women in the cell had now been joined by two men. One of the men carried a book with a black leather cover, the other had a black leather bag in his hand.

'Shall we pray together?' the prison chaplain asked. 'Or perhaps you would prefer me to read you something from the Bible.'

Margaret smiled at him. 'You're very kind but . . .'

'It's the least I can do.'

'. . . but God deserted me long ago.'

'You should never think that, my child,' the chaplain said. 'He will never desert you.'

'Then perhaps I've deserted him,' Margaret replied. 'In either case, your prayers won't be necessary.'

The doctor placed his leather bag on the table and unzipped it. He reached inside it and produced a bottle of brandy and a glass.

'Would you like a drink?' he asked. 'You're entitled to one, you know. Under the rules.'

Margaret shook her head. Whatever else they might say about her – and they would say many things – they would never be able to claim that she went to her death with the stink of alcohol on her breath.

'What time is it?' she asked.

'There's plenty of time yet,' the plump warden said.

They kept offering her things she didn't want, Margaret thought angrily.

A prayer.

A glass of brandy.

But when she *did* want something – wanted to know the bloody time, the simple bloody time – they denied her.

'It is not too late to change your mind about praying,' the chaplain said.

'It's been too late for a long while,' Margaret told him.

The cell door opened, and the room was suddenly full of people.

So it's eight o'clock, Margaret thought. It's finally eight o'clock.

She recognized the governor, but the other three new arrivals were strangers to her. One of these strangers took her arms and placed them behind her back. Though she had not willed it, she found that her fingers were interlocking. And then she felt the leather strap binding her wrists together.

The two wardresses had crossed the room and were moving the wardrobe. She wondered why they were doing that, then saw that it was in order to reveal a doorway she had never even suspected existed.

If I'd known about that, I could have escaped, she thought, almost whimsically.

She could not have been more wrong, she soon discovered, for when the wardresses each took an arm and led her through the doorway she saw that it did not lead to freedom at all, but a second empty cell. And beyond that was a third room – the execution chamber, which the governor had promised her was not far away.

The gallows were not what she had been expecting. They looked more like a very thick set of goalposts than an instrument of death, and had it not been for the chain and rope hanging from the crossbeam, she might have thought that she still had further to go.

There was a trapdoor just below the noose, and as her

wardresses were manoeuvring her on to it, she noticed that a 'T' had been marked out in chalk.

So that my feet are in the right place, she thought, marvelling at how calm she appeared to be.

The man who had bound her wrists together now placed the white hood over her head, while a second man bent down and tied a leather strap around her ankles. Then she felt the noose being slipped over the hood and something pressing – not too severely – against the angle of her jaw.

It had all been so quick, she thought. There had been no time for fear, no time for doubts – no time to change her mind ~~her mind~~ and tell all these people what had really happened to her husband.

She was right about the speed of events. From the moment the executioner had entered the room until the point at which he removed the safety pin from the base of the operating lever and the trapdoors flew open, a mere *seventeen seconds* had passed.

The prison doctor and the governor walked slowly down the stairs to the cell below the execution chamber. The doctor didn't make a move to examine the hanging woman. There would have been no point. It was his job to confirm that she was dead, and he knew that for several minutes yet her heart would still be beating weakly.

The doctor took out his packet of Players' Navy Cut and offered it to the governor.

'How many executions is this we've attended together?' he asked, as he held a match under the other man's cigarette.

'Do you *really* need to ask me that?' the governor replied, inhaling deeply.

'No,' the doctor admitted. 'No, I don't. This is our fourth. Do you think you'll ever get used to it?'

'Not a chance,' the governor said. 'Will you?'

'Probably not,' the doctor conceded.

They smoked their Players in silence, and then the doctor placed his stethoscope against the woman's chest and pronounced her dead. They left the room, locking it behind them. It would stay locked for an hour, then the executioner would return, remove the body and prepare it for the autopsy and inquest that were required by law following a hanging. He would also, at some point, measure the amount by which the neck had been stretched.

Sometimes that elongation could be more than two inches.

At nine fifteen a senior warder appeared at the gate of the prison and pinned to it a notice that announced that Margaret Dodds, in accordance with the law, had been executed at eight o'clock precisely. The waiting crowd pushed and strained to see the notice for themselves, though they must already have known exactly what it would say.

Charlie Woodend did not join in the tussle. As far as he was concerned, he had done his duty by Mr Earnshaw, and was already walking back towards the railway station.

He had reached an important conclusion while he had been standing there in the rain outside Strangeways. If hanging was to continue, he had decided – and there was no indication that it wouldn't – then it was vital that those in charge of murder investigations should catch the right man or woman. For while it might be morally wrong to hang a guilty person, it would be nothing short of a human tragedy to hang an innocent one.

Yes, what the English police forces needed, he thought, was to recruit men who were decent and honest, hardworking and imaginative. And, catching a glimpse of his own reflection in a shop window, he was fairly confident that he was looking at one such man.

One

As she walked briskly along the platform towards the waiting train, Jane Hartley was well aware that several pairs of men's eyes were following her movements, and that most of those eyes were fixed on the swaying of her rump. She knew that most women of forty would have welcomed such attention – that, indeed, the knowledge would have resulted in an extra spring in their step – but as her colleagues and associates had long since learned, she was *not* most women. True, she had long since ceased whirling round and confronting her watchers – long since stopped taking pleasure in reducing them, through her carefully chosen words, to embarrassed, bumbling wrecks – but that had been due more to expedience than to inclination.

It was nearly twenty years since she had been to the North, and had it not been for this one compelling reason, she would not have been there now. She was eager for the train to take her away from Manchester – far too many unhappy memories still lurked there – yet at the same time she dreaded it delivering her to Whitebridge. But there was no help for it – not if she were to achieve the goal she had set herself. And she *always* achieved her goals.

She drew level with the first-class carriages and slowed down so that she could examine each one in turn. Ideally she hoped to find an empty carriage, but, failing that, she would settle for one occupied exclusively by women. If that proved not to be available, she would seek out a carriage containing both men and women. Her final fallback position would be to share a carriage with several men. If the only choices before her were either to sit opposite a lone man or stand in the corridor, then she would prefer the corridor.

She was in luck and found a carriage that was completely – perfectly – empty. With eight seats all to herself, she could spread out her papers and get some work done on the hour-long journey.

Once she had made herself comfortable in the carriage, she opened the expensive leather briefcase – a gift from the members of her chambers to mark her last, spectacular, victory in the Old Bailey. She ran her slim fingers over the brief that her clerk had handed to her just as she was leaving the office. It was an important case – a case which would benefit both her bank balance and her already considerable reputation – and she'd been hoping the instructing solicitor would pass it her way. Yet now she actually had it in her hands, she found she could not summon up her customary enthusiasm.

She reached into the briefcase again and took out the copy of the *Manchester Guardian* that she had bought from the newsagent's on the station.

Much of the paper was devoted to the Profumo Affair, which was only to be expected, given that it was the biggest scandal to hit the English political establishment since the war. She had met John Profumo socially on several occasions and had been quite impressed with him at the time. Now, however, as more of the scandal leaked out every day, she was beginning to see what a bloody fool the ex-minister really was.

He'd had everything a man could want – wealth, a beautiful wife, the important position of Secretary of War in the government. There had even been talk of him being the next Prime Minister. And he had destroyed it all by embarking on a torrid relationship with Christine Keeler, a young woman who even the most charitable of newspapers had called 'a showgirl'.

Had he bothered to check who else she was sleeping with, he would have discovered that another of her 'friends' was the Russian Naval Attaché. But he'd taken *no* such precautions. Instead, like most men, he had kept his brain firmly in his underwear.

Even so, he might have survived the scandal if he had not lied to the House of Commons – had not told all the members of parliament gathered there that he did not even know Miss Keeler. Yet the lie had been told, and there was no going back on it. And now the government, which had been in power for twelve long years, looked to be in imminent danger of collapse.

Jane Hartley quickly and impatiently scanned the paper. She had very little interest in the doings of John Profumo, but there was one name, connected only peripherally with the minister, that she *was* hoping to see.

There it was – not in the lead story but in one of the articles related to it! Jane Hartley lit a cigarette, and began to read.

MINISTER CALLS FOR 'BUSINESS AS USUAL'

The wheels of government could not be expected to grind to a halt simply because of press interest in the Profumo case, Eric Sharpe, Home Office Minister in the House of Lords said last night.

Lord Sharpe, 63, who was first elected to parliament as MP for Whitebridge in 1935, went on to attack what he called 'the less responsible elements of the press' and added that any journalist hoping to uncover further scandals was 'doing no more than whistling in the wind'.

Our Parliamentary Correspondent writes: 'It is clear from the statement that Lord Sharpe was speaking on behalf of a government walking a tightrope and only too well aware that one more unfortunate disclosure could cause it to lose its balance completely.'

15

The picture that accompanied the article had the same grainy quality as most newspaper photographs, but it was still clear enough to give a fairly accurate impression of Sharpe. The noble lord was staring directly into the camera, as if to demonstrate that whatever others might wish to hide, *he* certainly had nothing to fear. He wore his years well, and his white hair (which he had allowed to grow unfashionably long) gave him the air of a patrician.

'You fake!' Jane Hartley said. 'You complete bloody fake!'

She drew heavily on her cigarette, and then, with almost surgical precision, placed the glowing tip of it against the photograph. The cigarette end all but obscured Sharpe's face from her, but she still had the satisfaction of seeing the edge of the paper around it turn brown and then begin to glow red.

She pressed harder, and the slim cigarette buckled. She could feel the heat beginning to scorch her fingertips, and could smell the acrid smoke as it snaked unpleasantly up her nostrils. She knew she should stop what she was doing, but she didn't want to.

She didn't want to!

There was the sound of the carriage door being opened, and then the paper was snatched violently out of her hands.

She looked up. The man who had grabbed the newspaper from her was wearing a ticket collector's uniform. He flung the paper to the floor and stamped on it several times.

'What the hell do you think you were doing?' he demanded.

'I'm . . . I'm not sure,' she said. 'I think I must have fallen asleep.'

'You didn't look *to me* as if you'd fallen asleep,' the ticket collector said aggressively. 'You looked *to me* as if you were deliberately setting fire to that newspaper.'

'Now why should I have wanted to do that?' Jane Hartley

asked, regaining just enough control of herself to slip into her courtroom manner. 'Do I look like a pyromaniac?'

'A what?'

'Would you mind opening the window a little?' she asked, the tone of her voice making clear that it was not a request.

'I . . .'

'The window!'

Almost as if he were surprised to find himself doing it, the guard stepped past her and opened the window.

'That's far enough!' she said, when he'd slid it about halfway down. 'And now I expect you would like to see my ticket.'

'I still want to know—'

'Here it is,' she said, holding the ticket out.

The collector took the ticket off her, but barely gave it a glance. 'I mean, from what I saw out in the corridor—'

'Is it in order?' she asked firmly.

'What?'

'My ticket! Is it in order?'

Reluctantly, the collector looked down at it again. 'Yes, it seems all right,' he admitted.

Jane Hartley held out her hand. 'In that case, you can give it back to me, can't you?'

The collector handed her ticket. 'By rights, you know, I should make a repor—' he began.

'Thank you. You may go now,' Jane Hartley interrupted him.

'Look, missus . . .' the ticket collector blustered.

'Miss!' she corrected him. '*Miss* Jane Hartley, *Queen's Counsel.*'

The words gave him pause for thought. 'You're a lawyer, are you?' he said.

She smiled suddenly – a courtroom trick she knew would throw him further off balance. 'Yes, I'm a lawyer,' she said. 'Quite a famous one, as a matter of fact. But I like to keep quiet about that when I'm travelling.' She paused for the two beats necessary for her words to have their required effect. 'Now, if you wouldn't mind, I would appreciate a little privacy.'

'Uh . . . of course,' the ticket collector said, leaving the carriage in the same dazed way that she had observed so many witnesses step down from the witness box.

The smile stayed on her lips until she was sure he had gone, then quickly slipped away. It was a good thing that he had come in when he did, she thought, because she had almost certainly lost control. And she must not do that. If she were to succeed in her mission, she must learn to keep the same tight grip on herself in Whitebridge as she always achieved in the courtroom.

She bent down, picked up the newspaper, and smoothed it out. The photograph of Eric Sharpe was now framed by the imprint of the ticket collector's boot, but the only real damage had been done by her cigarette. She gazed down in satisfaction at the burn mark, which had once been his head. By the time she had finished with Lord Eric Sharpe, she promised herself, he would feel worse than he looked.

They had left Manchester far behind, and she turned towards the window in order to watch the once-familiar countryside sweep past. The first time she had gone after Sharpe, it had been with all the haste and inexperience of a young barrister whose mind was already fully occupied with her work and her forthcoming marriage. This time, she had planned it all out carefully in advance – marshalling all her evidence, working out all the possible directions that her enemy's counterattack might come from. This time, she would *not* fail.

The moorland had disappeared, and she was once more gazing at the backs of terraced houses. The train was starting to slow, and she knew that it must already be approaching Whitebridge Station. Despite her previous resolve, she felt a sudden urge to sink down into her seat and not to move so much as an inch until the train had pulled out of Whitebridge again and was heading for Preston.

And why not? she asked herself. Why put yourself through all that suffering again? It can't change anything, you know. The past is dead and buried.

But she knew that was not true – knew that the past that she held in her head was as real and vivid as it had ever been. Even if that were not so – even if she could find a way to numb the pain that had been eating away at her for nearly thirty years – there were other factors to be taken into consideration.

Debts had to be paid, whatever it cost her. She owed a debt to the even-handed justice that she had sworn to uphold when she had been admitted to the bar. And she owed a debt to her mother – a debt that, however successful she was, she could only *begin* to repay.

The train juddered to a halt. Through the window she could see the chipped enamel sign which announced that she had arrived at Whitebridge. Other passengers had already started to disembark and we're signalling for porters. The guard, walking up and down the platform, would soon be waving his flag and blowing his whistle. She had only to sit there for a little while longer and the matter would be taken out of her hands.

She climbed to her feet and reached shakily for the door handle.

Two

The room he was sitting in reminded Charlie Woodend of the one in *Great Expectations* where Pip first meets Miss Haversham. It wasn't an analogy that would have occurred to most people, he supposed. For a start, there was no crumbling three-tiered cake and no decayed wedding breakfast laid out for guests who had never arrived. Nor was there any evidence of a mad old bat parading around in a tattered lace dress. In fact, with its conference table and desk lamps, the place did not look the least Dickensian. But it *felt* it – at least to Woodend.

He glanced quickly around the table at the other five members of the committee he had been unwillingly co-opted on to. Like Miss Haversham, they had all refused to accept that time had moved on. Like her, they blamed their present misery on the past misdemeanours of others. He heard them complaining constantly during the committee's numerous tea breaks:

'If Shithouse Radcliffe hadn't blocked my promotion that time, I could have been Chief Constable by now . . .'

'If I'd have got the credit for the Simpson Murder Case that I really deserved . . .'

No modern bobby was as tough as they'd been. There wasn't an inspector in Mid Lancashire who showed half the initiative they'd displayed when they'd held that rank. If they were only twenty years younger, they'd show the lot of them.

'Any comment to make on that, Charlie?' asked the chief superintendent who was serving as chairman of the committee.

'I think the rest of you have already summed it up nicely, sir,' Woodend replied, wondering – but only briefly – what the topic under discussion that morning actually was.

Didn't they realize that nobody would ever read this report they were putting together? he asked himself. And even if they *did* realize, did they actually *care*? Probably not. It was a cushy life, sitting on your arse all day and swilling back tea. And it was a hell of a sight easier to criticize other *working* bobbies than to get off that arse and do some of the work yourself.

How on earth had he landed up in this asylum for the terminally incompetent? the Chief Inspector wondered.

But he already knew the answer to that. He was there because – during the course of an investigation the previous winter – he'd uncovered evidence of corruption on the part of several town councillors, more than one successful local businessman and – most importantly – a very senior police officer.

He was there because he had neither accepted the bribe that had been offered him, nor given the guilty parties time to cover their tracks. Instead, he had brought the whole rotten structure of deceit and dishonesty crashing down around their heads.

And though his bosses had agreed that what he had done had *needed* to be done, they still didn't like the fact that he had *done* it. He was there, in other words, because they didn't want him upsetting any more apple carts.

'It's twenty-five to twelve,' the chairman said, glancing at his watch. 'Doesn't seem much point in starting any new business before lunch. If it's all right with the rest of you chaps, I suggest we break now and resume again at, say, half-past two.'

The other men around the table nodded. Of course it was all right with them, Woodend thought. Why wouldn't it be all right with them? They'd all forgotten what it was like to be a real policeman.

But he bloody hadn't!

*   *   *

21

As she sat looking at Chief Constable Henry Marlowe across his impressive teak desk, Jane Hartley found herself unable to decide whether he was sneakier than he was slimy – or slimier than he was sneaky. Whichever he turned out to be, she would be glad when the interview was over.

'I don't often get the chance to see ordinary members of the general public, Miss Hartley,' Marlowe said condescendingly.

'I'm sure you virtually *never* get to see them,' Jane Hartley replied. 'But then I'm *not* an ordinary member of the general public, am I? Because if I was, I wouldn't be sitting here now.'

Marlowe shifted uncomfortably in his padded seat. 'I'm not sure I see your point, Miss Hartley.'

'The matter I'm about to bring to your attention is one that I first raised nearly twenty years ago,' Jane Hartley said.

'Really?'

'Indeed. *Then*, my complaint didn't even go beyond the duty inspector, whereas *now*, I'm talking to the chief constable. And why is that, do you think? Because the case has become more important over time? Highly unlikely. In fact, the reverse is normally true – the more a case moves towards being ancient history, the less interest there is in it. So what has changed?'

She fell silent and leant back in her chair. Marlowe waited for her to speak again, and, when it was plain she wasn't going to, he sighed and said, 'What do *you* think has changed?'

Jane Hartley affected a puzzled look, which slowly melted into one of surprised revelation.

'Why, if anything's changed, it must be me!' she said, with mock incredulity. 'I was a nobody then – and I'm a famous lawyer now.'

'I don't like being threatened, Miss Hartley – not even by famous lawyers,' Marlowe said in a voice that was almost a growl.

Jane Hartley's answering laugh was as light as the gentle clink of a pair of cyanide bottles.

'You misunderstand me,' she said.

'Do I?'

'Of course. If I were threatening you, I'd have pointed out that I have some very influential contacts in the world of politics – especially at the Home Office. Or I might have mentioned that I have powerful friends in the national press – friends who, if I asked them to, would launch a campaign to crucify you. I might even have said it would be unwise of you to displease someone who has a very good chance of becoming the first female high court judge. But I really don't want to give the impression that I've done any of that, Chief Constable.'

'Then what *do* you want?'

'I want you to investigate a miscarriage of justice which has been a blot on the record of this police force for over a quarter of a century.'

'I assume that you're acting on behalf of some client with a personal interest in this case,' Marlowe said.

'Then you assume wrongly,' Jane Harley replied.

'So who are you representing? Surely not one of those bleeding-heart liberal organizations that have nothing better to do with their time than cause trouble for hard-working police officers?'

'Not them, either. I'm representing myself and my own interests.'

'Are you indeed? And just who's supposed to have suffered as a result of this miscarriage of justice, then?'

Jane Hartley gave him a look that would have melted steel. 'My mother!' she said.

The attractive blonde woman, with the nose that was just a little bit too big to have been home-grown Lancashire, had been standing at the bar of the Drum and Monkey for more than five minutes. If no one came to join her soon, the travelling salesman (surgical supports) at the other end of the bar decided, he might just chance his arm and see if he could pick her up.

The entry of the big man in the hairy sports jacket and cavalry-twill trousers put a sudden end to any hopes that the salesman had been nurturing. It was obvious that the blonde had been waiting for him, and that – though he was considerably older than she was – there was a very definite familiarity and intimacy between them. The surgical supports salesman quickly turned away before the new arrival – whom he thought seemed *very* big indeed – noticed that he was staring and offered to rearrange his face with a ham-like fist.

Unaware of the salesman's disappointment, Woodend bought a pint for himself and a vodka for Monika Paniatowski, then led his sergeant over to a corner table.

'What are you workin' on at the moment, Monika?' he asked, trying his best to sound interested.

Paniatowski shrugged. 'Breaking and entering cases mostly. I suppose somebody's got to do it, but it's no more than PC Plod stuff really. How much longer will you be serving on this committee? I'm bursting to get back to doing some real police work.'

Woodend sighed. 'In that case, you'd better see Mr Hoskins about bein' reassigned.'

'And just what's that supposed to mean?'

'It means that when this committee's finished its so-called task, there'll be another one formed that I'll be expected to serve on. And another one after that. And so on – all the way to retirement. I warned you this might happen, Monika. As far as the brass in the Mid Lancs force is concerned, I'm a leper. An' the longer you hang around with me, the more chance there is you'll catch the disease yourself. So get out from under. Do it while you still can.'

'And leave you to your fate?'

'You can't help me, Monika, however much you might want to,' Woodend said sadly. 'Nobody can.'

'So you're perfectly content to be a committee man for the rest of your career?'

'No,' Woodend said. 'I'm not content at all. That's why I'm goin' to put my papers in.'

'You're resigning? And what will you do instead?'

'Buggered if I know,' Woodend admitted. 'But it can't be any worse than this.'

A uniformed constable came in through the main door, looked around him, then walked over to the table where Woodend and Monika were sitting.

'Mr Marlowe would like to see you, sir,' he said.

'Is that a fact?' Woodend replied. 'An' did he give you sort of any idea of *when* he'd like this rare an' historic encounter to take place?'

'Yes, sir. He said you should come right away.'

Unlike Jane Hartley, Woodend had already made up his mind about the Chief Constable. Marlowe might do a pretty good slimy, he had decided long ago, but the Chief Constable's sneakiness had attained such heights that it would put the wisest, most cunning old fox to shame. None of which explained why – after months of pretending that his chief inspector simply didn't exist – Marlowe felt such an urgent need to talk to him now. Nor did it explain why he looked genuinely frightened.

'Thirty years ago there was a particularly nasty murder here in Whitebridge,' the Chief Constable said. 'A man called Fred Dodds, a highly thought of local businessman by all accounts – got himself battered to death. The officer in charge of the case arrested his wife, a woman called—'

'Margaret Dodds,' Woodend interrupted.

The Chief Constable's eyes narrowed in a way that could have been either defensive or suspicious – but was probably both.

'How could you possibly know about that?' he demanded. 'You wouldn't even have been on the Force then.'

25

'No, I wasn't,' Woodend agreed, wondering if the man who had instructed him to stand outside Strangeways Prison, that wet early morning, was still alive.

'Anyway, Margaret Dodds had a daughter by a previous marriage, name of Jane,' Marlowe continued. 'Jane went to live with her aunt for a few years, then won a scholarship to Oxford, where she read law. She wasn't called Dodds herself. She'd kept her real father's name – which was Hartley.'

Given the drama Marlowe had infused his last few words with, it was obvious to Woodend that the name was expected to mean something to him. He repeated it silently. Hartley . . . Jane Hartley.

'The QC?' he asked.

'The very same. Jane Hartley, who gets front page headlines every time she takes on a case – and not just because she's a woman.'

'So what's her problem?' Woodend asked.

'Her problem is that she thinks her mother was framed.'

Woodend shrugged. 'Nobody likes to think they've got a murderer in the family.'

'But not everybody is as determined to *prove* that they don't. Jane Hartley has done some background research herself, and has also put private detectives on the job.'

'An' has she come up with any real proof that her mother was innocent of the crime?'

'No, but she's come up with enough unanswered questions to suggest that there might be proof out there, if only we're prepared to look for it. And that's what I want you to do.'

'But the case is thirty years old,' Woodend protested. 'Half the witnesses are probably dead by now. Bloody hell, the officer who investigated the case is most likely kickin' up daisies himself.'

'That's where you're wrong,' Marlowe said heavily. 'The officer in question is very much alive.'

'An' livin' in Whitebridge?'

'I believe he's still got a house here, but he spends most of his time in London.'

'Then he can't still be on the Force.'

'No, he isn't,' Marlowe agreed. 'In fact, he resigned shortly after Margaret Dodds was hanged – and got himself elected to parliament.

'For where?' Woodend asked. 'The horseshoe or the hoof?'

'He won as a Conservative,' the Chief Constable said.

The horseshoe then. The constituency which ran round the more prosperous edges of Whitebridge, and ensured that, despite solid Labour support in the town itself, there would always be at least one Conservative Member of Parliament elected in the area.

The current Tory MP, Archibald Heatherington, would have been no more than a lad in short trousers back then, Woodend thought. Besides, Heatherington had been a chartered accountant, not a bobby, before he was elected to parliament. So who had served as the MP for the horseshoe before him?

'Sharpe!' Woodend said. 'Eric Sharpe!'

The Chief Constable nodded sombrely. 'Or Lord Sharpe of Whitebridge, as he is now,' he agreed.

'An' Jane Hartley thinks he fitted up her mother for the murder of her stepfather?'

'That's right.'

Jane Hartley probably had some very influential friends she could call on for support if she needed to, Woodend thought. But Eric Sharpe – who was both a peer of the realm and a government minister – could do the same and, in addition, had clout *in his own right*. All of which meant that whatever way a new investigation into the Margaret Dodds murder case went, the officer in charge of it was virtually certain to make himself at least one powerful enemy.

The case was a poisoned chalice if ever he'd seen one. Which was why, of course, it was being handed to him.

Three

M aking a quick and accurate assessment of people she had just met for the first time was an essential basic skill in Jane Hartley's line of work, and thus she found no difficulty at all in forming an opinion of the two police officers sitting opposite her in the interview room.

The man, Woodend, was pushing fifty, she guessed. He was, as she would have said when she lived in Lancashire herself, 'a big bugger', broad as well as tall, with features that looked as if they had been chiselled out by a sculptor who had quite considerable skill but was working against the clock. In her experience, men his size either gave off an air of aggression, which came from a realization of their own power, or else a diffidence, which sprang from exactly the same source. Woodend seemed to fall into neither of these two camps, and Jane was forced into the impression that if he had been nine inches shorter, he would still have been exactly the same man.

His assistant was more of an enigma. Monika Paniatowski must have been a pretty child, as Jane had been her-self, yet the sergeant – and again she found a parallel – didn't exude the impression of having had the easy childhood which pretty children come to expect as a right. In her own case, that was easily explained – her child-hood had been destroyed by her mother's execution – but she needed to discover what had gone wrong with Paniatowski's.

'Are you a local woman?' she asked, embarking on what,

in cross-examination at the Old Bailey, was usually called 'a fishing expedition'.

'It depends what you mean by local,' Paniatowski said. 'I've lived in Lancashire since I was nine.'

'And before then?'

'Before then, I didn't.'

There was a moment's awkward silence, then Woodend said, 'Monika and her mother spent most of the last war being chased around central Europe by the Nazis.'

'I see,' Jane Hartley said thoughtfully.

'Not that it's any of your business,' Monika told her.

Woodend cleared his throat. 'Shall we get down to the matter in hand?' he suggested. 'As I understand it, Miss Hartley – it is *Miss*, isn't it?'

Most other men would have asked the question in a sneering way, Jane Hartley thought. Woodend seemed only to be seeking information.

'Yes, it's "Miss",' she said. 'For a while I was called Mrs Jarvis, but after the divorce I reverted to my maiden name.'

'Who divorced who?'

'That's really not any of your concern,' Jane Hartley said stonily.

Woodend smiled good-naturedly. 'You just been checking out our Monika here,' he said, 'an' I've no doubt that as soon as you've left the station, you'll be checkin' me out, too. Don't we have the right to know a little bit about you?'

Despite herself, Jane Hartley found she was returning the smile. 'I suppose so,' she conceded. 'He divorced me for mental cruelty. But that was just a matter of mutual convenience, agreed on beforehand by both sides.'

'Meanin'?'

'Meaning that neither of us had committed adultery, and neither of us wanted to wait the inordinate length of time it would have taken to establish grounds on the basis of desertion. We wanted a divorce because, though it was nobody's fault, the marriage simply wasn't working any more. Mental cruelty was the only way open to us.'

'You could have divorced *him* on those grounds, rather than havin' him divorce you,' Woodend pointed out.

'True, but we both knew that I was mentally tougher than he was, and therefore better able to stand the strain.' An unexpectedly impish grin suddenly appeared on Jane Hartley's face. 'Besides, it didn't do my reputation around the courts any harm to be known as a bit of a harridan.' Her expression changed again and became very businesslike. 'Can we deal with my reason for being here, now?'

'Aye. Why not?' Woodend said thoughtfully.

'My grandfather was a vicar, and my mother was brought up in a quiet country parish,' Jane Hartley said crisply. 'No doubt she was expected to marry a nice young curate and become a vicar's wife herself, but she had other plans. She won a scholarship to Somerville College, Oxford, which was something of an achievement in the 1920s, when places for women were at a premium. She read philosophy – one of the most demanding courses available. She returned to Whitebridge to teach at one of the local schools, but during her first year there she met my father, and they were married.'

'What was your father's job?'

'He was a clerk at the Empire Mill.' Jane Hartley's eyes flashed with sudden anger. 'I know what you're thinking – that she married below her. That was what her family thought, as well. But my mother was above such petty distinctions as social class.'

'Actually, I wasn't thinkin' that at all,' Woodend said mildly. 'I was just wonderin' if your dad knew mine. My dad was a tackler at the same mill. An' he didn't think much of social distinctions either – which is somethin' that's rubbed off on me.'

Jane Hartley flushed slightly. 'I'm sorry to have mis-read you and caused offence. I won't make the same mistake again.'

'Don't worry about it, lass,' Woodend said. 'Get on with your story.'

'When a teacher married in those days, she was obliged to resign from her post. For a while my mother stayed at home – my parents had a tied company cottage near the mill – but when I was born they soon realized that my father's wages were no longer enough to maintain the family. So my mother got a job as assistant to the mill manager.'

Woodend thought back, once more, to his lonely vigil outside Strangeways Prison. 'She worked for Seth Earnshaw, did she?' he asked.

'That's right. Do you know him?'

'Used to. The last time I saw him was at my dad's funeral. I imagine he's been six feet under for some time himself.'

'That's where you're wrong,' Jane Hartley said. 'He's well into his eighties, but he's still very much alive. I get a card from him every Christmas, and another one on my birthday.'

'Good of him to remember after all this time,' Woodend said. 'So how long was your mother actually workin' for him?'

'Until two years after my father's death. Then she resigned and married Fred Dodds.'

'How old would you have been when these two important events took place?'

'I was five years old when my father died, seven when my mother married Dodds.'

'An' nine when . . . when . . .'

'When my mother was hanged,' Jane Hartley said. 'It's all right, Chief Inspector, you can say the words. I'd never have got as far as I have with this thing if I'd been squeamish.'

Woodend nodded. 'I imagine your mother marryin' Dodds brought about some big changes in both your lives.'

'It did. My mother could give up work, and we moved from our tiny cottage to a detached house on Hebden Brow.'

'Was it a happy marriage?'

'How would I know?' Jane Hartley asked awkwardly. 'I was only a child at the time.'

'You were seven when your mother got married, an' nine when Dodds was killed. You must remember somethin'.'

'No I . . . I really don't remember anything at all.'

Woodend sighed, and turned to his sergeant.

'How old were you when you first saw the man who became your stepfather, Monika?' he asked.

'Eight,' Paniatowski said dully.

She knew she was being used, and knew too that if anyone but Charlie Woodend – her boss and mentor – had tried this on, she'd have told him where he could stuff it.

'Describe that meetin' for me, if you will,' Woodend said.

'It was in Berlin,' Paniatowski said. 'We were walking up Kurfürstendamm, towards a soup kitchen. A jeep pulled up beside us. There was a sergeant at the wheel and a captain sitting in the back. The captain was Arthur Jones, the man who became my stepfather. He asked my mother if she spoke English, and when she said she did, he told her he was lost. She gave him directions, and then—'

'That's enough about Berlin,' Woodend interrupted. 'Do you think you know whether or not your mother's second marriage was a happy one?'

'I don't want to talk about it.'

'An' I'm not askin' you to. All I want to find out is whether *you* know if the marriage was happy.'

'I know.'

Woodend turned his attention back to Jane Hartley. 'You get the point, Miss Hartley? Monika remembers a lot. An' so do you!'

'*Monika* also said that she didn't want to talk about it,' Jane Hartley replied, cuttingly.

'An' that's her right,' Woodend agreed. 'But Monika isn't askin' me to investigate her stepfather's death an' her mother's execution.'

Jane Hartley looked down at her hands. 'If I tell you what I remember, do you promise it won't bias you?'

'I can't promise anythin'. But I still need to know.'

Jane Hartley nodded, giving in to the inevitable. 'It seemed to be a good match at first. They appeared to be very happy. Then the arguments started.' She shuddered. 'They were bloody.'

'Are you sayin' that they came to blows?'

'No, I'm almost sure they didn't. But they did a lot of screaming at the tops of their voices. And I know that some of the crockery got smashed, because I kept stepping on the evidence.'

'But you didn't see anythin' bein' thrown yourself?'

'No, I used to go and hide in the cupboard under the stairs,' Jane Hartley admitted, almost guiltily. 'I'm not sure this question and answer method is really getting us anywhere,' she continued, with a new resolve in her voice. 'If you don't mind, I'd prefer just to lay out the facts.'

'All right,' Woodend agreed.

Jane Hartley took a deep breath. 'Fred Dodds died as a result of multiple blows to his head with a hammer that was subsequently identified as being his property. He was killed in the lounge of his own home, and the police doctor estimated his time of death as between seven thirty and eight thirty. At the time he was killed, he was alone.'

She gave Woodend a defiant, challenging look, but the Chief Inspector said nothing.

'I was staying with my aunt – my father's sister – at the time,' Jane Hartley continued. 'My mother's absence is explained by the fact that she'd gone out for a walk. When she returned home *at nine o'clock,* she found her second husband lying there, and immediately called the police. She never expected to be arrested, but she was. The Crown's case was based on circumstantial evidence. She couldn't prove – at least to the police's satisfaction – that she hadn't been in the house when Fred Dodds died. Her fingerprints were on the hammer but, as you must know, she could easily have picked that hammer up without even realizing it. There was blood on her dress, but naturally she would have touched her husband to make sure that he was dead. She had no motive to kill him and—'

'I thought she did,' Woodend interrupted. 'I thought the Crown claimed she did it for the money.'

'How could you possibly know that?' Jane Hartley demanded angrily. Then, as Marlowe had done earlier, she added, 'You couldn't have been a policeman at the time!'

'I remember readin' all about it in the papers,' Woodend said, unwilling, at this stage in the proceedings, to reveal his own connection with the case. 'I am right about the money, aren't I?'

'You're right in so far as that's what the Crown prosecutors claimed,' Jane Hartley agreed.

'An' you're sayin' they were lyin'?'

'I'm saying they were *wrong*. Look, there had been some talk of my mother and Fred Dodds getting a divorce, and the prosecution hypothesized from that that she must have been worried about being thrown out on the street without a penny to her name.'

'So *he* was divorcin' *her*?'

'It hadn't got to that stage. It was all still talk.'

'All right. But what was the talk *about*? What were the grounds he was *thinkin'* of divorcin' her on?'

'His friends claimed that he told them he suspected her of having an affair. But he had absolutely no proof of it. He couldn't even say who it was she was supposed to be having an affair *with*.'

Jane Hartley spread out her hands in a gesture of help-lessness that acknowledged the fact that she knew she was rapidly losing the battle to convince him of her case.

'Look, Chief Inspector,' she continued, 'I have had a team of private detectives working on this, and they've come up with all kinds of details which bring the verdict into question.'

'Like what?'

'Inconsistencies in witness statements. Evidence that there were other witnesses who might have been able to give my mother an alibi – or at least establish a reasonable doubt – but who, for some reason, were never called to the stand. Some clear indications that police investigation was hasty, slipshod and perhaps deliberately misleading . . .'

'Bent bobbies tamperin' with the evidence,' Woodend said with a heavy sigh. 'I'd have expected you to come up with somethin' a little better than that old chestnut.'

'But what if it's *true*?' Jane Hartley demanded hotly. 'What if Chief Inspector Eric Sharpe really did behave in that way?'

'Why should he have?'

'Because he needed a conviction in a hurry, and he didn't care *who* took the fall.'

Woodend shook his head. 'It's true that no bobby's ever happy about leavin' a murder unsolved,' he conceded, 'but I've never yet met one who was in a mad rush to close the case. We like to make sure our evidence is as solid as it can possibly be, because if there's one thing worse on a policeman's record than failin' to make an arrest at all, it's arrestin' somebody who then gets off.'

'There were special circumstances in Eric Sharpe's case. He didn't care about whatever reputation he had within the Force, because he was planning to leave all that behind him. What he *did* desperately want was to become a Member of Parliament, and he was only a few months away from appearing before the local Conservative Party selection board. He knew competition was going to be stiff, and knew that if he was going to stand out above the other candidates he needed something that would give him an edge. He couldn't have asked for anything better than Fred Dodd's murder.'

'*Dodd's* murder?' Woodend asked. 'Or *any* murder?'

'Dodd's murder! My stepfather was not only an important man in this town, he was an important man in this town's *Conservative Party*. The members of that selection board were all friends of his. They were bound to look favourably on the policeman who had brought his killer to justice.'

'So you're sayin' that Eric Sharpe framed your mother just to get himself elected? That would make him—'

'That would make him a murderer himself,' Jane Hartley interrupted. 'Is that so incredible? You must have known a lot of murderers in your time, Chief Inspector. Can you honestly say that any of their motives would have been enough to make *you* kill?'

'I like to think that, apart from protecting my daughter, there's *no* motive that would make me kill,' Woodend said.

But he knew what she meant. Over the years he had met any number of murderers whose explanations of the motives which had driven them to kill had seemed so totally trivial that he'd been tempted to believe that they were nothing more than a shield behind which to hide the real motive. But rarely had that turned out to be the case – because however pathetic the reasons had seemed to him, they had been truly compelling in the eyes of the killer.

'Besides, I'm not saying that Sharpe actually ever saw things in such stark terms,' Jane Hartley continued. 'He probably convinced himself that my mother really was the murderer and that tinkering with the evidence was necessary, if justice was to be served.' She looked straight into Woodend's eyes. 'We can convince ourselves of anything if we really want to, can't we?'

36

'Aye, we can,' Woodend agreed, meeting her gaze with his own. 'We can convince ourselves that we're different to all the other people who've lived through the same sort of experience that we have. We can convince ourselves that the police, and the prosecutor an' the judge an' the jury were all wrong – an' that only we are right.'

Jane Hartley did not even blink. 'Perhaps that's true,' she said. 'Perhaps my mother really did kill her second husband. But if that is the case, it shouldn't be too difficult to prove, should it?'

'Shouldn't be too difficult to prove? After *thirty years*?' Woodend asked. 'It should be bloody near impossible. Besides, are you really sure that you want me to *prove* anythin'? As things stand, you can remember your mother as a victim of mistaken justice. That's tragic enough – but it's probably a lot easier than knowin' for a fact that she was a cold-blooded killer who murdered her own husband for his money.'

'Perhaps she was cold-blooded, but she certainly wasn't stupid,' Jane Hartley said. 'She'd won a scholarship to Oxford. She'd been a teacher, and had run Mr Earnshaw's office practically single-handed. If she really had wanted to kill Fred Dodds, don't you think she would have contrived to do it in such a way that she wouldn't automatically become the prime suspect?'

She had a point, Woodend decided, and realized that the same thought had been nagging away in the back of *his* mind ever since that morning outside Strangeways Prison. Still, Jane Hartley was taking a big gamble in opening up the whole can of worms again.

'Are you certain you want to know the truth?' he asked. 'Are you sure you're strong enough?'

'I'm sure!' Jane Hartley said.

Then you're an exceptional case, Woodend thought – because in your place I don't think *I'd* have the courage.

Four

The landlord of the Drum and Monkey glanced into the public bar and saw that the corner table was occupied by Paniatowski and Woodend. A moment later a third person joined them, the youthful inspector who always looked as if he should be a company director rather than a bobby.

So the old firm was back in business, the landlord thought. Well, he'd known they couldn't be kept down for ever.

He signalled to his new barman to come over to him. 'See them three buggers sittin' in the corner?' he said.

'Yes, Mr Roberts?'

'Well, they'll be wantin' a pint of best bitter, a half of bitter an' a vodka as soon as you can. An' take 'em a repeat order every twenty minutes, whether they ask for it or not.'

The barman looked dubious. 'You sure about that? What if they feel like a change from their usual drinks? People do, you know.'

'Then the age of miracles will truly have to come to pass before my very eyes,' the landlord said.

'Beg your pardon?'

'Listen lad, the Beatles may eventually stop having hits, the sky may fall down on us, the government may even start listenin' to the ordinary feller in the street one day – but whatever happens, that table over there will still want a pint of best bitter, a half of bitter an' a vodka.'

'You know best, Mr Roberts,' the barman said.

'You're bloody right I do,' the landlord agreed. 'That's

why I'm the one standin' behind the bar an' you're the one waitin' on tables.'

Woodend looked at his team. 'We're out on a limb with this one,' he said.

'Well, that'll certainly be no novelty for us, will it?' Detective Inspector Bob Rutter replied.

'The best solution all round would be if we could prove that Margaret Dodds really *did* kill her husband,' Woodend said. 'That would certainly let Lord Sharpe off the hook. An' while Jane Hartley might not *like* our findings, she'd have no grounds for causin' any more trouble or holdin' a grudge against us. The problem is, there's a lot to be said for Miss Hartley's argument that her mother would have had to be incredibly stupid to think she could kill her husband in that manner an' hope to get away with it. So where does that leave us?'

'With the assumption that Margaret Dodds was telling the truth,' Paniatowski said. 'That she was out of the house, taking a walk, when her husband was murdered.'

'Was the murderer hopin' that she'd take the blame?' Woodend asked.

'Perhaps,' Rutter said. 'Then again, it might never have entered his head that she would be arrested – but once she *was* arrested, he certainly wasn't going to stick his own neck in the noose just to keep hers out of it.'

'*He?*' Woodend said. 'What makes you think it was a man?'

Rutter picked up his leather briefcase, and flicked open the catch. '*These* are what made me think it,' he said, laying a number of photographs out on the table. 'I found them in the investigation file.'

Woodend looked down at the pictures of the dead man and then whistled softly. 'Bloody hell fire, Bob!' he said. 'Fred Dodds wasn't so much attacked as *mashed*!'

It was hardly an exaggeration. What they were looking at was only identifiable as a face by the fact that it had hair on top and was attached to the rest of the body by a neck. Though it was impossible to say exactly how *many* blows had been struck with the hammer, the assault appeared to have been both sustained and relentless.

'So the reason you assume the attacker must have been a man is that you don't think a woman would have had the strength?' Woodend asked Rutter. 'Is that right?'

'Yes.'

'I disagree,' Paniatowski said.

Rutter shot her a look that carried with it not only his customary dislike of her but also the implication that the *only* reason she disagreed was because the suggestion had come from him.

Woodend sighed. He still harboured some small hope that Rutter and Paniatowski would eventually learn to get on, but the longer they worked together, the less likely that seemed. Rutter saw Paniatowski's approach to policing as slapdash and buccaneer, Paniatowski saw Rutter's as clerical and bureaucratic. Neither was fair to the other – though there was a grain of truth in both their criticisms – and neither seemed willing to grasp the point that it was the very diversity of the team which made it so effective. They disliked each other, and that was that. And they would all have to learn to live with it as best they could.

'What makes you think it *could* have been a woman, Monika?' Woodend asked, returning to the immediate problem.

'Dodds must have been dead long before he ended up in that state,' Paniatowski said. 'And even the murderer – if he or she had stopped to think about it – should have realized that.'

'So?'

'The fact that the murderer *didn't* stop to think shows it was a *frenzied* attack. And when people lose control like this killer obviously did, they can summon up reserves of strength they didn't even know they had.'

'Bob?' Woodend asked.

'I suppose it's possible,' Rutter conceded.

'So we're lookin' for a man or a woman who really *hated* Dodds,' Woodend said. 'Of course, that could point the finger straight back at his missus.'

'But it doesn't have to,' Paniatowski countered.

'No,' Woodend agreed. 'It doesn't have to. Did you find anythin' besides the photographs in the investigation file, Bob?'

'A surprising amount,' Rutter said. 'I've not had time to go through the whole thing yet, but I thought you might find this interesting.'

The 'this' he referred to was a transcript of Margaret Dodds' interview with Chief Inspector Eric Sharpe. Holding it so Paniatowski could read it as well, Woodend ran his eyes over the sheet of typewritten paper.

DCI Sharpe: Before we begin, can you confirm that you've been cautioned and advised that you have the right to have a lawyer present?

Margaret Dodds: Yes, I can confirm that.

DCI: Would you please tell me where you were between the hours of seven thirty and nine o'clock this evening.

MD: I went for a walk.

DCI: Where did you go?

MD: I don't know. I was deep in thought. I didn't notice where I was going.

DCI: What were you thinking about?

MD: Personal matters.

DCI: What personal matters?

MD: I'd prefer not to say.

DCI: You do realize you've been charged with *murder*, don't you?

MD: Yes, I do. But I'd still prefer not to say.

DCI: Did anybody see you on this 'walk' of yours?

41

MD: I have no idea.

DCI: What happened when you got home?

MD: I found my husband dead on the lounge floor.

DCI: Found him dead? You didn't kill him yourself?

MD: No.

DCI: You didn't pick up the hammer and smash his skull in?

MD: I've already said I didn't kill him.

DCI: There was blood all over your dress. We found your prints on the hammer!

MD: I didn't kill him. And it doesn't matter how many questions you ask me, or how often you ask them, that's the only answer you'll get from me. I *didn't kill him.*

'What do you make of that, Monika?' Woodend asked.

'I think DCI Sharpe certainly wasn't doing his job as it should have been done.'

'How'd you mean?'

'He was far too blunt. Far too direct. He was supposed to be building a case. He should have been trying to make his suspect open up to him – getting her to give him all the information she could, so he could tie up the loose ends. And he simply wasn't doing that.'

'The printed word always looks cold and heartless,' Woodend pointed out. 'Maybe if you'd been there yourself – heard the tone of his voice – seen the look on his face—'

'No interrogation that *you've* ever conducted would read anything like that,' Paniatowski interrupted.

'The sergeant's right,' Rutter agreed reluctantly. 'Based on the evidence of this transcript, I'd have to say that Sharpe wasn't looking for answers.'

'Then what *was* he doin'?'

'The very opposite. He was trying to make Margaret Dodds retreat into herself.'

'An' why would he want to do that?'

'Because he didn't want his nice neat case spoiled by the accused opening her mouth too much and starting to sound innocent?'

Woodend nodded gloomily.

'It's looking less and less likely that we're goin' to find the *convenient* solution to this case, isn't it, sir?' Paniatowski asked.

'Aye,' Woodend agreed. 'What's lookin' *most* likely is that we'll end up with the worst of both worlds – provin' that Sharpe didn't do his job, but not havin' a clue as to what really *did* happen that night.' He took a long swig of his pint. 'Still, we'll have to soldier on as best we can,' he continued stoically.

'And how big is our army?' Rutter asked.

Woodend grinned, slightly awkwardly. 'You're lookin' at it, lad.'

'Just us!'

'That's right.'

'But this is a murder inquiry!' Rutter protested.

'So they tell me. But we've cracked murders before usin' just the three of us.'

'Yes, but they've been *recent* murders. This one's thirty years old. The trail's so cold that—'

'That you could use it to chill Monika's vodka,' Woodend interrupted. 'I know. An' believe me, if I thought they'd give me any more men, I'd ask for them. But Mr Marlowe's as likely to give me a bigger team as he is to nominate me for Pope. So you'll just have to double up – take on two or three jobs each.'

Paniatowski and Rutter exchanged glances that could almost have been called mutually sympathetic, but Woodend had no illusions that common adversity would keep them united for long.

'The main thrust of all our investigations will be into Fred Dodds' background,' the Chief Inspector continued. 'If there's anybody out there who would have taken a special pleasure in his death, we need to know about them. Now the additional tasks. Bob, I want you to go through the records of the police investigation an' the trial with a fine-toothed comb. I want to know which of the witnesses we should be questionin' again . . .'

'If they're still alive,' Rutter said.

'Well, there won't be much use talking to them if they're dead,' Woodend said dryly. 'In addition, we need to know which of DCI Sharpe's conclusions are worth a second examination. Got that?'

Rutter nodded. It was the kind of painstaking work he was good at, and – though he would never have admitted it – rather enjoyed.

'Monika, I want you to come up with as much of the background as you can on Margaret Dodds an' her two husbands. An' while you're at it, see what you can discover about Jane Hartley QC.'

'Why her?' Monika Paniatowski asked. 'She was only a kid at the time of Dodds' death.'

'But she's not a kid *now*,' Woodend pointed out. 'She's a powerful woman with a lot of clout in all the right places. Whether we like it or not, she's the one we're actually workin' for – an' I always think it's a good idea to find out as much as I can about my boss.'

'Fair point,' Paniatowski agreed.

'What about you, sir?' Rutter asked, doing his best to keep a slight smile of anticipation from creeping to his lips.

'What about me?' Woodend countered.

'Will you be doubling up on anything?'

'As a matter of fact, I will. I was brought up on gramophone records as big as hubcaps, an' tea that was so strong you could stand your spoon up in it. You two young sprogs, on the other hand, are more used to 45 rpm discs an' your frothy coffee. The world in which this case occurred is so alien to you that it's no more than a blank canvas at the moment. The deeper you get into the investigation, of course, the clearer the picture you'll have of how the central characters thought an' acted. But the background will still be empty. It'll be my job to fill that background in. Only I can't do that for the pair of you until I've regained some of my own feelin' for the time, now can I?'

'I suppose not,' Rutter agreed.

'So that's what I'll be doin' in my spare time – attemptin' to regain a feelin' for the time.'

Rutter gave up the battle to hide his smile. 'In other words, what you'll be doing is "cloggin'-it" around Whitebridge, trying your best to remember just what life was like here before the war?' he suggested.

'Exactly!' Woodend agreed.

Five

The brass plate next to the front door read:

Peninsula Trading Company Ltd
Founded 1923
Branches in Whitebridge, London
Penang and Kuala Lumpur

Woodend chuckled. Whitebridge, *then* London, he noted. That was typical of the businessmen he remembered from his childhood. It wasn't that they had thought their home town to be the centre of the universe – it was that they had *known* it was.

Woodend turned to his sergeant. 'I suppose we'd better see if anybody's in, Monika,' he said.

Paniatowski nodded. She pressed the doorbell, and listened for a ringing from inside. When it was plain there wasn't going to be one, she lifted the knocker and rapped on the door. This time she was rewarded with the sound of slightly hesitant footfalls in the corridor.

The door was opened by a man in his late sixties. He might once have had the lean and hungry face of a hard-bitten entrepreneur, but age had given him both the shape and expression of a rather absent-minded Santa Claus.

'Yes?' the old man asked, as if he were slightly surprised to find them standing there.

'We're here to see Mr Bithwaite,' Paniatowski said.

'That's me.'

'If it's not convenient at the moment, then we can—' Paniatowski began.

'But of course it's convenient,' the old man said enthusiastically. 'More than convenient. *Do* come in.'

'Don't you want to know who we are, or why we're here?' Woodend wondered.

'I suppose so,' Bithwaite said, and then – as if he were worried such an answer may have offended them – he quickly added, 'at least, I want to know if you want to *tell* me.'

'We're from the police,' Woodend said. 'We'd like to talk to you about Fred Dodds.'

A puzzled look crossed Bithwaite's rosy face. 'Fred Dodds?' he repeated. 'But he's been dead for years.' He shrugged. 'Still, why *not* talk about old Fred? It will certainly help to pass the time.'

He led them into an office just to the left of the front door. A big, old-fashioned mahogany desk – badly in need of polishing – dominated much of the room. On the wall behind it hung a map of the world that showed boundaries long since redrawn and empires that had faded away. The air smelled slightly of must, and the sun, which streamed in through the window, was muted somewhat by the thin layer of grime on the window.

Two small leather armchairs, both of them losing a little of their horsehair stuffing, were positioned in front of the desk, and it was on these that Bithwaite bade his guests to sit.

'I'd order up some coffee for you, but I'm afraid my girl Friday only comes in two days a week – and this doesn't happen to be one of those days,' he said apologetically.

'I take it business isn't doin' too well,' said Woodend sympathetically.

Bithwaite smiled. 'If business was going any slower, it would be moving in reverse. The sort of work we used to do before the war has been gradually taken over by the big corporations. There's no room in this world of ours for a

Merchant Prince any more. You'd have to be a Merchant *Emperor* to survive now.'

'I'm sorry,' Woodend said.

'Don't be,' the older man told him. 'I did well enough *before* the war. Even up to the middle fifties I was making a comfortable living. And I have a very nice little nest-egg tucked away for when I do eventually retire.'

'Then why are you . . . ?'

'Why am I still working?'

'Well . . . yes.'

'Because I still enjoy it, I suppose. This place may not look like much now, but it's a monument to my working life and, sitting here behind my desk, I can remember how things used to be. And that is what you wish to talk about, isn't it? How things used to be?'

Woodend grinned good-naturedly. 'That's right, sir. What can you tell us about Fred Dodds?'

'Oh, I could tell you many things,' Bithwaite said. 'Where would you like me to start?'

'How about when you first met him?'

'That would be when he and his partner interviewed me for the post of Chief Clerk, towards the end of 1923.'

'His partner?' Woodend said. 'I don't remember readin' anythin' about a partner in the papers.'

'That's because, by the time Mr Dodds died, the partnership between him and Mr Cuthburtson had been dissolved for over three years.'

'Is that so?' Woodend asked pensively.

'It is indeed. The break-up came as quite a surprise – at least, it did to me.'

'An' why was that?'

'They'd seemed ideally matched, you see. Mr Cuthburtson was a staid, unimaginative sort of man, with both feet firmly on the ground. Mr Dodds, on the other hand, had a certain flair – a certain cavalier attitude – about him.'

'Wasn't that a problem?'

'No, not at all. In fact, it was a positive advantage. You needed both kinds of men in the sort of business this was back then.'

'Why is that?'

'Well, for example, Mr Cuthburtson hated the idea of travel. He had a young family, which he wanted to get home to every night. Besides, he was always at his happiest dealing with the detailed paperwork – he loved reading all those columns of figures. Mr Dodds was just the reverse – hated figures, was prepared to pack a suitcase at the drop of a hat. A perfect partnership in many ways. And what made the eventual break-up even more surprising was that they weren't just partners – they were great friends as well.'

'Great friends?'

'Absolutely. Of course, they both had their own lives to lead, but that didn't preclude them socializing with each other. Mr Dodds was living on his own at the time, and so Mr Cuthburtson used to invite him round to his house every Sunday for luncheon. And in return, Mr Dodds would take the entire Cuthburtson family out on occasional expeditions to the seaside or the Lake District.'

'So if everythin' was so tickety-boo, why *did* the partnership break up?' Woodend asked.

'I never found out,' Bithwaite confessed. 'As I said, it was all very sudden. One moment everything was going along swimmingly. The next they were not only dissolving their agreement – they couldn't even stand the sight of one another. They even went so far as to refuse to be in the same room when the final papers were signed.'

'You must have *some* suspicions about what went wrong,' Woodend persisted.

'Not really,' Bithwaite replied. 'The best theory I could come up with was that Mr Cuthburtson was fiddling the books in some way, and Mr Dodds found out about it. But since Mr Dodds never took any interest in the accounts himself, it's hard to see how he *could* have found out.'

'Still, from what you say, if anybody *did* force anybody else out of the business, it was Dodds forcin' out Cuthburtson,' Woodend said.

'Yes, I think I'd have to agree with you there.'

So Cuthburtson loses the business he's helped to establish, and a couple of years later Fred Dodds is found beaten to death by somebody who obviously hated his guts, Woodend thought. He wondered if there was anything in DCI Sharpe's records about *that*.

'Do you happen to know where Cuthburtson lives now?' asked Paniatowski, whose mind seemed to be running along roughly the same lines.

'No, but I can tell you where he and his family went after the partnership broke up,' Bithwaite said.

'An' where was that?' Woodend asked.

'Canada.'

'Canada!'

'That's right. Within a couple of months of the final papers being signed, they'd emigrated. I think that perhaps Mr Cuthburtson wanted to leave the unpleasant memories of the past behind him. You know, make a clean start in some completely new place.'

'An' nobody's heard from him since?'

'I haven't, certainly.'

'Did you become a partner after Cuthburtson had gone?'

Bithwaite laughed. 'Good heavens, no. I might have taken a lot of the burden of Mr Cuthburtson's work on my own shoulders, but my position in the company was essentially unchanged until I bought the whole thing outright.'

'An' when was that?'

'After Mr Dodds death.'

'Bought it outright, after Mr Dodds' death,' Woodend repeated. 'The company was very much a goin' concern back then, from what you've said.'

'That's right.'

'So it must have been very expensive.'

'Not really,' Bithwaite said.

'No?'

'There was a depression on. People were cautious. They thought twice before investing whatever cash they'd managed to salvage from the Great Crash in a new business. And a certain amount of superstition came into it, too. The owner had been brutally murdered – perhaps the business itself was unlucky.'

'But those considerations didn't bother you?'

'To a certain extent, they did. But remember, I'd seen the business from the *inside*. I knew that, even in hard times, I'd have to be the unluckiest man alive *not* to make it work. Besides, the executors of the will eventually dropped the asking price so much that I just couldn't resist it.'

'Tell us more about Dodds as a man,' Woodend suggested.

Bithwaite gave the matter some thought. 'He could be very charming,' he said. 'Quite the gentleman, in fact. But there were occasions when he forgot himself – and then his rough edges tended to show through.'

'Rough edges?'

Bithwaite looked embarrassed.

'How can I express this without seeming like a snob?' he wondered aloud. 'I'm not exactly out of the top drawer myself, but my father was a senior clerk in a highly respected solicitor's office, and I was educated at King Edward's Grammar School. Whereas Mr Dodds . . . Mr Dodds . . .'

'Whereas Mr Dodds' father was a mill worker, an' he went to an elementary school?' Woodend suggested.

'I couldn't say about that. I don't *know* what his father did for a living, because the family weren't from round here. But Mr Dodds' rough edges must have come from somewhere, and I would seriously doubt that his father was the kind of man one could comfortably have invited to dinner.'

'Where *was* Mr Dodds from?' Paniatowski asked.

'Simcaster, I believe. He always *claimed* he'd attended Simcaster Grammar School.'

'But you think he was lyin'?' Woodend said.

'I suppose I had no real reason to disbelieve him,' Bithwaite admitted. 'He just didn't have the *stamp* of a grammar school boy on him.' He paused for a second, as if he'd suddenly retrieved a long-forgotten memory. 'He used to sit there examining his hands.'

'He did what?'

'He'd sit behind his desk, examining his hands. Especially his fingernails. It was almost as if he couldn't quite believe they were really clean.'

'What about women?' Woodend asked.

'*What* about them?'

'Unattached man with plenty of money. Loads of charm – even if he wasn't quite a gentleman. Your Mr Dodds seemed to have had all the qualities to make him a perfect ladies' man.'

'I really wouldn't know about that,' Bithwaite said, almost haughtily. 'He certainly never brought any "ladies" here. In fact, I wasn't even aware of the existence of the lady who became *Mrs* Dodds until a week or so before the wedding.'

'She wasn't exactly the sort of woman you'd have expected him to marry, was she?' Woodend said.

'I beg your pardon!'

'Daughter of a vicar, degree from Oxford. I'd have thought she'd have been a little too refined for his taste.'

'You misunderstand him,' Bithwaite said. 'She was the perfect choice for just those reasons. As I see it, she represented a step up the ladder. Money can't buy you breeding, but it can buy you *people* who have breeding.'

'You didn't like him much, did you?' Woodend said. 'In fact, from what you've said I'd guess you positively despised the man.'

A sudden change came over Bithwaite's face. The

avuncular softness drained from his eyes and was replaced by the mongoose-sharpness of a man who had traded in rubber and tin.

'It's been so pleasant to have someone to talk to that it never occurred to me to wonder *why* you're asking all these questions,' he said in the voice of a younger, harder man. 'Well, I'm asking now.'

'We're givin' the murder of Fred Dodds the quick once-over,' Woodend said.

'For what reason? The murderer was arrested and hanged. Isn't that the end of it?' The trader's eyes flashed. 'Unless, of course, you suspect that someone else killed him.'

'It's certainly not an idea I'm willin' to rule out at the moment,' Woodend admitted.

Bithwaite stood up and walked around his desk towards the door. 'You've been here longer than I'd realized,' he said. 'I'm falling behind with my tasks, and so I'm afraid – ' he pointedly opened the door to the corridor – 'that I'm going to have to ask you to leave now.'

'I wonder if we could just ask—' Woodend began.

'I told you as much as I know,' Bithwaite said firmly. 'See yourselves out. And please make sure to close the front door properly behind you.'

Six

I t was just after midday. In the lounge bar of the Drum and Monkey, young men in suits drank bottles of Bass and ate either triangular-shaped ham sandwiches or chicken and chips from the basket. The public bar, just a few feet away from the lounge, was an entirely different story. Here, most of the men were dressed in greasy or paint-stained overalls, and drank pints. They ate pickled eggs, and expected their ham butties – never *sandwiches* – to be oblong in shape, just as God intended. It was, Rutter had learned long ago, his boss's natural environment, and though he still called it 'the public', he thought of it as 'Woodend Land'.

The two of them had been sitting at their usual table in the public for nearly a quarter of an hour, and for most of that time the Chief Inspector had been outlining to Rutter his interview with Bithwaite. Now, he came to the end of his tale, took a deep slug of his pint, and asked, 'So what do you think?'

'I think that it might well be worth contacting the Canadian Mounties,' Rutter replied.

'To see if Cuthburtson's still alive?'

'And to find out if they know whether or not he made a short trip to England in the summer of 1934.'

'Do you think that's likely, lad?'

'Yes, I do,' Rutter said. 'Imagine this. Dodds finds some way to eject Cuthburtson from the business that they started together. At first, Cuthburtson's bloody furious. Then he calms down, and starts to tell himself that what happened was probably for the best. It's not a defeat at all, he decides. It's more an opportunity to make a new start. But it doesn't work out quite like that.'

'Why doesn't it?'

'Either because he's not the success in Canada that he thought he would be, or he *is* a success but the memory of Dodds having shafted him is still gnawing away at his insides. He knows he'll have no peace of mind until he's had his revenge, so he comes back to Whitebridge and kills his old partner. And not just kills him – pulverizes his skull. Because that's how deep his anger runs.'

'An' he's prepared to let Margaret Dodds, an innocent party, swing for what he's done?'

'It wouldn't be the first time a man's been too weak to face up to the consequences of his actions,' Rutter pointed out. 'Besides, who's to say he even knew Margaret Dodds had been *arrested*, let alone convicted?'

'How could he not?'

'Because he's timed the whole thing very carefully – including his escape – and within a couple of hours of killing Fred Dodds, he's stepping on to a steamer in Liverpool bound for Canada.'

'An' between then an' the time Margaret Dodds is hanged, he never picks up a newspaper? Isn't that a bit unlikely?'

'Even if he does read the papers, there's still no guarantee he would have found out. Look, sir, if there's a murder in Whitebridge, you can be pretty sure that the local Lancashire papers will splash it across the front page. But in Manchester – which is only thirty miles away – the story doesn't merit more than a few paragraphs towards the back of the paper. And the further away from the crime scene you get, the less interest there is in it. The nationals may not mention it at all, and if they don't, why should the foreign papers?'

'You've got a point,' Woodend agreed. 'So Cuthburtson's a possibility. But he's not the only one, is he? Isn't it equally possible that Mr Bithwaite could turn out to be our killer?'

'No, not at all,' Rutter said firmly.

'Why not?'

'Because if he was the murderer, he'd never have told you as much as he did.'

Woodend smiled indulgently. 'Ah, youth!'

'What do you mean by that?' Rutter asked, sounding slightly offended.

'Just that growin' older tends to change the way you look at life,' Woodend replied.

'You mean, you get more cynical?'

'No, I don't mean that at all. It's more to do with time an' memory than attitude.'

'Go on,' Rutter said.

'The things I did as a kid are more vivid to me now than they've ever been,' Woodend said. 'I can remember the first soapbox car I ever had. An' I mean remember it *in every detail*. I can still feel that rough string in my hands. I can still smell the rubber of the tyres. On the other hand, there's parts of the war which are becomin' so distant that they're startin' to seem like they happened to somebody else. An' in a way, they did. Because while the kids we once were will always be locked up somewhere inside us, I'm certainly not the same man as I was on that Normandy beach in 1944.'

'But how does that apply to Bithwaite?'

'Back in 1934 he was workin' for a man he didn't like – a man he didn't even consider his equal. It was tearin' him apart. Then he began to see a solution to his problem. If he killed Dodds, there was a good chance he could step into the bastard's shoes himself. At the time, he had so much rage in him that he murdered Dodds in a particularly violent way. But thirty years have passed since then. He's an old man now. He doesn't experience the same depths of passion as he used to, an' when he talks about Dodds it's almost like he's describin' a dream – a dream in which the murder plays only a small, terminal part. Then I press the wrong button by sayin' that he couldn't stand Dodds, could he? It doesn't really make him feel guilty – it's very difficult to feel guilty about somethin' you did half a lifetime ago – but it does put him on his guard, an' he switches from being a jovial old duffer to a feller who can't wait to get us out of his office.'

'So Bithwaite's the one you're putting your money on?'

'I'm certainly not pullin' him out of the race at this stage. Which is not to say I'm willin' to dismiss Cuthburtson, either. Put through that inquiry to the Mounties, and then see whether you can find out any more about the causes of the ill feelin' that sprung up between the partners.'

'It won't be easy after all this time,' Rutter told him.

'Nothin's easy after all this time,' Woodend agreed. 'But you have to play the cards you've been given as best you can.'

Rutter grinned. 'You're getting very philosophical today,' he said. 'Where's Paniatowski, by the way?'

'It wouldn't do you any harm to call her "Monika" now and again,' Woodend pointed out.

Rutter grimaced. 'All right, sir. If it makes you any happier – where's *Monika*?'

'I've sent her up to Hebden Row, to find out what she can about the married life of the Doddses,' Woodend said. He glanced towards the door, and frowned. 'Fasten your seatbelts. It's goin' to be a bumpy night.'

'What?'

'Bette Davis in *All About Eve*,' Woodend said, with mock despair. 'Another thing that you're too bloody young to remember.'

'I still don't see . . .'

'Prepare yourself for an unexpected – an' definitely *unwanted* – visitor,' Woodend told him. He looked up. 'Good afternoon, Miss Hartley. Why don't you take a seat?'

Jane Hartley sat. She was dressed in a severely cut beige suit with a definite masculine feel to it. Her hair was tied in a tight bun at the back of her head, and there was a look of fierce determination – but also, Woodend thought, of vulnerability – on her face.

'I take it that you've got some new information which you wanted to give us?' Woodend said.

The question seemed to knock Jane Hartley off balance. 'No,' she said. 'No I don't have any new . . . I just thought . . .'

'So why are you here?' Woodend said, speaking crisply though not unkindly. 'You surely can't expect any results from us yet. We've been on the case for less than a day.'

'So you are *on* the case?' Jane Hartley countered.

'Meanin' what?'

'Meaning you are actually investigating.'

'Yes.'

'Because it would be a mistake just to try and fob me off, you know.' Jane Hartley's eyes narrowed. 'A very, very grave mistake.'

Woodend sighed. 'We all know what a big important lawyer you are, Miss Hartley,' he said. 'An' trust me on this, we're all far too frightened of you not to follow out your wishes to the letter.' He grinned. 'Now we've got that out of the way, would you like a drink?'

Jane Hartley coloured slightly. 'Yes . . . I mean no. It's a little early in the day for me.'

But you'd like one, wouldn't you? the Chief Inspector thought, noticing the way her eyes strayed towards the optics. You'd *really* like one.

'Why do you think your mother decided to marry Fred Dodds?' he said aloud.

'I beg your pardon?'

'We know more about Fred Dodds now than we did when we talked to you yesterday. I can't say that what we've learned has impressed us all that much. He seemed to be a rough an' ready sort. So I was wonderin' why your mother – an Oxford-educated parson's daughter – should have chosen to marry a man like him.'

'Perhaps she'd fallen in love with him,' Jane Hartley said, instantly defensive.

'Perhaps she had,' Woodend agreed. 'But by all accounts, he wasn't a very wise choice. Besides, I can't help askin' myself how they ever got to meet in the first place.'

'Why *shouldn't* they have met?'

'Well, because he was a reasonably successful business-man who probably moved in quite prominent social circles.'

'And?'

'An' she was nothin' more than a humble filin' clerk, who can't have got about town much, because she had a little kid at home to look after.'

'What are you implying?' Jane Hartley demanded, the flush in her cheeks now more the result of anger than embarrassment. 'That she tracked him down like some kind of big game hunter? That she was tired of living in a small cottage on a meagre salary, and set her sights on a man – any man – with money? That she decided *I'd* have a better chance in life if she was married to someone who could buy me my opportunities? Is that what you're saying?'

'No, not me,' Woodend countered softly. 'Truth is, I rather think it's what *you're* sayin'.'

The tower of rage that Jane Hartley had built for herself cracked, and then crumbled.

'I don't *know* why my mother married him,' she said in a voice that could almost have belonged to a little girl. 'I was too young then to understand what was going on – and that's the truth, whatever *you* seem to think. I admit that I have wondered since if she did it for the money – if she did it for me – but that shouldn't make any difference, should it? We've already agreed that she couldn't have killed him, because if she had, she'd have gone about it in a much cleverer way. We have agreed that,' she continued, sounding increasingly desperate, 'haven't we?'

'I'm certainly willin' to agree that it would be surprisin' if an intelligent woman like her was responsible for such a crude murder,' Woodend said cautiously.

'You still haven't answered my question – and you know it!'

'I'd like to tell you what you *want* to hear, lass,' Woodend said. 'But at this stage in the investigation I couldn't even swear that *you* didn't kill Fred Dodds. You'll just have to learn to be patient.'

Jane Hartley nodded, and it was obvious to him that she was fighting a losing battle to hold back her tears.

'I'll try be patient,' she promised, 'but it's a very hard thing to do when you seem to have been waiting for an answer for most your life.'

'Aye, I can see that,' Woodend said.

'And if I'm to be patient, then first I need to know that I trust you. I *can* trust you, can't I?'

'It would be easy enough for me to say yes, but it wouldn't mean anythin',' Woodend told her.

'Why wouldn't it?'

'Because the trust can't come from me – it has to come from deep inside you.'

Jane Hartley gazed at him – through tear-streaked eyes – for well over a minute.

'I *do* trust you,' she said finally. 'I believe you'll uncover the truth – whatever it takes.'

'An' whoever I have to hurt,' Woodend reminded her.

'Yes,' Jane Hartley agreed. 'I believe you'll uncover the truth whoever you have to hurt.'

Seven

Neither the passage of time nor the machinations of man had treated Hebden Brow very kindly, Monika Paniatowski thought. Thirty years earlier, when Margaret Dodds lived there, it must have stood on the very edge of Whitebridge. The houses would all have been single family residences, probably owned by mill managers, successful doctors, and businessmen who were still not *quite* rich enough to buy themselves houses which had grounds, rather than gardens. Then, the moors would have sloped gently upwards, away from the backs of the houses, while the rest of the town climbed aspiringly towards their fronts. But that golden age was long gone. Now most of the houses themselves had been converted into flats, and the untrammelled wilderness behind them had been conquered by a brash new council estate.

Paniatowski stood at the front door of *the* house – the one in which Fred Dodds had met his bloody end – and examined the four bell pulls. It was unlikely, she decided, that anyone living in the house now had known the Doddses. In fact, given the transient nature of both fame and infamy, it was unlikely that any of them had even *heard* of the notorious hammer murderer and her victim-husband. So was there even any point in asking?

'You! Young woman! Are you from the council?' asked a husky voice to her left.

Monika turned towards the driveway of the next house. The speaker had short white hair, and at first Monika thought

it was a man. Then she noticed that below the severe tweed
jacket were an equally severe tweed skirt and a pair of strong
legs clad in sensible woollen stockings.

'Are you deaf?' the woman demanded. 'I asked you if
you were from the council.'

'Why should I be?' Monika countered.

'Because after all the letters of complaint I've written to
the town hall, I've a right to expect them to get off their
backsides and send somebody round.'

'Well, I'm afraid I'm *not* from the council,' Monika
confessed. 'I'm from the police.'

'Really?' the woman asked sceptically.

'Really,' Monika assured her.

'So what exactly is your position in the Force? Are you
some kind of officer-wallah or something?'

'No, I'm a detective sergeant.'

'The Major – that's my husband – always used to maintain
that you should never send a woman to do a man's job. But I
suppose times change, whether we want them to or not.' The
tweedy woman sighed. 'Still, if there's one thing I learned
on the North West Frontier, it's to work with whatever
authority is around,' she continued, brightening a little,
'and I'm sure that a few days behind bars will do those
hooligans a great deal more good than a strongly worded
letter from some jack-in-office down at the town hall would
ever have done.'

'I'm not sure I'm following you,' Monika confessed. 'A
few days behind bars would do *who* more good?'

'Those bohemians in the upstairs flat next door. The ones
who play their filthy jazz music until nearly dawn,' the
woman said. 'You really are remarkably poorly informed
for an officer of the law, you know.'

'I'm not here about your neighbours,' Paniatowski said.

'You're not?'

'At least, not about the neighbours you've got now.'

A look of comprehension came to the tweedy woman's

weather-beaten face. 'You want to ask about the Dodds family,' she said.

'That's right. Did you know them?'

'Far better than I ever wished to,' the woman replied. She glanced quickly up and down the street. 'We'd better go inside, because the people who live around here nowadays can smell a police officer from a mile away – and if they see me talking to one now, they'll only think that the Major's been threatening to horsewhip someone again.'

The woman – Mrs Fortesque – led Paniatowski into her living room. There was a tigerskin rug on the floor, and garish Indian prints hung from the walls.

'We moved in here in 1931, the Major and I,' she said, indicating to the detective sergeant that she should sit down. 'In those days it was generally understood that if a soldier was prepared to serve his twenty-five years – and was willing to live fairly modestly after that – he should be able to retire in his late forties. Which is what the Major did. He came from land-owning stock in this area, so when we left British India, this is where we put down our roots.'

'And you said you knew the Doddses,' Paniatowski prompted.

'That's right. It's entirely due to them that Hebden Brow went into such decline.'

'Because of the way they behaved when they were living here?'

'That, too! But what I'm really talking about is what happened as a result of the murder. How would you feel about buying a house in which you knew someone had been recently battered to death on the lounge carpet?'

'I wouldn't really fancy the idea.'

'No, and neither did anyone else. The house stayed empty until the end of the war. Then, what with all the damage done to housing in general by Jerry's bombing, plus the fact that people suddenly had more money in their pockets, there was a strong demand for accommodation. That was when some bright spark got the idea of turning the house next door into flats. As soon as we got a whiff of it, of course, the Major and I tried to buy the place ourselves.'

'Why?'

'Because we knew that the sort of people who took the flats would not be the sort we were used to living side by side with. Unfortunately, we couldn't meet the asking price, even when we'd scraped together all the capital we could lay our hands on. So we had no choice but to sit back and watch as the commercial travellers and assistant shop managers moved in. And once the rot had started, it soon spread. Our other neighbours didn't like the change any more than we did. They sold their houses – to property developers naturally, since they were the ones who were offering the highest price – and that really sealed the neighbourhood's fate.'

'Why didn't you move yourself?' Paniatowski asked – aware that it had nothing to do with her investigation, but still curious.

Mrs Fortesque looked embarrassed. 'The Major was a very dependable soldier,' she said. 'Not as showy as some I could mention, but he did his duty well enough.'

'I'm afraid I don't see . . .'

'The strain of helping to run an empire was starting to tell on him even during our last couple of years in India. By the time we needed to sell this house, his nerve had gone completely. He just couldn't stand the idea of any upheaval, you see. So here we stayed.'

There was a short, somewhat embarrassing silence, then Paniatowski said, 'You were going to tell me about the Doddses.'

'That's right, the Doddses. Mr Dodds was some sort of importer-exporter. Claimed to be quite keen on the Conservative Party, though I'm not sure how genuine that was.'

'You think he was putting on an act?'

'I think he wanted to get on in the world – meet the right people. He would have liked to be a gentleman, you see. Even tried to pretend that he already *was* one, though as far as I was concerned he was about as convincing as a punkah-wallah wearing spats and a monocle.'

Which was roughly what Mr Bithwaite had said, Paniatowski thought.

'What about Mrs Dodds?' she asked.

'Different kettle of fish entirely. It was obvious that she'd been brought up in what we used to call "genteel poverty".'

'So they were very different?'

'Yes, not that that's *necessarily* a bad thing. Nowadays people talk far too much about the *romance* of marriage, and far too little about what each of the partners can contribute to it. My own marriage was as much an arranged one as any of the Indian marriages that we presume to look down on, but still the Major and I . . .' She paused. 'I do go on, don't I? Must be something to do with my age.'

'I don't mind,' Paniatowski said, only a *little* insincerely.

'Well, I *do* mind. People are willing enough to call the old gaga as it is, without us wandering off the point and giving them more fuel for their fires. So – to get back *on* the point – what was I saying?'

'That the Doddses were very different to each other?'

'That's right. That may have been the reason they decided to get married – because each of them could bring a different strength to that marriage. She, you see, gave him a little more class. And in return, he gave Margaret and Jane financial security.'

Mr Bithwaite, in slightly less charitable terms, had said basically the same thing, Paniatowski thought.

'So you remember Jane, do you?' she asked.

'Of course I remember her. She'd be hard to forget. She was a beautiful child. The Major and I never felt any urge to have any children of our own, yet we'd catch each other looking doe-eyed at little Jane.'

'Was it a happy marriage?'

There was a faint tapping on the door. 'If you'll excuse me a moment, that'll be the Major,' Mrs Fortesque said.

She stood up, walked across the lounge, and opened the door to reveal a frail old man with a bald head and a huge white moustache.

'Have you had a good rest, Major dear?' Mrs Fortesque asked, raising her voice slightly.

The old man looked slightly panicked, as if such a question were far too complicated for him to answer.

'A good rest?' Mrs Fortesque repeated.

'Yes . . . I . . . I . . .'

'Well then, come and sit down, Major dear. I'll make you a nice cup of tea as soon as I've finished talking to this young woman.'

The Major crossed the lounge in a slow shuffle, while his wife followed closely behind him in case her help was needed. The walk appeared to exhaust the old man, and he sank gratefully into an overstuffed leather armchair, which all but swallowed him up.

Mrs Fortesque returned to her own seat opposite Paniatowski's.

'You were asking if the Doddses' marriage was a happy one,' she said. 'It seemed to be happy enough when they first moved in, but then they started having loud arguments – or, at least, she was loud.'

'What were they arguing about?'

'I'm not the kind of person who eavesdrops on her neighbours' disputes,' Mrs Fortesque said, with a hint of reproach in her voice. 'Whenever it got heated enough for me to hear, I turned the wireless on.'

'Do you remember anything about the night on which Mr Dodds was murdered?'

'Not likely to forget, am I, not with all the fuss it caused.'

'So what can you tell me?'

'We must have had half the Whitebridge police force outside the front door,' Mrs Fortesque said.

'No, I don't mean that. I meant *before* that.'

'Before?'

'Did anything unusual happen?'

Mrs Fortesque laughed. 'Not anything you'd call unusual in this day and age.'

'But something you would have called unusual *back then*?'

'Yes, I suppose I would,' Mrs Fortesque said. 'In 1934, the motor car was still something of a novelty, you see. Even quite rich people regarded an automobile as a luxury. I don't think there were more than two or three of them on this entire brow. And we certainly weren't used to them driving past the house at a hundred miles an hour, as we are now.'

'Go on,' Paniatowski said encouragingly.

'I heard two cars that night. I wasn't paying particular attention, but I'd have said that they were about half an hour apart. And both of them stopped very close to here. I wouldn't be willing to swear to it under oath, but I'm almost certain they pulled up next door.'

'Did they stay long?'

'No. Not more than a minute each time.'

'Jane!' Major Fortesque said suddenly. 'They came for little Jane!'

A look that was half compassion, half irritation, swept across Mrs Fortesque's face.

'Who did, Major dear?' she asked, turning towards her husband. 'Who came for her?'

'They took her away,' the old man said.

'We're talking about the night Mr Dodds was murdered,' Mrs Fortesque said patiently.

'*Why* did they take her away?' the Major mumbled.

Mrs Fortesque turned back to Paniatowski. 'He'd grown

quite fond of Jane,' she explained. 'He took it very badly when he couldn't see her any more.'

'Was Jane here on the night her stepfather was murdered?' Paniatowski asked.

'Shouldn't that information be somewhere in your records?' Mrs Fortesque asked. Her eyes suddenly narrowed with realization and suspicion. 'You're not trying to test my memory, are you?'

'No, I . . .'

'Not trying to find out whether or not I'm any more than just a batty old lady?'

'No, of course not,' Paniatowski lied.

'Then, in answer to your question, no, Jane wasn't here on the night her stepfather was murdered. She was spending a week with her aunt – the one who adopted her after her mother was hanged. She'd been gone about three days when Frederick Dodds was killed. There! Have I passed the test which you protest – a little too loudly in my opinion – that you never set me?'

'I . . . er . . . really, I'd have asked anybody, of any age, the same question,' Paniatowski said, hoping that she was not blushing as much as she thought she deserved to be.

She searched her mind for some distraction – anything to steer the conversation away from the fact that she'd tried to trick the old woman and been thoroughly caught out.

'How . . . how long was it between the second car going away and the police arriving?' she asked.

'I don't think it can have been more than ten minutes. I might be wrong, of course. Thirty years is a long time to remember something like that, especially . . .' and she gave Paniatowski a look that showed that she had not forgotten and still not quite forgiven, '. . . especially for a batty old lady like I am.'

'I'm sure you're right,' Paniatowski said.

'But don't take my word for it,' the old lady continued relentlessly. 'If you want to be certain, you can always read the statement I made to the police at the time, now can't you?'

'Yes, I suppose I can,' Paniatowski agreed.

At least, I can read it if it's still there, she thought. I can read it if, in the interest of making the case against Margaret Dodds tidier and more straightforward, it hasn't been removed and destroyed by Chief Inspector Sharpe.

Eight

B ob Rutter placed the documents which Jane Hartley's private detectives had prepared for her at the left-hand edge of his desk, and the documentation from Chief Inspector Sharpe's investigation to his right.

The difference between the two sets of papers was striking. The barrister's detectives had produced a small series of concise reports, each one typed (with double spacing) on foolscap paper, and presented in a crisp new folder. There were considerably more documents from the original investigation. They were yellow with age, and thick with dust. Some were typed, some handwritten, some typed with handwritten annotations in the margins. They were stacked in a tower that both dwarfed the newer collection of documents and – given the tower's tendency to sway – threatened to bury them.

Rutter picked up one of the newer files and began to look for something he could cross-reference with similar material from the earlier investigation. It took him no time at all to decide that Harold Brunskill would provide him with as good a starting point as any.

Brunskill himself was long since dead, Jane Hartley's detectives reported. However, they had spoken to the deceased man's daughter. She quite clearly recalled that shortly after Margaret Dodds' arrest her father had gone to the police station, to volunteer the information that he had seen the very same woman some distance away from Hebden Brow at the time the murder was supposed to have taken place.

70

The daughter had never learned what happened during her father's interview with the police. She had tried to ask him about it on a number of occasions, she told the private detectives, but he had immediately become guarded and insisted that she let the matter drop.

Whatever the result of the interview, Rutter thought, it was significant that Brunskill – whose statement could have raised reasonable doubt in the minds of the jury – had never been called to give evidence.

So what *had* occurred during the interview, he asked himself as he reached across to the perilous tower of the earlier investigation. And would any evidence of it still be in existence?

He was moderately surprised to discover that there was indeed a record of it – to find, in fact, a handwritten report on the subject near the top of the stack.

INTERVIEW WITH HAROLD BRUNSKILL

Harold Brunskill (53) of 17 Bradshaw Row, Whitebridge, was questioned as to his claim that he had seen Margaret Dodds coming out of the telephone box in front of St Mary's Church at approximately the time Frederick Dodds met his death. Since the church is a mile away from the Dodds family home, it was decided that his claim should be investigated more fully.

Brunskill has a long criminal record, and at first it was suspected that he might have been bribed by friends of Margaret Dodds to provide her with an alibi. However, this suspicion was probably unfounded, since within minutes of the interview starting Brunskill made the totally unsolicited statement that he now thought that he had made a mistake. He had indeed seen a woman resembling Margaret Dodds, he admitted, but looking at the photograph he now saw in front of him, he felt that the resemblance was not close.

Besides, he had confused his dates, and it was the day *before* the murder that he had seen the woman. I asked him if he was sure of that, and he said that he was. I asked him how he had come to make such a mistake, and he explained that the doctor had prescribed him heart pills, which sometimes made him confused. Finally, just to make certain that it was his *initial* statement which was incorrect, I asked if it would help if I were to place MD outside the church, on the spot where he at first he claimed to have seen her, and have him stand on the spot from which he had made the observation. He said it would not, as he was now sure both that he had made the observation on another day and the woman he had seen had not been MD. He apologized for having wasted my time.

The signature at the bottom of the page was DCI Sharpe.

It was not a perfect report by any means, Rutter thought. But given that it had been written back in the Old Stone Age of policing, it was not half bad. And it certainly suggested that, whatever Jane Hartley's detectives might have thought, this witness at least had seen nothing that might help her case.

Rutter put the file to one side and began a fresh search, totally ignorant of the knowledge that – some two hundred miles away from Whitebridge – thoughts of Harold Brunskill were simultaneously engaging another mind.

Lord Sharpe stood on the Embankment, his back to the Houses of Parliament. His eyes were fixed on the grey swirling water of the Thames, but in his head he was picturing Brunskill as he had looked on that late afternoon in 1934.

Brunskill had been a scruffy individual – battered boots, darned shirt and a greasy flat cap. He had not even bothered to shave before presenting himself at the police station. And there in the interview room – standing, because he had not been invited to sit down – he seemed so frightened that Sharpe thought there was a distinct possibility he would piss himself.

The man had had no self-respect, the former chief inspector thought – no self-respect at all.

'*So you're here to put Margaret Dodds in the clear for this murder, are you, Harry?*' Sharpe asked, *deliberately injecting a nasty, threatening edge into his voice.*

Brunskill nervously fingered the cap he was holding with both his hands. '*I wouldn't put it quite like that, Mr Sharpe.*'

'*Then how would you put it?*'

'*I . . . I just thought I'd better tell you what I saw.*'

'*Now that was really kind and thoughtful of you, Harry. And I want you to know that, caught up in the middle of a murder inquiry as I am, I have all the time in the world to listen to toe-rags like you.*'

'*Do . . . do you want me to say what it was I saw?*'

Sharpe sighed theatrically. '*Yes, I suppose you might as well, now that you're here.*'

'*I saw the woman. She was just comin' out of the phone box in front of St Mary's. I looked up at the church clock. It was twenty-past eight.*'

'*How convenient that you chose to check on the time just at that moment,*' *Sharpe said, disbelievingly.*

'*It's the truth, Mr Sharpe!*'

'*Now when you say you saw* the *woman coming out of the phone box, I assume that what you mean is that you saw a woman.*'

'*Beg pardon, Mr Sharpe?*'

'*A woman, not* the *woman.*'

'*No, it was her all right, Mr Sharpe. Mrs Dodds. She was wearing a black an' white check frock, just like the one she was wearin' in the picture of her bein' arrested in the newspaper.*'

Sharpe took a packet of cigarettes out of his pocket, but despite the look of expectation in Brunskill's eyes, he did not offer him one.

'How far away from her were you, Harry?' he asked, slipping one of the cigarettes between his lips and lighting it up.

'How far? Couldn't have been more than a few yards.'

'Were you wearing your glasses?'

'I don't have no glasses, Mr Sharpe.'

'So you got only a blurred picture of her at best.'

'The reason I don't have no glasses is because I don't need *'em. I've never been one to wear out my eyes by readin'.'*

Sharpe took a long, thoughtful drag on his cigarette. 'There's one thing I don't understand, Harry.'

'An' what's that, Mr Sharpe?'

'Before today, you've never voluntarily entered a police station in your life. Why the sudden change of heart?'

'I . . . I think it was the birth of my grandson that did it.'

'Is that supposed to make sense to me?'

'Probably not. You see, Mr Sharpe, he's a beautiful little kid. He reminds me of his mother at his age.'

'Very touching, I'm sure,' Sharpe said with a sneer.

'I never saw much of our Bessie when she was growin' up, like, because I was always doin' time. An' if I go down again with my record, it'll be for a ten stretch.'

'At least a ten stretch,' Sharpe agreed. 'At the very least. Get to the point, Harry.'

'I don't want to lose out on my grandson like I lost out on my daughter. I want to take him fishin'. I want to see his eyes light up when I give him his Christmas presents.'

'Do you know, I'm almost in tears.'

'So I've got to stay out of trouble, haven't I, Mr Sharpe? More than that – I've got to be a model citizen. That's why

I'm here. Because I'm doin' my duty – just like a model citizen should.'

Sharpe nodded. 'A model citizen,' he repeated. 'So you've not committed any new crimes recently?'

'No. I swear I haven't. Not since little Wilf was born.'

'You haven't done any shoplifting?'

'No.'

'You haven't received any stolen property?'

'No.'

'How about burglaries?'

'I told you, I—'

'Do you know that row of big houses not far from St Mary's Church?' Sharpe interrupted.

'I've seen 'em,' Brunskill said defensively.

'Must be lots of rich pickings for a burglar in places like them.'

'Maybe there is, but—'

'On the night of the murder, one of those houses was broken into. We don't have any suspects for the crime at the moment, but now we know that you were in the vicinity at the time, well . . .'

Sharpe let his words trail off into nothingness. Brunskill, he noted, was sweating.

'I haven't heard of no burglaries in any of them houses, Mr Sharpe,' Brunskill said.

The DCI nodded. 'That's because none has been officially reported – yet! But one could be reported, Harry, if you get my meaning. You do get my meaning, don't you?'

Brunskill bowed his head. 'Yes, I get your meanin', Mr Sharpe,' he mumbled.

'So let me ask you again,' Sharpe said. 'Where exactly were you at eight twenty on the night of the murder of Frederick Dodds?'

'I . . . I was at home.'

'You're sure of that?'

'I didn't leave the house all day.'

Sharpe smiled. 'That's just what I thought you'd say, Harry,' he told the other man.

The deep groan of a tug's hooter wrenched Sharpe out of his recollections and deposited him squarely in the middle of his present cold reality.

It was thirty years since that interview with scruffy little Harry Brunskill, he reminded himself – long enough for the past to fade almost to invisibility, for words spoken and actions taken to be all but forgotten. In truth, he had thought that was just what *had* happened. And then he'd got that warning phone call from Chief Constable Henry Marlowe, and had felt all the certainties he'd built his life and career on begin to slip away.

The woman had been *guilty*, despite the fact that some of the evidence might have seemed to suggest otherwise. Any policeman who had been assigned to the case would have come to that conclusion. And even if there was a slight, remote – almost infinitesimal – chance that she hadn't killed her husband, did any of that really matter now?

If she'd lived, she would probably have led an unremarkable life, whereas her death had helped him to be elected to parliament, from where he had been able to help hundreds – perhaps thousands – of women just like Margaret Dodds. Yes, it had been a more than fair exchange. If she had, in fact, been sacrificed, then it had all been for a very good cause.

Big Ben struck the hour, and Sharpe looked up at the clock – just as Harry Brunskill must have looked up at St Mary's clock all those years ago.

Even now, there *shouldn't* be a problem. The officer in charge of the case should, by rights, recognize the fact that Sharpe had once been in the Force himself – and thus do him the professional courtesy of granting his investigation a clean bill of health; and no doubt most officers would. But Charlie Woodend – so Sharpe had learned from his contacts in Scotland Yard – was unquestionably *not* most officers.

The mess needed to be cleared up, Eric Sharpe told

himself. And it needed to be cleaned up in the *right* way. Because if it were not, it could bring him down. And whatever his personal wishes in the matter – however much he might wish to spare his colleagues – the situation was such that he would not go down alone.

Nine

Woodend had been driving around the old part of town, more or less aimlessly, for the best part of an hour. Now, as dusk began to fall, he decided it was probably time to stretch his legs a little. He turned left up Grimshaw Street, and was almost surprised to discover that the cinder track that ran from the end of the street down to the old canal was just where it had always been.

He parked his Wolseley at the end of the track, and as he climbed out of it he felt the cinders crunch beneath his feet. He'd been back in Whitebridge for over two years, he reminded himself. Two years! And never once – until now – had he contemplated paying a visit to the part of the town in which he'd grown up.

He wondered why that should be. Was it, perhaps, because he was not self-indulgent enough to roll around nostalgically in his past? Or could it be that looking back would only serve to remind him of how long his journey had been thus far – and how comparatively little of it there was left?

'You're gettin' philosophical again, Charlie,' he said out loud. 'It'll be the death of you yet.'

He lit up a cigarette and turned to face the old Empire Mill. It was still the massive structure he remembered, towering over the surrounding area and making all the buildings close to it look as tiny and fragile as doll's houses. Its original red brick had been turned black by a century of industrial filth, yet that only seemed to add to its power – transmuting it from a mere man-made object into something as solid and immovable as a mountain.

Woodend let his gaze shift to the chimney stack, which – on the whimsy of an industrial architect now long dead – had been built as an exact replica of a bell tower that was to be found in Florence. What kind of brain had it taken to come up with such an idea – to decide to recreate one of the glories of Renaissance Italy within the confines of a dark satanic mill?

There was nowt as queer as folk, the Chief Inspector thought – and that was a fact.

His own father had started working at this mill at fourteen, on the very day he had left school. Back then, it had been a true symbol of British industry, turning out cotton cloth by the mile. Charlie himself had been taken around the mill as a boy, and had bathed in the warm glow of the respect that his father – who was no more than a common tackler – was shown by both workers and bosses alike. He remembered gazing up at the machinery, wondering how *anything* could be so powerful. He recalled, still a little guiltily, stealing for himself some of the pride that the workers took in knowing that the cloth they made covered the whole world.

It had seemed to him then that anything so majestic was sure to go on for ever. He had, of course, been completely wrong. Even by the time Sam Woodend died – just a couple of weeks short of his fifty-second birthday – the mill had become a shadow of its old self. And now, a quarter of a century beyond that, the place stood empty against the skyline – a monument to its own former glory, a stark reminder that even the greatest empire in the world had been built on shifting sands.

Not that the building was *quite* empty, he noted. For just as the corpse of a mighty beast will soon be invaded by scavengers, so too it was now possible to buy mass-produced Pakistani carpets, retread car tyres and second-hand furniture from the smaller businesses that had sprung up within the shell of the once-vast one.

Woodend turned his back on the mill to face the streets that surrounded it – row upon row of terraced houses running in long, straight lines. They no longer served as the homes of mill workers, but the road names still reflected their golden past – Calcutta Street, Rawalpindi Row, Bombay Terrace. They, too, were living on borrowed time. Soon they would be gone – cleared away to make space for housing estates with every modern convenience.

And a good thing too, the Chief Inspector thought – though he could not but feel a pang of regret for the sense of community that would, inevitably, be destroyed in the process.

He walked to the end of one of these cobbled streets – streets built for clogs, not shoes with leather soles – and reached a pub called the Red Lion. It, at least, did not look much changed since the days when he himself had stood at the counter – puffing on a Park Drive and trying desperately to act as if he were eighteen. He pushed the door open and entered the public bar.

As Bob Rutter drove around the corner, he saw his young-executive semi-detached house up ahead of him. In the earlier years of his marriage, it had not been unusual for him to find the house in complete darkness. It wasn't that the place had been empty – Maria would invariably be waiting for him, with his evening meal bubbling away on the stove – it was simply that the electric light was neither a help nor a hindrance to his wife. But things had changed since the baby had been born. Now, looking up at the nursery window, he could see a night light burning.

Maria was waiting for him at the front door. They kissed, then he followed her down the hall. She was so well aware of the obstacles in her own little kingdom, he thought, that anyone who had not met her before could be excused for assuming that she could see. He knew there had been people who'd never imagined that he would marry her once she'd gone blind. Perhaps she'd even thought it herself. But he'd never had any doubts. He'd loved her then, and he loved her still.

'Dinner will be about fifteen minutes,' she said. 'I expect you'd like a beer first.'

'I'd sell my soul for one,' he admitted.

She brought his drink, then sat down next to him. 'What's the problem?' she asked.

She could always tell when he was troubled. 'It's just something Cloggin'-it Charlie said to me today,' he admitted.

'What about?'

'Do *you* think I'm unfair to Paniatowski?'

'Unfair?'

'Perhaps that's not the right word. Do you think I'm unduly antagonistic to her? Am I less tolerant of her than I would be of another sergeant?'

'Do you know any other female sergeants to *be* tolerant of?'

He'd been thinking in terms of rank, not sex, and Maria's comment took him by surprise. 'Are you saying I'm against her because she's a *woman*?'

'Perhaps. You don't fancy her, do you?'

'Of course not! Why do you ask that?'

'It's just that sometimes the way the pair of you act reminds me of school children.'

'I don't see any comparison at all,' he said, slightly huffily.

'Perhaps if you hadn't attended an all-boys school you would. In a *normal* school, you could always tell when a boy had a crush on a girl, because he'd be horrible to her. He'd punch her on the arm, or dip her pigtail in the ink well.'

He could either be amused or annoyed. He decided on amusement. 'You're not jealous, are you?'

'I didn't think I was. Now I'm not so sure.'

'Do you think that wicked old witch Sergeant Paniatowski is trying to steal your big boy away from you?' he asked, lapsing into baby talk.

'No, but . . .'

'The only crush I feel for Paniatowski is a desire to crush her windpipe now and again. And that's mild in comparison to what I suspect she'd like to do to me.'

Maria smiled. 'I was on the point of becoming silly, wasn't I?'

'Yes,' Rutter agreed. 'But there's no need to apologize for it. I like it if you get jealous occasionally. It shows I'm wanted.'

They had wine with their dinner – a Rioja specially imported for Maria's father. They talked about the baby and the Margaret Dodds case. It was towards the end of the meal that she said, 'Do you think there is any chance you'll be able to take Sunday off?'

'It all depends on how the case goes. Why do you ask?'

'I thought we might drive out into the countryside,' Maria said. 'Like we used to.'

Like they used to!

They'd climb to the top of a hill, and claim all they saw below them as their personal fiefdom. They could still do that, he supposed. True, Maria couldn't see, but she could smell and hear. And when he described things to her, she could draw on her old memories. But it just wasn't the same any more. She could imagine a skylark, but she couldn't see the *particular* skylark he was watching – couldn't share in this unique moment with him.

Didn't it distress her that they had lost something they once had together? he wondered. Because it certainly bloody well distressed him!

'Well, what about it?' Maria asked. 'Do you fancy a drive in the country on Sunday?'

Rutter felt a sudden stabbing pain in his chest. 'I told you, it depends on how the case goes,' he said, sounding harsher than he'd intended.

Most of the drinkers in the Red Lion that night had probably been no more than babies when the Empire Mill had finally shut down its machinery, Woodend thought. But there was *one* very old man – sitting alone in the corner and sipping slowly and carefully at a glass of Guinness – who looked vaguely familiar.

The Chief Inspector bought a pint of bitter and a bottle of stout, then made his way over to the table.

'Do you mind if I join you?' he asked.

The old man ran his watery eyes up and down the Chief Inspector's frame. 'Tha's Sam Woodend's lad, Charlie,' he said.

'That's right, I am.'

The old man nodded. 'I've read about thy doin's in the paper. Tha's a big, important bobby now, isn't tha?'

'Well, a bobby, anyway,' Woodend admitted.

'So why is tha standin' there like a long streak o' piss? Take the weight off thy feet, lad.'

Woodend sat down. 'I've bought this for you,' he said, sliding the Guinness across the table.

'Aye, I didn't think tha'd bought it for tha'sen,' the old man said. 'Tha doesn't remember me, does tha?'

'Not the name,' Woodend admitted.

'I'm Zachariah Clegg. I used to go whippet racin' with thy dad. One year I nearly had a regional champion.'

'Would you mind if I asked you a few questions?' Woodend said.

Clegg glanced down at the Guinness. 'I'm not so green as to have thought that come free,' he said. 'What is it tha want to know, lad?'

'I was wonderin' if you remembered Robert Hartley.'

'Which Robert Hartley? I've known a number of 'em in

my time. Is't tha talking about him whose wife was hanged for the murder of her second husband?'

'That's the man.'

'Aye, I remember him,' Zachariah Clegg said. 'He were a good-lookin' man, were Rob. Clever, an' all. He could have ended up as one of the bosses if he'd set his mind to it. But he never had the drive, tha sees, even though his missus did all she could to push him forward. So he ended up clerkin' in the office, an' earnin' not much more than a mill hand.'

'Margaret had ambitions for him, did she?' Woodend asked.

'I've just said as much, haven't I? She were a teacher when they met. An' I think she set her cap at him more because of what he could *become* than because of what he were then.'

'So he must have been somethin' of a disappointment to her?'

The old man sighed. 'Life's full of disappointments, lad,' he said. 'If that whippet of mine hadn't gone an' got lame just before the big race over in Accrington—'

'How did Rob Hartley die?' Woodend interrupted.

'It were an accident.'

'What kind of accident?'

'A tragic one.'

'They all are,' Woodend said, stifling his impatience. 'How did this particular tragic one occur?'

'It were the booze what caused it. Rob'd not been much of a drinker when he were a lad, but for the last couple of years of his life, he were hittin' the bottle regular – an' not just after workin' hours neither. Anyway, this partic'lar afternoon he must have done a fair amount of cork sniffin', because when the head clerk sent him down the mill floor on some errand or other, he missed his footin' on the steps an' broke his neck.'

'He couldn't have been pushed, could he?'

The old man gave him a hard stare. 'What makes thee ask that?'

'I'm a bobby,' Woodend said. 'It's my job to be suspicious whenever there's a sudden death.'

'Well, tha's wastin' thy time on this one,' Zachariah Clegg said. 'He fell, right enough. There was more than dozen witnesses.'

'Was there any compensation for his widow?'

'There might well have been, if it hadn't been all his own fault. But tha couldn't very well put the blame on the mill when he were lyin' there stinkin' like a distillery.'

'So his widow got nothin'?'

'She still had her own job. She worked for Mr Earnshaw, tha knows.'

'So I've heard.'

'An' I have heard tell that the gaffer slipped her a few extra bob now an' again, out of the goodness of his heart an' from his own pocket. Still, without her husband's wages comin' in an' all, her an' the kiddie wasn't exactly livin' in the lap of luxury.'

'It was lucky for her that she met Fred Dodds then, wasn't it?' Woodend said.

'Lucky!' the old man said contemptuously. 'I suppose *some* folk might call it luck.'

'An' what would *you* call it?'

'Tha never asked me what caused Rob Hartley to start drinkin',' the old man said.

'No, I didn't,' Woodend agreed. 'What was the reason?'

'There's some as believe it was because he were disappointed that he didn't get that promotion what he put in for.'

'But you think that's wrong?'

'I think it were *her* that were disappointed.'

'I'm not sure I'm followin' you,' Woodend admitted.

'She gave up on him, didn't she?'

'How do you mean?'

'They was still married – still livin' in the same house – but she wanted nothin' more to do with him as a *man*. Well, that state of affairs couldn't go on for long, could it? I don't suppose that after a while it bothered Rob much that he weren't gettin' his end away, because by then he'd found out what good company a bottle can be. But she was still a young woman, an' young women need a proper seein' to every now an' again.'

'You're sayin' that she took a lover?'

'I don't know about that, but she certainly found herself a fancy man!'

'An' Rob didn't like that?'

'Even though he weren't up to doin' job himself any longer, he still took it hard that some bugger else had stepped into his clogs.'

'Do you have any idea who this fancy man might be?'

The old man shook his head, though in disbelief rather than in denial. 'Tha's not very bright for a boss bobby, ist tha?' he asked. 'It should be as plain as the nose on tha face who the fancy man was.'

'So what *was* his name?' Woodend probed stoically.

'Well, nobody can say for sure, because she was right careful about it. But the rumour goin' round the mill was that she were seein' Fred Dodds. An' if you believe what you hear, that weren't only time she strayed, neither.'

'You mean, there was someone *before* Dodds?'

'Nay, lad, *after* him.'

'After him, she was in prison.'

'*Durin'* him, then, if that's what you prefer.'

'Do you have any idea who this other man was?'

'Nay, but the lad what told me said *he* knew.'

'Then why wouldn't he tell you?'

'Said he didn't want to cause no trouble.'

'Maybe he was just pullin' your leg,' Woodend suggested.

The old man stiffened. 'I were never a Todmorton goat!' he said, sounding offended.

'A what?'

'Tha doesn't know the term?' Clegg asked, slightly contemptuously. 'Tha dad would've done!'

'Explain it to me.'

'There was always lads in the mill who'd believe whatever they were told, an' a lot of them came from Todmorton. The rest of the lads used to have a joke at their expense. When I think of the stories we'd come up with! An' them lads would take it as gospel truth. We were all laughin' at them, an' they never knew it. That's why we called them goats – because they'd swallow anythin'.'

'I see.'

'Tha'd never call a mate a Todmorton goat, because it was one o' the biggest insults you could come up with. An' I'm not best pleased to have a mate's son call me it, neither.'

'I never meant to suggest—'

'Besides, I've got more than just my mate's word for it. Did tha ever know Tommy Frisk?'

'No, I don't think I did.'

'Tommy couldn't do heavy work on account of his gammy leg, so he did odd jobs – window cleanin', sweepin' up, an' the like – for one of the solicitors in town. An' he heard things.'

'What kinds of things?'

The old man seemed to have regained some of his good humour, and smiled. 'Is tha sure I'm not treatin' thee like a Todmorton goat?' he asked.

Woodend grinned back at him. 'I'll take that chance.'

'One day shortly before he was murdered, Fred Dodds went to see this solicitor. He said he wanted a divorce, an' when the solicitor asked what the grounds was, he told him the grounds was adultery!'

Ten

J ane Hartley knew that she was dreaming. Or perhaps she only *thought* she knew. Or knew for *some of the time* and not for the rest.

Whatever!

Dream or reality, there was no doubt in her mind that this was her wedding night, and she was in a gorgeous bedroom in a luxury hotel that overlooked a romantic Italian lake.

The wedding had been perfect – as smooth as the silk in the revealing nightgown she'd just slipped into. Her head of chambers had agreed to give her away, and had led her down the aisle with a confidence and assurance that had made backing out seem almost impossible. The best man, her new husband's brother, had not lost the ring (as best men always seem to do in stories) but had handed it over to Ralph at just the right time. The bridesmaids, Ralph's three sisters, had looked lovely in their lilac dresses.

His mother had cried, his sisters had cried, Jane's Aunt Helen had cried. She and Ralph had danced the first dance at their reception and she had felt like Ginger Rogers to his Fred Astaire. Everybody agreed that – as justly befitted the union of a rising young barrister and an incredibly successful young businessman – it had been the wedding of the season. She had enjoyed it all so much that if Ralph had not literally dragged her away, they would have missed their plane.

Now, with the ceremony already hours behind them, she could hear the sounds of Ralph in the bathroom. He was brushing his teeth, and though she knew him to be the most fastidious of men, there was no doubt that tonight he was rushing through the whole process of preparing for bed.

She was not surprised at his haste. All their friends assumed that he had bedded her long ago – but all their friends were wrong. She had made it clear from the start that he would have to wait until they were married, and Ralph – dear, sweet Ralph – had told her that he did not mind, even though it must have been absolute torture for him. Well, now they were married, and she was determined to make it up to him – to prove that all the waiting had been worthwhile.

The bathroom door swung open, and Ralph stepped into the room. He, too, was wearing silk – blue silk pyjama bottoms. His torso was well muscled, his arms thick and strong. And he was an extraordinarily handsome man – everybody agreed about that.

He looked down at her and smiled. 'I've waited so long for this moment, my darling,' he said. 'I love you. I really do.'

No longer in the Italy of her honeymoon, but now lying in her lonely Whitebridge hotel bed, Jane felt a sudden sense of dread sweep over her. For she knew – from so many previous terrible experiences – that this was always the point at which the mood of the dream changed.

She pulled the bedding more tightly around her and prayed – as much as she *could* pray in her unconscious state – that this time it would be different. But she knew deep down that it wouldn't be – that it never was.

Her picture of the honeymoon suite had been so clear and sharp before, but now it started to change.

The furniture began to sway.

The colours of the room all melted into one another until she was seeing everything through a muddy red filter.

The voices were even worse.

When Ralph spoke again, his voice was deep, pained, and almost unintelligible – like the sound of a wounded beast moaning into a bucket.

When she answered her new husband, it was like the screech of a hysterical trapped bird.

His mouth began to move again, and Jane felt an overwhelming urge to damage him – to make him suffer.

She let her gaze travel slowly – contemptuously – down the length of his body, until it finally came to rest on his crotch. She did not even need to think of what words to say. They came naturally, spilling like poison from her mouth. She watched his expression move through all its inevitable stages – first shock, then disbelief, then hurt.

It was the final stage she hated the most – the one in which he began to make excuses for her.

She had been working very hard recently, he pointed out in his wounded beast roar. Besides, her last case had been so unpleasant that it must have been emotionally draining. And however much she had prepared herself for it, being married – being part of a couple – was bound to be a shock.

She felt nothing but disgust for his delaying tactics. Yet, she let him continue because – though he did not realize it himself – all he was doing was giving her more ammunition for her next attack.

Finally he came to the end of his plea on her behalf, and it was Jane's turn to speak.

How dare he find excuses for her, she demanded. Didn't he realize just how weak – how truly pathetic – he had sounded? If he couldn't be a man, could he at least try to act like one?

Ralph made one more attempt to pull them back from the brink of a disastrous first night together, but she was having none of it. She showered him with even more venom until – finally – he saw no other choice open to him but to act like the man she had challenged him to be.

It was always after Ralph had hit her the third or fourth time that she awoke from the dream and found herself lying between crumpled sheets, her body drenched in sweat, her lip and right eye both aching without any apparent cause. For the first few moments she did not normally even know where she was, then her eyes would focus on the walls of her bedroom, or her hotel room – and she would burst into tears.

And so it was that night – the first night she had spent in Whitebridge for so many years.

She could handle the nightmares, she told herself, as she hugged her legs to her and buried her face between her knees.

She *had* to handle them! There was simply no choice!

Because it wasn't being married to Ralph that had brought nightmares into her life. They had always been there – like huge carrion crows following in her wake.

She reached up and switched on the light. She had only to turn her head to see her bedside cabinet, yet she was afraid to – afraid that while she had been suffering on her own mental rack, a dark goblin had crept into the room and stolen her one source of solace.

She did turn – and gasped with relief when she saw that the whisky bottle was just where she'd left it.

'There should be a red cross on this bottle, you know,' she said, as if she were addressing some benevolent – though invisible – presence in the corner of room. 'Yes, a bright red cross. Because as God is my witness, it's the best medicine I've ever had.'

It was an old joke of hers, one which she recognized had not been very funny even the first time she'd cracked it. But she laughed anyway.

She poured herself a stiff Scotch. Her friends all said that she drank too much, but she paid no attention to their warnings. Why should she? They weren't *real* friends! *Real* friends would never have turned on her like ravening wolves when she split up with Ralph.

'He's the best thing that's ever happened to you,' she said, mimicking the mock concern in their voices. 'He's gone out of his way to try and make things work between you – but you have to make an effort too, Jane.'

Who did they think they were? How could they possibly even begin to understand the strain she was under? Let them try having a mother hanged for a murder she didn't commit, and then see how *they* handled marriage.

She took a deep gulp of her whisky. Everything would be all right if she could just clear her mother's name, she told herself. She wouldn't have to drink so much then. She wouldn't need to bury herself in her work, taking on more cases than anyone could reasonably handle. She could learn to trust people. She might even get married again.

Yet before any of that could happen, the police must first play *their* part. And she wasn't sure that they would! True, she had told Woodend that she trusted him. And when she was speaking the words, she had believed what she was saying. But that had been in daylight, in a pub full of people. Now, sitting in a room just beyond the reach of the claws of darkness – and alone! – she was no longer so certain.

How could she be sure that Woodend would do anything more than just go through the motions? she wondered desperately. Then she picked up the phone and dialled a London number.

Monika Paniatowski paced up and down the living room of her flat, a cigarette in one hand and a glass of vodka in the other.

She had gone to bed earlier than usual that evening, but the moment her head had touched the pillow an itching had begun to develop in her right calf. She had resisted the urge to scratch it, and instead had charged her mind with the task of willing it away. It had been a battle her mind was destined to lose. The itch had quickly colonized her other leg and then launched a two-pronged attack that had swept up through her hips, past her waist and into her torso. And soon it seemed as if a thousand tiny men on delicate feather skates had turned her back into their own personal rink.

She'd got up and taken first a hot shower and then a cold

one. Neither of them had helped, and nor – as yet – had the vodka. It was almost as if her body had decided to defy the laws of medicine and had caught chicken pox for a second time.

She knew where the cause of her nervousness lay – in Jane-Bloody-Hartley – but she had no idea why the woman should have had such an effect on her.

Yes, Hartley was powerful. Yes, she probably had enough influence to get the team well and truly screwed if she wasn't happy with the way they carried out the investigation. But there was nothing new in that. Working with Charlie Woodend had always been like riding shotgun on a stagecoach that perpetually travelled through hostile Indian territory. So what the hell *was* different this time?

Perhaps it was not so much Hartley herself as her own reaction to the bloody woman, Monika reasoned.

If ever two women had been poles apart on almost every count, then those two women were herself and Jane Hartley. They differed in age, income, home bases, personal histories, temperaments and tastes. Even their superficial points of contact served to do no more than widen the divide between them: though they had both built up their careers in the law, Monika's job was catching the criminals and Jane Hartley's to persuade gullible juries to set them free.

Yet their relationship – if they could even be said to have one – wasn't something that could be summed up using only cold, neutral facts. Though she was an only child herself, she felt a sort of bond with Hartley, which she could only imagine might resemble a relationship between siblings. Thus she could dislike Jane, and at the same time feel a strange sort of affection for her. She could resent the fact that Hartley was making the team jump through hoops, yet still experience a perverse, almost proprietorial, pride that the woman had the power to do so.

It was very, very confusing – and Paniatowski wished it would all go away.

*   *   *

When her bedside phone rang, Elizabeth Driver was attempting to sleep off a heavy early evening's drinking session with her fellow hacks in the Coach and Horses, so it was scarcely surprising that her only response to the ringing was an irritated, 'Yes?' rasped into the mouthpiece.

'That is Elizabeth Driver, isn't it?' asked her female caller. '*The* Elizabeth Driver? The crime reporter for the *Daily Globe*?'

'Yes. Who's calling?' the journalist demanded.

'I don't think we've ever met, but—'

'If we've never met, then how the hell have you got hold of my number? The bloody thing's unlisted!'

'I have friends in some extremely influential places,' her caller said, apparently unperturbed. 'As I was saying before you interrupted me, I don't think we've ever met, but I do know you by your reputation – as I'm sure you know me by mine.'

The caller was either a crank or a potential goldmine of rich information – and if she'd been a crank she'd never have found where to ring. Driver's fingers began to tingle, as they always did when she sensed a story in the making.

'You still haven't told me your name,' the journalist said.

'Haven't I? It's Jane Hartley.'

'The QC?'

'That's right.'

Elizabeth Driver looked up towards heaven and mouthed a silent 'thank you'. 'What can I do for you, Miss Hartley?' she asked aloud.

'Has your paper gone to press yet?'

Driver looked across at the bedside clock. A quarter to twelve. 'No, as a matter of fact, it hasn't. The first edition won't be printed for another hour. Why do you ask?'

'Because if you can guarantee me front page coverage tomorrow, I'm prepared to give you an exclusive story.'

The tingling in Driver's fingers had become a positive electric shock. 'Go on,' she said, trying not to sound *too* eager.

'I'm in Whitebridge, Lancashire,' Jane Hartley said. 'Do you know the place?'

'Yes, I know it,' Driver confirmed. '*Why* are you there? Why would *anybody* be there?'

'I'm investigating what I believe to have been a miscarriage of justice in a murder case.'

'Miscarriage of justice?'

'I'm convinced that a woman who was hanged for murder nearly thirty years ago was innocent of the crime. I've handed over some fresh evidence to the police, and I'm not convinced they're planning to take it seriously. But if you run it as a big story, they won't have any choice, will they?'

Elizabeth Driver felt the tingle start to drain away from her fingers.

'I'm not sure I *can* run it as a *big* story,' she said dubiously. 'You see, to be on the front page of the *Globe*, it's got to be something really special. The murder of a child, for example. Or a crime that involves somebody famous.'

'Is Lord Eric Sharpe famous enough for you?' Jane Hartley asked hopefully.

Driver caught herself shaking her head. 'Doubtful.'

'You do know who he is?'

'Yes, *I* know who he is. He's the Home Office Minister in the House of Lords. The problem is, my readers won't have heard of him. They don't take much of an interest in politics.'

There was silence from the other end of the line, but to Driver it was a *telling* silence.

She's not as confident as she likes to pretend she is, the reporter thought. Not even half as confident!

'How about me?' Jane Hartley asked reluctantly. 'Will your readers know my name?'

'Well, yes, you're certainly famous enough,' Driver said,

feeling the tingle start to return. 'We've done several big spreads on the trials you've been involved in. But in order for the story to fly at this stage of the proceedings, you'd still need to have a personal involvement with the case.'

Another uncertain pause.

'The woman who was hanged was my mother,' Jane Hartley said tightly, as if she were forcing the words out of her mouth.

Bloody hell fire! Elizabeth Driver thought. Bloody *buggering* hell fire! The story would certainly be a big one. It could even be huge.

'You'd better give me some more details,' she said, crisply. 'What's the name of the cop who's supposed to be re-opening the case?'

'His name is Chief Inspector Woodend.'

'*Cloggin'-it Charlie* Woodend?'

'Do you know him?'

Did she know Charlie Woodend? The man who had lost her her job at the *Maltham Chronicle* just because she'd muddied the waters of his investigation a little with her publicity stunt! The man who *could* have given her an exclusive on the *Maddox Row* case, but instead had chosen to treat her as if she were just another reporter.

'Oh yes, I know him,' she said. 'Charlie and I have crossed swords any number of times.'

'So you won't mind if this story causes some unpleasantness between you and him?'

Elizabeth Driver did not have to look in the mirror to know that she was smiling as broadly as the proverbial village idiot.

'Mind?' she said. 'No, I won't mind. Getting up Woodend's nose will be the icing on the cake.'

Eleven

'Have either of you two seen this mornin's *Daily Globe*?'
Woodend asked, shaking a copy of the offending paper
at the other members of his team the moment they walked
through his office door.

Rutter shook his head, and Paniatowski said, 'Not yet.'

'Then sit down an' be instructed,' Woodend told them. He
smoothed the crumpled paper out on the desk in front of him.
'It starts with the headline, "QC DEMANDS JUSTICE FOR HER
DEAD MOTHER!" an' there's a picture of Jane Hartley – complete with wig an' gown – standin' outside the Old Bailey.'

He turned the paper around so that Rutter and Paniatowski
could both look at it.

'They'll have pulled the photograph from their files,'
Rutter said. 'It's nothing to do with this story.'

'No, but given how determined an' serious she's lookin',
it's a perfect match for Elizabeth Driver's purple prose,'
Woodend said. 'Listen to this. "Bravely fightin' back her
tears, the normally fierce and formidable Jane Hartley,
Britain's battlin' woman QC, told me last night of her
struggle to finally set the record straight on her own mother's
execution. 'The police failed to consider all the facts properly
durin' their first investigation, and I do not believe they are
doin' any better now,' Miss Hartley said, with a catch in her
throat'." Got that! *With a catch in her throat!*'

Rutter and Paniatowski nodded.

'"I took her hand to comfort her",' Woodend continued,
'"an' felt the sorrow which she had kept imprisoned for

97

so long flow from her body to mine." *Took her hand to comfort her!*' He swept the newspaper off his desk in disgust. 'There's several more paragraphs along the same lines, but you get the general idea.'

'It didn't happen quite like that, did it?' Rutter asked.

'No, it didn't. Elizabeth Driver's in London an' Jane Hartley's still in Whitebridge – so if there was any hand-holdin' goin' on, they must both have bloody long arms. But that's not to say they haven't spoken over the phone.'

'It certainly reads as if it came straight from the horse's mouth,' Rutter said.

'Aye, an' it's landed us straight in stuff that comes out of the other end of the horse,' Woodend said. 'Doesn't Jane Hartley realize that in gettin' this story printed she's made our job – the job *she* wants done – all that much more difficult?'

'And even more importantly – at least from a personal point of view – doesn't she realize what the story will do to her own reputation?' asked Rutter, who always tried to keep half an eye on *his* own career prospects, even as he willingly flew off on one of Woodend's kamikaze missions.

'Aye, this certainly could harm her,' Woodend agreed.

'Harm her!' Rutter said. '*Harm* her? It could *ruin* her! How many top solicitors will want to brief her as their barrister, knowing that her mother was hanged for murder? And how do you think the other members of her chambers will react? They'll *hate* the publicity. They'll probably vote to kick her out of the practice. What's the matter with her? Doesn't she care?'

'No, she doesn't care,' Monika Paniatowski said, with an absolute certainty which took both Rutter and Woodend by surprise.

'What do you mean by that, Monika?' the Chief Inspector asked.

'I mean exactly what I said. Jane Hartley doesn't care if she loses her reputation. She doesn't care if she loses her job. There's something much more fundamental at stake for her here. She's fighting a battle for her very survival – and the cornerstone of that battle is the investigation into her mother's trial and execution. Whatever else she has to sacrifice, that investigation *must* go ahead.'

A troubled frown came to Woodend's brow.

'Was there somethin' significant that I missed durin' our meetin' with Miss Hartley?' he asked. 'Somethin' you've been keepin' back from me?'

'I don't think so,' Paniatowski replied.

'An' have you seen her again, on your own, since the three of us had that meetin' the day before yesterday?'

'No.'

'Then why is that while I'm still at the stage of tryin' to work out exactly what it is that makes her tick, you seem to think you've got right inside her head? Because you do think that, don't you, Monika?'

'Yes, I suppose I do,' said Paniatowski, looking as puzzled as a second-string runner who unexpectedly finds herself at the head of the pack.

'An' why is that? Because you're both women?'

Paniatowski shook her head. 'No, I don't think that's the explanation.'

'Then what is?'

'I don't know,' Paniatowski confessed. 'I'd tell you if I did – but I really don't.' She thought for a second – searching the corners of her brain for some answer that would satisfy her boss. 'Maybe it's because we both lost our fathers when we were very young.'

Woodend nodded, as if he was assured. But he wasn't. Something very strange was going on with Monika – and he wished he knew what it was.

'Let's move on,' he suggested. 'Why did Jane Hartley choose this particular moment to go off on this crusade of hers, Monika?'

Paniatowski consulted her notebook. 'Strictly speaking,

she didn't. This is her *second* attempt to have the case re-opened. The first was when she'd just been admitted to the bar.'

Woodend did a quick mental calculation. 'But that was nearly twenty years ago. Why such a long gap between that first attempt an' her second?'

Paniatowski shrugged. 'The first time she was a nobody, and so she got nowhere. Perhaps she learned a lesson from that, and didn't try again until she was sure she had plenty of clout.'

'But she's had clout for *years*,' Woodend said, unconvinced. 'Remember how she got that French count acquitted of murderin' his wife, even though there were his fingerprints on the gun and her blood on his clothes? What year would that be, Bob?'

'57, I think,' Rutter supplied.

'Right, well ever since 1957, everythin' the woman's done has been headline news. An' that's all the clout *anybody* needs.' He lit up a cigarette and took a thoughtful drag. 'There has to be somethin' else that's acted as a trigger to make her move on it now. Has anythin' significant happened recently in her *personal* life, Monika?'

Paniatowski consulted her notebook again. 'Helen Hartley, the aunt who brought her up, died about six months ago.'

'That'd be her father's sister, would it?'

'That's right.'

'So bein' Robert Hartley's sister, she presumably lived locally?'

Paniatowski shook her head. 'She was living in Whitebridge at the time Fred Dodds was murdered. After Margaret Dodds' death, she sold up and moved down south. To Hastings. I expect she wanted to take Jane as far away from the tragedy as possible.'

'I expect she did,' Woodend agreed. He turned to Rutter. 'Have *you* got anythin' interestin' to report on the way Eric Sharpe carried out his investigation, Bob?'

'Nothing that's likely to please Jane Hartley,' Rutter said.

'By which you mean that you've not found any evidence which suggests that there might have been a cover-up?'

'By which I mean just that,' Rutter agreed. 'The records of the investigation are not the most professional job I've ever seen, but they're certainly one of the most comprehensive.' He reached into his briefcase, took out a sheaf of papers, and laid them on the desk in front of Woodend. 'Look at this.'

It was an inventory of the contents of the living room of the house on Hebden Brow. Woodend quickly ran his eyes down the list.

> Packet of Embassy Cigarettes (three smoked, stubs in the ashtray – see below)
> Box of England's Glory matches
> Ashtray (souvenir of Fleetwood)
> Ball of wool (light blue)
> Knitting needle
> Magazine (*Woman*, 16th June)
> *Daily Herald* (15th June), corner of page containing crossword ripped out
> Pair of pinking scissors
> One shilling and threepence (1/3d) recovered from back of sofa (sixpenny piece, threepenny piece, four pennies, four ha'pennies) . . .

'The list goes on for another six pages,' Rutter said. 'It must have taken someone hours to compile.'

'Aye, it must,' Woodend replied. 'An' it's just the sort of list *I'd* have compiled.'

'It is?'

'Definitely. Especially if I wanted to convince any future auditors that I'd been completely open – while at the same time I was tryin' to hide a vital piece of evidence.'

'The old needle in the haystack?' Paniatowski suggested.

'Aye, that's it,' Woodend agreed. 'An' the trick is to make sure your haystack is *so* bloody big that, rather than sift through it, the searcher's likely to persuade himself the needle must be somewhere else.'

'Is that meant to be a dig at me, sir?' Rutter asked, sounding just a little offended.

'Nay, lad,' Woodend assured him. 'I was speakin' in general terms – of ordinary mortals. I've worked with *you* long enough to know that even if it looks like hay and feels like hay, you still won't be convinced it *is* hay until you've found some horse that's willin' to eat it.' He paused for a second. 'Movin' on again, I think it's about time I told you about an old whippet fancier I talked to last night in the Red Lion.'

Twelve

Jane Hartley had awoken that morning with an Olympic-class hangover, but in the time it had taken her to read the career-suicide note she had dictated over the phone to Elizabeth Driver – and was now writ large on the front page of the *Daily Globe* – the waves of pain had already begun to ebb away.

She glanced at the whisky bottle, still sitting comfortingly on her bedside table. It was tempting to speed up the process of her recovery by having just one drink – a hair of the dog that had bitten her – but she knew that once she started she wouldn't be able to stop.

She lit a cigarette and wondered how she would fill the time until the hour when it would be possible to persuade herself that it would be all right to have just one small Scotch. She could work, she supposed – she had a case bulging with briefs – but she was not sure whether her clients, having read the papers, would still want her to represent them. Besides, for the first time in twenty years she did not *feel* like doing any work. The problem was, though, that she didn't feel like doing *anything else*, either.

She found herself thinking about Aunt Helen. She had really loved that woman. It had been Helen who had comforted her when she'd fallen down and grazed her knee, Helen who had encouraged her to apply for Oxford, Helen who had shared her joy when Ralph had proposed – and the heartbreak when the marriage collapsed. In so many ways, her aunt had been as much of a mother as any little girl had the right to expect.

Yet . . . yet there had somehow always been a wall between them. It hadn't been a wall of her making – Jane was sure of that. No, it was Aunt Helen who had – carefully and deliberately – built the wall herself.

And why? For what purpose?

Because Helen had not dared to let her niece see her as she really was?

Because somewhere beneath that soft, gentle exterior a monster had been hunkering down?

Jane had tried so many ways to breech that wall. And when that had failed, she had attempted – with her questions – to at least see over the top of it.

'*Are you glad I came to live with you, Auntie Helen?*'

'*Of course I am, my little pet.*'

'*Then why do you look so sad?*'

'*I'm thinking of your mummy, I suppose. Thinking what a pity it is that she should never have had the joy of seeing you grow up.*'

'*Was my mummy a bad person?*'

'*No, of course she wasn't.*'

'*Then why did she have to die?*'

'*You shouldn't think about it, Jane. It will drive you mad if you think about it. It will drive us both mad!*'

The more she had questioned, the higher and thicker the wall had seemed to grow. And so Helen had died with the mystery still unsolved – the barrier still in place.

Jane remembered the sense of grief that had overwhelmed her as she stood by her aunt's grave. She had mourned not just for what she had lost, but for what had never really been hers to lose – what had been denied to her even before she could take full possession of it.

She had been entitled to a mother who would stay with her until she was ready to fly the nest. She had been entitled to an aunt who was not driven mainly by the fear of intimacy. These things had been *stolen* from her!

She wondered where the thief was now. Wondered if he

had read the morning papers and finally understood that she was as determined to destroy his life as he had been to destroy hers.

Lord Sharpe crossed the central concourse of Euston Station with a copy of that morning's *Daily Globe* in his hand.

The bitch! he thought. The bloody vindictive bitch!

He understood revenge. He was something of an expert in it himself. But what he could not even *begin* to understand was the kind of revenge that would also ruin the person taking it.

The woman must be mad. There was no other explanation for it.

He passed the WH Smith's newspaper stall, and saw the tall stack of *Daily Globe*'s waiting to be sold. He scanned the station, tried to estimate how many of his fellow passengers had already bought the filthy rag, and decided there was a depressingly large number of them.

His thoughts travelled back to the conversation he had had with the government chief whip earlier that morning. The whip had looked across his desk with eyes that showed kindly concern. Sharpe had not been fooled. He knew the whip for what he really was – a man whose task was to clean up other people's messes, a pest controller posing as a kindly uncle.

'This really is rather unfortunate, Eric,' the whip had said.

'I know,' Sharpe had replied, in the voice of an errant schoolboy brought up before the stern headmaster.

'Your work for the party has earned you at least a minor place in the history of this century. It would be a great pity to lose that – to feature only in the gallery of infamy – would it not?'

'Yes.'

'Is your conscience clear, Eric?'

'Of course it is.'

'None of what I've read in the papers is true? There is nothing reprehensible in your investigation of the Margaret Dodds case?'

'Nothing.'

The whip had favoured him with a ghostly, thin smile. 'Then go up to Whitebridge, Eric. Bury this thing before it buries you.'

And that was what he was doing on Euston Station. Going up to bloody Whitebridge. Trying to bury this thing before it buried him.

As he walked towards the ticket barrier, he let his mind rove over the pitfalls that might lie ahead.

It was possible, of course, that the new investigating team would have found nothing they could use against him. More than possible – because even in his headlong rush for a seat in parliament, he had still taken the time to pause and cover his tracks.

On the other hand, what he had learned from his contacts at the Yard about this bugger Charlie Woodend inclined him to take a more pessimistic view.

So what was the worst Woodend and his team could come up with, and how might he deal with it?

Witnesses like Brunskill – the toe-rag who claimed to have seen Margaret Dodds outside St Mary's Church – might have been a problem a few years ago, but the chances were that they were all either dead or gaga now.

The physical evidence, what little there had been, could only work in his favour.

So, the real danger didn't come from anything he had done, so much as from the things he had chosen *not* to do. And there were enough of those around to land him in a sticky situation.

Like the dead coalman, he thought with a shudder. He hoped to Christ they hadn't found out about the dead coalman!

Thirteen

Woodend stood in the toilet stall, draining his bladder and thinking about a course he had once attended in the police college at Hendon.

He was remembering one particular lecture given by a chief superintendent who had appeared on television so many times that he could almost have been called a celebrity. In his lecture, this chief superintendent had chosen to compare the task of a senior detective involved in a major criminal investigation with that of a chef preparing a meal.

'Both must deal with a number of ingredients which seem to have no value on their own,' the man had said. 'Both must be able to see how these ingredients can be blended together to produce the desired result – in the chef's case a culinary masterpiece, in our case a solution to a crime.'

Most of the audience had loved the analogy, and had applauded furiously at the end of the lecture. Woodend himself had been far from impressed, because though the concept had the advantage of appealing simplicity, that very simplicity was also, it seemed to him, a serious flaw.

For a start, he had argued later with his colleagues in the pub, the chef not only knew exactly what it was he wished to make, but also which ingredients would be required for the task. The bobby, on the other hand, was aware that some kind of dish would ultimately have to be produced, but he had no idea what it would look or smell like – or even which of the many ingredients he had been given he would eventually use.

This current case – the Fred Dodds murder – was a good example of what he'd been saying back then, he thought as he washed his hands vigorously in the sink. Was the stuff that the team had already gathered up going to be of any use – or were they still at the stage of starting to cook their omelette without having any eggs?

He walked back down the corridor to his office. Paniatowski and Rutter were sitting just where he had left them, as silent as two people who didn't speak each other's languages and were waiting for the interpreter to arrive.

Woodend slid behind his desk. 'Well, based on what I was told in the pub last night, do we now have a clearer picture of Margaret Dodds than we had yesterday?' he asked.

'Yes, I think so,' Rutter said.

'Then tell us what your impression is.'

Rutter nodded. 'I think the best way to express it is to say that if Margaret Dodds had been a man, she'd have been the kind of man who didn't know how to keep his trousers buttoned.'

'If she *had* been a man, you'd never have made that comment,' Paniatowski said sharply. 'Either you wouldn't have *cared* how she behaved, or you'd have admired her for it. It's only because she was a woman that you object to her having a lover.'

'*A* lover!' Rutter repeated, clearly stung by her comments. 'We're not talking about *a* lover here, Sergeant Paniatowski. From what the boss has told us, it appears to have been common knowledge around Whitebridge that she was having an affair with Fred Dodds while she was still married to Robert Hartley—'

'Truly a scarlet woman!' Paniatowski said. 'Seems to me that hanging was too good for her!'

'And that the ink on her second wedding certificate was barely dry before she was betraying Dodds with someone else,' Rutter said, ignoring the interruption. 'That's *two* lovers we're pretty sure of already, and I'd be willing to bet that we'll uncover a few more during the course of the investigation. The woman just couldn't seem to get enough of it.'

'Are you really as obsessed with sex as you sound?' Paniatowski asked, an angry edge to her voice.

'Monika!' Woodend cautioned.

'Well, is he?' Paniatowski demanded. 'Are you, Inspector?'

'No, I'm not,' Rutter said. 'But your friend Margaret Dodds certainly seems to have been.'

Paniatowski shook her head in exasperation.

'That's complete bollocks!' she said. 'And I'll tell you why. Firstly, it's bollocks because, despite what you've just said, we have no actual proof that Margaret had *any* affairs. Secondly, it's bollocks because even if you are right about *what* she did, you may well be wrong about *why* she did it. Lust isn't the only thing that can drive a woman into a man's arms, you know.'

A slight, uncharacteristic sneer played on Rutter's lips. 'You're surely not suggesting she did it for money, are you?'

'No, I'm bloody not!' Paniatowski retorted. 'I'm suggesting that in a lot of affairs there's an element of comfort – at least on the woman's part. If Margaret was seeing another man just before Fred was murdered, then perhaps it was because she was finding life with her husband unbearable.'

'And what about Robert? Did she find life with him unbearable, too? If she did, it doesn't say much for her choice in husbands.'

'Some women *do* make bad choices,' Paniatowski agreed. 'That doesn't mean they have to be either nymphomaniacs or prostitutes.'

'But it doesn't exclude them from those categories, either,' Rutter pointed out.

'I'm glad I don't see life through your eyes,' Paniatowski told him. 'I really am!'

Any minute now, one of two things were going to happen, Woodend thought. Either Rutter would say something he'd really regret later – or Paniatowski would decide to find out just how easy it was to choke the life from a man who had considerable height and weight advantage over her.

'I think we're goin' a bit off track here,' the Chief Inspector said. 'Let's assume for the moment that this second lover does, in fact, exist. What are the chances that he was the one who topped Fred Dodds?'

'It's a possibility,' Rutter conceded. 'Perhaps the lover came around to the house and asked Dodds to set Margaret free. They had an argument and the lover, in a rage, killed Dodds with his own hammer.'

'And Margaret – the nymphomaniac – just stood there and watched it, I suppose,' Paniatowski said.

'Perhaps she *wasn't* there,' Rutter replied. 'Perhaps at least that part of her story was true, and she really did go out for a walk.'

'So she comes back to the house either in the middle of the attack, or just at the end of it?' Woodend asked.

'That's right. And the reason she waits before calling the police is to give her lover time to get away.'

'The lover – if he existed – had no need to ask for Margaret's freedom,' Paniatowski said. 'Fred had already told his friends that he was thinking of divorcing her.'

'But if he did that, she wouldn't get the money,' Rutter countered.

'Money's no good to a dead woman,' Paniatowski said.

'Maybe she thought she could get away with it.'

'As Jane Hartley herself pointed out, her mother wasn't a stupid woman,' Woodend said. 'She'd have known it was too big a risk.'

'Then maybe she wasn't the one who made the decision to run it,' argued Rutter, unwilling to give up the theory without a struggle. 'Maybe the lover *did* kill Fred for the money, but without consulting Margaret first. That would explain why the only thing she would say in her statement was, "I didn't kill him." She didn't! The lover did!'

'She didn't kill Fred, but she took the blame for his death?' Paniatowski asked sceptically.

'Yes! Because she loved the man too much to give him up to the police.'

'Five minutes ago you were saying the only thing she was interested in was sex, now you're saying she was willing to die for love! I wish you'd make your mind up.'

'What about other suspects?' Woodend asked.

'You mean Cuthburtson and Bithwaite?' Rutter said.

'Aye, they'll do for a start,' Woodend agreed. 'Cuthburtson may have had a grudge against Dodds for kickin' him out of the business, an' Bithwaite certainly benefited from his death.'

'But in 1934 Bithwaite was only the chief clerk,' Monika Paniatowski said. 'Would he have been able to run a car on his salary?'

'You're thinkin' about the two cars that your mate Mrs Fortesque says stopped in front of the house on the night of the murder?'

'That's right.'

'It might be a lead, but it might just as easily be a red herrin',' Woodend said. 'Maybe Mrs Fortesque was wrong about the time when the cars stopped. Maybe she was wrong about the day. An' even if she got the day an' the time right, perhaps they didn't stop in front of the Doddses' house at all, but another house a little further down the road.'

'Even so, there should be a record of them,' Rutter said, giving his reluctant backing to Paniatowski.

'An' there isn't?'

'I've only had time to skim through the documentation so far, but I think that if there'd have been any report on a couple of cars, I'd have noticed it.'

'There certainly *should* be a report,' Woodend mused,

'because Mrs Fortesque is quite adamant that she told the police, isn't she, Monika?'

But Paniatowski was staring at the wall, and if she heard what he said she gave no indication of it.

'Are you with us, Monika?' Woodend asked.

'I . . . uh . . . what?'

'You want to tell us what's on your mind?'

'I was thinking over my interview with Mrs Fortesque. I've got this uneasy feeling that there's something important I missed out on – something about the cars. The problem is, I can't quite pin it down.'

'You've got your notes, haven't you?'

'Yes, but I didn't make them during the interview, because I thought that would put Mrs Fortesque off.'

'So when did you make them?'

'As soon as I'd left the Fortesques' house, I sat in the car and wrote down everything I could remember. But even at that time, I got the feeling that there was something else I should have been including.'

'You best plan is just to forget about it for the moment,' Woodend advised. 'Give your brain some quiet time, an' it'll probably work it out on its own.' He lit up a cigarette. 'Now where was I?'

'You were talking about the cars,' Rutter prompted.

'Aye, the cars. We still don't know how much – or how *little* – faith we can put in Eric Sharpe's records. But if there really is no mention of the two vehicles in any of his reports, then it'd probably be best to take *everythin'* he says with a very large pinch of salt.' He paused to take a drag on his Capstan. 'But enough of that for the moment,' he continued. 'Have either of you got any plans for this afternoon? A game of tennis, perhaps? Or maybe just a quiet ramble in the countryside?'

Rutter and Paniatowski grinned, as he'd intended them to.

'I thought I'd drive over to Simcaster,' Rutter said.

'Oh aye? An' what's brought on this sudden yearnin' for an expedition into foreign parts?'

'It's where Fred Dodds was brought up. I might be able to fill in a few of the gaps we have in his background.'

'Good plan,' Woodend agreed. 'What about you, Monika?'

'I'll be doing my background check on *Margaret* Dodds.'

'An' where will that take you?'

'To Blakebrook. Her father was the vicar there.'

'Join the modern police force an' see the world,' Woodend said. 'Right, you'd better get on with it then.'

Rutter and Paniatowski rose to their feet and were almost at the door when Woodend said, 'Actually, Monika, I'd appreciate it if you'd give me just a couple of minutes more of your time.'

Rutter stepped out into the corridor, closing the door behind him, and Paniatowski returned to her seat.

'Yes, sir?' the sergeant said.

'What was that all about?' Woodend asked.

'What was what all about?'

'You know very well,' Woodend told her. 'What made you have a go at Inspector Rutter?'

'You've always told us we should speak our minds on this team,' Paniatowski reminded him. 'You said that the fact we could have a proper argument with the gloves off was what made us good.'

'A proper argument *about the case*, Monika,' Woodend said softly. 'But that wasn't what you were doin'. You were takin' ever opportunity you could to have a pop at Bob.'

'He makes me sick!'

'A lot of people make *me* sick, but when they outrank me, I have enough common sense to hold my tongue.' He paused. 'Well, usually I have, anyway,' he added honestly.

'So when it comes down to it, you're just like all the others,' Paniatowski said bitterly. 'An inspector's worth more than a sergeant simply *because* he's an inspector.'

'An' *now* you're takin' a pop at me,' Woodend said.

'Would you like me to tell you what I think the real problem is?'

'Why ask my permission? You're the boss. If you want to talk, then I have to listen.'

'Maybe I'd better start by tellin' you what the problem *isn't*,' Woodend said, ignoring the insubordination. 'It isn't Inspector Rutter. Bob may be a bit conservative for your taste – sometimes he's a bit conservative for mine – but he's a good bobby, an' you bloody know it. It isn't your workin' relationship with him, either. You're not a match made in heaven, but you've cracked enough cases together to know that you can be a good team when you want to be. So what *is* the problem?'

'I thought you were about to tell me. That's why I'm sitting here with bated breath and my tongue hanging out.'

'The problem is this case. Or rather, the way you're approachin' this case. You're gettin' far too involved.'

'You used to say that a good bobby always gets involved.'

'I still say it. A good bobby always wants to see justice done, but it shouldn't be cold, blind justice. He should always hold on to his humanity. That's not what's happenin' here, Monika. You've stopped bein' the sympathetic outsider who's just lookin' in – the audience of one who's tryin' to make sense of the plot. You've stepped on to the stage, an' you're startin' to behave like one of the actors.'

'Now that is clever,' Paniatowski said in mock admiration. 'No wonder you're a chief inspector.'

'If you carry on like this, you're headin' for a fall,' Woodend said. 'I'll protect you for as long as I can, but there's only so much that even I can do. Do you understand what I'm sayin', Monika? Try to take a step back from this case. An' when you start walkin' again, for God's sake tread carefully.'

Paniatowski's face had grown gradually more impassive, and it was becoming plain to Woodend that if he'd been expecting a response, he was going to be disappointed.

'Have you finished, sir?' the sergeant asked. 'Can I go now?'

Woodend sighed heavily. 'Yes, Monika, you can go now,' he said.

Fourteen

The visitor – who was not entirely unexpected – arrived at Woodend's office door a few minutes after Paniatowski had made her graceless exit. The man was in his mid-sixties, Woodend estimated. He must once have had an athletic build, but now his good appearance owed more to the skilful cut of his expensive suit than it did to rigorous physical exercise. His skin shone, his white hair flowed over his collar in a patrician mane, and he had dark brown eyes that were quick, rather than intelligent. If Hollywood had been looking for someone to cast in the role of the noble lord, he would have been its man.

Eric Sharpe glanced quickly round the office, then held his hand out to Woodend. 'Well, that is a relief,' he said.

'What is?' the Chief Inspector asked.

'You are! I was dreadin' havin' to waste my time talkin' to some snotty-nosed little university graduate who'd learned all his policin' from books, but I can tell just by the cut of your jib that you're exactly the kind of old-fashioned bobby I used to be.'

Woodend favoured him with a ghost of a smile, invited him to sit down, and offered him a Capstan Full Strength.

Lord Sharpe accepted the cigarette, took a deep drag on it, then settled back comfortably in his chair.

'I expect you're wonderin' why I'm here,' he said.

'I assume that it's got somethin' to do with the Margaret Dodds case,' Woodend said.

'You've hit the nail right on the head there, Charlie,'

Sharpe said. He paused for a second. 'You don't *mind* if I call you Charlie, do you?'

'No, I don't mind, Lord Sharpe,' Woodend assured him.

'An' please, if I'm to call you Charlie, then you must call me Eric. Bein' ennobled can be quite useful in some social situations – I never have to queue for theatre tickets these days, for instance – but even though I've been "lordin' it" for years now, the title still doesn't always sit too comfortably on the shoulders of a lad whose dad was nowt but a mill worker.'

Woodend looked puzzled. 'Now that is strange,' he said.

'What is?'

'Your dad *wasn't* a mill worker. He was the station master at Whitebridge railway station. He had his own office, an' a lass whose job it was to brew up for him.'

Sharpe's crafty eyes suddenly hardened. 'You've been checking up on me,' he said accusingly.

'Aye, I have,' Woodend agreed. 'An' you've been checkin' up on me. That's how you know my dad *did* work in the mills.'

For a moment it looked as if Sharpe was unsure exactly how to react. Then he threw back his head and laughed as if he were genuinely amused.

'You've caught me out, fair an' square,' he said. 'It's an old politician's trick, is that.'

'What? Pretendin' to come from the same background as the person you're talkin' to?'

'That's right. There's no harm in it, you know.'

'Isn't there?'

'Of course not. To tell you the truth, I do it more for the sake of the fellers I'm talkin' to than for my own. People get a bit tongue-tied when they're dealin' with a lord, an' it puts them more at their ease to realize I'm an ordinary chap, much like themselves.'

'I see,' Woodend said, noncommittally.

Sharpe grinned ruefully. 'Still an' all, I should never have tried that trick on with a smart bobby like you – a man who, but for a few years difference in our ages, could have been one of my colleagues. I'm sorry, Charlie!'

'We all make mistakes. Think nothin' of it,' Woodend said. 'Now, just what can I do for you, Lord—'

'Eric!'

'What can I do for you, Eric?'

'It's more a question of what *I* can do for *you*,' Sharpe said. 'I was in on the Dodds case from the very start. In fact, I was the first officer to reach the crime scene. So I thought I might be able to fill you in on some of the background – an' perhaps point you in the right direction.'

'That's very kind of you,' Woodend said.

But he was thinking: The man's actin' like he's never read that article in the *Globe* – like he doesn't know that *he's* as much a subject of the investigation as the murderer is.

'So what have you come up with so far, Charlie?' Sharpe asked.

Woodend shrugged. 'It's early days yet, Eric. You know yourself how long it takes to get to grips with a case.'

Sharpe frowned. 'That's certainly true of *some* of the cases I've handled – but I would have thought this one was really pretty straightforward. Quite frankly, it should never have been re-opened. Indeed, if the hysterical bloody woman who's kickin' up all the fuss had been anythin' other than a QC, it *wouldn't* have been re-opened.'

'Maybe so. But the fact that you think she's a hysterical bloody woman doesn't mean that there's nothin' *to* investigate.'

Sharpe shook his head slowly from side to side. 'You're wastin' your time on this one, Charlie. Margaret Dodds was guilty as charged.'

'So why did she do it?'

Sharpe made some pretence of thinking. 'I can't really remember all the details,' he said. 'After all, thirty years is a hell of a long time, you know – especially – ' he paused to laugh self-deprecatingly – 'especially when you're gettin' as long in the tooth as I am.'

'But it was your last major case before you went into parliament, wasn't it? Surely you've still got at least a vague memory of it,' Woodend coaxed.

'Maybe I can recall bits here an' there,' Sharpe conceded. 'As far as I remember, she killed her husband for his money.'

'It wasn't a very clever murder, was it?'

'She didn't strike me as a particularly clever woman. Besides, as you know yourself, greed can make people do some incredibly stupid things.'

'That's true,' Woodend agreed. 'If people want anythin' badly enough, they'll as often as not cut corners. Either that or they'll go ahead without givin' proper consideration to the consequences of their actions.'

Sharpe gave him another hard stare. 'We are still talking about Margaret Dodds here, aren't we?'

'I was talkin' in general terms,' Woodend said. 'But I agree that it could certainly apply to the murder of Fred Dodds.'

Sharpe leant forward. 'Cards on the table, Charlie. How long will it take you to wrap this whole thing up, so that I can turn my attention to more important matters?'

'You seem to have lost your accent,' Woodend said.

'I beg your pardon?'

'When you first came in here, you were droppin' your Gs, an' soundin' like a true son of Whitebridge. Now you're talkin' more like a man who feels quite at home in influential London circles.'

'I *do* feel at home in influential London circles,' Sharpe said, his voice hardening. 'And you still haven't answered my question.'

'What happened to the record of the interview you conducted with Mrs Fortesque, Lord Sharpe?'

'Mrs Fortesque? Who's she?'

'She's the woman who lived next door to the Doddses. Still lives there, as a matter of fact. On the night of the murder, she heard two cars stop in front of the Doddses' house, not more than half an hour apart. She thought the occurrence was important enough to mention it to the police.'

'So what?'

'There should have been a report on it. Now you'll not have met my lad Inspector Rutter, but take it from me he's a conscientious bobby both by nature an' trainin'. An' yet he can't find hide nor hair of any such document.'

Sharpe waved his hand airily. 'Paperwork sometimes gets lost, Charlie. You should know that. After thirty long years, I'm surprised there's only *one* report missing.'

'We don't know it *is* only one,' Woodend said. 'In fact, we're reasonably sure it isn't.'

'Since there was no overall index of all the documents, I don't see how you can possibly say that.'

'Now that is interestin'.'

'What is?'

'You say you can't remember even some of the broad details of the case, but you *do* remember a minor clerical detail like the fact there was no overall index of contents.'

'This is outrageous!' Sharpe said.

'If I'd have been investigatin' the case, one thing that I'd have been certain to do was follow up on Mrs Fortesque's statement,' Woodend said.

'Perhaps I did follow it up. I don't remember.'

'I'd have interviewed all the residents of Hebden Brow, as well as the ones in the surroundin' area. I'd have found out whether or not they'd noticed the cars, too. Then I'd have got all the information I could from the registry in County Hall. I'd also have sent men to all the garages in Central Lancashire. It wouldn't have been as big a job as it would be today, because there weren't as many cars around then. But it would have been big enough. By the time I'd finished with that line of inquiry I'd have had a thick folder of information on cars. There's not a hint of any information *at all* in your records.'

'Perhaps you're right in what you implied,' Sharpe said. 'Perhaps I did cut a few corners in my eagerness to get a result. But it was the *right* result. I can assure you of that.'

'After the sloppy investigative work you allowed to go on, you can't assure me of *anythin'*,' Woodend told him.

'You do *read* the papers, don't you?' Sharpe demanded.

'Aye. When I get the time.'

'Well, in case you've missed this particular story, the government's facing a real crisis. It's all the fault of that idiot John Profumo. I don't object to him consorting with whores, but he should have had the sense to take some precautions to cover his back. Anyway, that's neither here nor there. The fact is, we're hanging on to power by a thread. One more scandal – or even the *appearance* of a scandal – and that thread will be broken.'

'That's not my concern,' Woodend said.

Sharpe sneered. 'Why? What are you – a strong Labour Party man or something?'

'As a matter of fact, I am,' Woodend said. 'But that has nothin' to do with the way I'm handlin' this case. I'd do exactly the same as I'm doin' now if Labour was in power.'

'You haven't thought this through – and that's a huge mistake,' Sharpe warned in a voice which reminded Woodend of the hiss of a poisonous snake. 'Very few people ever have the chance to bring a government down, but you have that power in your hands right now. No doubt that makes you feel a very big man. No doubt you're revelling in it like a pig rolling around in shit!'

'Maybe you'd feel like that in my situation, but I'm just—'

'Shut up!' Sharpe said. 'Shut up and listen! It's not just your chance to bring down the government – it's also a chance to make either powerful enemies or powerful friends. You could use some powerful friends right now, Charlie, because as things stand, your career is pretty much washed up. I could get you promotion, if I felt inclined that way. Maybe even a double promotion. You could be *Chief Superintendent* Woodend by the end of next week. You understand what I'm saying, don't you, Charlie?'

'Yes, I understand.'

'But what you can't even *begin* to understand is what I – and the people behind me – could do to you if you crossed us. You wouldn't just lose this job – we'd make sure you never got another one anywhere else. Your bank would suddenly demand you pay off your overdraft – which, I know for fact, you couldn't. So what would the bank do then? It would start legal proceedings to repossess that little cottage of yours. You'd soon find yourself with no job and no home – and that's even before we started to get *really* nasty.'

'I don't like makin' physical threats to old men like you,' Woodend told Sharpe, 'but if you're not out of my office within five seconds I'll knock your teeth so far down your throat that you'll have to stick your fingers up your arse to bite your nails.'

'You're still not thinking straight,' Sharpe said. 'You don't want to put everything you've ever worked for at risk, just for the sake of—'

'One . . .' Woodend counted. 'Two . . . three . . .'

It was on the count of four that Lord Sharpe stood up. He backed to the door and, with his eyes still on Woodend, groped for the handle. He pulled the door open, took a step backward, then paused on the threshold.

'You'll regret this,' he said, one foot still inside Woodend's office. 'I promise you, you'll regret this to your dying day.'

'At least I'll still be able to look myself in the eye when I'm shavin' in the mornin',' Woodend said. 'How long is it since *you've* been able to do that, "My Lord"?'

'You won't be able to *afford* a mirror to look into by the time we're through with you,' Sharpe told him.

The minister stepped fully into the corridor, and slammed the door hard behind him.

'Temper, temper!' Woodend said softly to himself.

Fifteen

B ob Rutter was all right *in himself* about parking in the space between the Rolls Royce and the Bentley, but he couldn't help but feel sympathy for his two-year-old Ford Cortina, which definitely seemed overawed by the experience.

He climbed out of the car, quickly put some distance between himself and it, then stopped to examine the Grand Hotel, Simcaster. It was a mid-Victorian structure and thus had all the attendant crenellations, small towers, and other fanciful additions that the tastes of the era had dictated. It was situated in an elevated position on the edge of Simcaster and faced north, so that its guests could look out over the moors – and imagine the lakes beyond them – rather than being forced to gaze down on the grimy cotton town.

Such guests no longer came. It was a long time since the hotel had catered for visiting British business magnates with cash in their pockets and a hunger for profits burning in their eyes. It had been at least forty years since any foreign dictator had strutted through the lobby, surrounded by his grim-faced bodyguards, and bragged about the mills he would set up with the cheap labour available to him, once he returned home.

Yes, times had changed, but the Grand – unlike many other businesses in Simcaster – had known how to adapt to those changes. Now, prosperous visitors came on most weekends, purely for pleasure – to breathe the country air, to play a round or two of golf, to conduct their illicit affairs far from the gaze of anyone who knew them. The Rotary Club, the Chamber of Commerce, the Conservative Association, and the Simcaster and District Hunt, regularly booked the place for their annual dinners and formal balls. And since it was still undoubtedly the poshest place in town, it had become the established watering hole for those members of the community who would rather not rub shoulders in a social context with men they would be ordering about at work the following morning.

Rutter nodded to the uniformed doorman, and stepped into the marble foyer. The Excelsior Bar was to his immediate left, and three well-dressed, self-satisfied men in their early sixties were already occupying a table near the window, just as they'd promised they would be.

Rutter walked across the room to the table. It was the bald, jovial-looking member of the trio who noticed him first.

'Watch out, lads!' he said in a stage whisper. 'The law's here!'

Rutter, who had not heard this particular joke much more than a thousand times before, smiled politely.

'At least, I *assume* it's the law,' the bald man continued. 'You *are* Inspector Rutter, aren't you?'

'That's right.'

'Then pull up a pew, and I'll perform the introductions. I'm Edward Bliss, solicitor of this parish. To my left we have Alfred Potter, the merciless capitalist owner of Potter Investments Ltd, and to my right is Philip Stokes, the best plumber in the county.'

'Plumber?' Rutter repeated, thinking he must have misheard.

'Waterworks specialist. If you ever have any problems with your prostate, he's the man to see,' Bliss explained. 'So tell me, how did you track us down? Or is that what you might call a professional secret?'

'No secret,' Rutter assured him. 'Simcaster Grammar School keeps excellent records on its past pupils. I simply asked the school secretary for the names of some of the men who had been in the same class as Fredrick Dodds.'

'And she came up with the three of us,' Alfred Potter said. 'Actually, I'm not sure we can be of much use to you.'

'You must have spent five years in the same classroom as Dodds,' Rutter pointed out.

'True,' Potter said awkwardly. 'But that's not to say we ever really got to know him.'

'His father was a coalman, for God's sake!' Dr Stokes said.

Bliss tut-tutted. 'A coal *merchant*, Philip,' he said reproachfully.

'Perhaps that's what he was by the time he enrolled his son in "Simmie", but it hadn't always been like that. I can remember him delivering coal to our house *personally* when I was five or six. My mother always used to tell the maid to watch him like a hawk while he tipped the coal into the cellar – just to make sure he didn't get away with delivering one bag too few.'

'Even so . . .' Bliss protested.

'His father might have been richer than any of ours by the time Fred came to Simmie, but all the money in the world won't quite wash away the coal dust from under your fingernails,' Stokes said remorselessly. 'Not that there was much of a chance to wash it away in Fred Dodds' case. If I remember rightly, Fred's father – who, typical of his class, had no vision at all – pulled Fred out of school to work on his wagons.'

'I . . . er . . . I think Philip may be giving you the wrong impression,' Bliss told Rutter.

'Are you saying there was no snobbery at Simcaster Grammar?' the inspector asked.

'Oh, there was snobbery all right,' Bliss said. 'Not that we'd have seen it in quite *those terms* before the First World War.'

'Then how would you have seen it?'

'As part of a social order in which everyone knew his place and stayed in it. You know how the hymn goes – "The rich man in his castle, the poor man at his gate, God made them high or lowly, And order'd their estate." That was pretty much the accepted wisdom in those days. But that's not the point.'

'Then what is?'

'It wasn't just a matter of class. We did, eventually, learn to accept some of the boys from more humble origins. And if they never quite became our "friends", then they were, at least, our "close acquaintances". But Fred Dodds would never have qualified for either of those titles – not even if he'd been *born* with a silver spoon in his mouth.'

'And why might that be?' Rutter asked.

'Because he was a freak,' Alfred Potter said. 'You must have known boys like him in your own schooldays – boys who stood out as being different, and were shunned by most of their contemporaries.'

Rutter thought back to his school, which, while it had not been as exclusive as 'Simmie', had at least been a grammar.

'Yes, there were a few of them,' he admitted. 'Usually, it was the ones who were no good at games. Was that Fred Dodds' problem?'

'By no means,' Bliss said. 'He was never what you'd call a team player, but he was quite an exceptional athlete – won the hurdles championship for three years running.'

'So what was wrong with him?'

'It's difficult to put one's finger on, especially after all these years,' Bliss admitted. 'I think it would be fair to say that he shunned us almost as much we shunned him. He never really tried to fit in – never aspired to be like the rest of us. He seemed quite content to spend all his time with Sidney Hill.'

'Who was he?' Rutter asked.

'Another freak,' Alfred Potter replied.

'And was he from the "wrong" social background, too?'

'No, as a matter of fact, his background was highly acceptable,' Potter said. 'His father was a rural dean. I believe, in fact, that he was elevated to a bishopric in the end.'

'So what drew Dodds and Sidney Hill together?'

'Again, it's very difficult to put a finger on that,' Bliss said. 'They seemed to share an interest – though it wasn't anything as commonplace as trainspotting or butterfly collecting.'

'Then what was it?'

'I don't know. But it certainly had to be *something*. They were always whispering conspiratorially to each other, you see. And even when the rest of us could hear what they were saying, we never seemed to understand them as well as they understood each other. It was almost as if they'd turned English into their own secret language – as if they'd given all the words a different meaning.'

'What about girlfriends?' Rutter asked.

Bliss chuckled, as if at a fond memory. 'None of us was what you'd exactly call "advanced" for our age. I suppose that came from attending an all-boys school. Even so, by the time we were fifteen we could all feel the sap rising in our loins. But not those two. Not Fred and Sidney. They'd turn up when the school organized a joint dance with Lady Margaret's College, but they'd show absolutely no interest at all in the "tottie".'

'Perhaps they were both . . . er . . .'

'Queers? Poofs? Bum bandits?' Dr Stokes supplied.

Rutter looked at him with dislike. 'Not being a medical man like yourself, I don't know all the scientific terms you have at your command,' he said. 'So to put it in simple, layman's terms, I was wondering if they might have been homosexuals.'

'Not a chance of that,' Bliss said firmly.

'How can you be so sure?'

The solicitor squirmed a little in his leather seat. 'Well, you can always tell, can't you?'

'No,' Rutter replied. 'You can't.'

Bliss exchanged a quick glance with the other two. 'We have a friend,' he said tentatively. 'Very nice chap indeed, and one of the driving forces behind the Lodge. He's been taking medication for his condition for over forty years, and I must say, it seems to have worked a treat.'

Woodend would have said, 'So a poof's all right is he – as long as he's also a Mason?'

Rutter said, 'If I understand you correctly, this friend of yours is, or was, a homosexual.'

'*Was*. Definitely *was*,' Bliss replied. 'In fact, I'm not sure he ever *practised* it at all. Just had a tendency towards it. No more than that.'

Woodend was right about the Masons, Rutter thought – a funny handshake excused a multitude of sins.

'How does this friend of yours fit into this conversation?' he asked.

'Can't you work it out for yourself?' Dr Stokes demanded.

'Possibly. But I'd prefer to hear it from you.'

'All right. If you must,' Bliss said resignedly. 'This friend of ours didn't think that either Dodds or Hill were homosexual.'

'That's scarcely what I'd call proof,' Rutter said.

'They can spot each other a mile away,' Alfred Potter said. 'That's the way they are.'

Rutter nodded, as if what they were saying made perfect logical sense. Then, when he saw the looks of mild relief on their faces, he said casually, 'You're holding something back, aren't you?'

Bliss sighed. 'When this person we were speaking of decided to take the cure, he gathered all his friends together.'

'In the Lodge?' Rutter guessed.

'As a matter of fact, I think it was. Anyway, he said that

some of us may have had our suspicions about him and others may have not, but he wanted to make a clean slate of it before all of us – to confess everything.'

'And that's when Hill and Dodds came up?'

'That's right. He said that towards the end of our school days, he'd approached both of them separately. Dodds punched him on the nose, and when Hill had finally understood what he was talking about, he was physically sick. Does that satisfy you?'

'More than it seems to have satisfied them,' said Rutter, allowing himself one small Woodendesque comment. 'I'd like to talk to this Sidney Hall. Does any of you know where I might find him?'

Dr Stokes smirked. 'You could try St Jude's churchyard,' he suggested.

'I beg your pardon?'

'He threw himself under the wheels of the Simcaster to Manchester express train. That would be in 1915, I think.'

'1916,' Potter corrected him.

'Whatever the date, he's been as dead as they get for well over forty years.'

'Does any of you know *why* he committed suicide?' Rutter asked.

'He was a freak,' Dr Stokes said. 'That's exactly the kind of thing that freaks do.'

Bliss gave his friend a reproachful look. 'I remember reading in the paper that it was something a mystery,' he said. 'There was certainly no suicide note, if memory serves.'

'Did any of you have any business dealings with Fred Dodds after you'd all left school?' Rutter asked, changing tack.

'Are you asking if we bought our coal from him?' Dr Stokes said, after draining most of a large whisky in one swallow. 'If I did, I really can't remember.'

It would almost be worth going back into uniform – if it

gave him a chance to arrest Stokes for drunk-driving, Rutter thought.

'I wasn't asking if you had any dealings with him while he was still a coalman,' he explained. 'I meant after that. When Dodds and his partner, Mr Cuthburtson, ran the Peninsula Trading Company over in Whitebridge.'

Stokes and Potter immediately shook their heads.

'What about you, Mr Bliss?' Rutter asked. 'Didn't you do any legal work for him when he was setting up his business?'

'As far as I can recall, Fred always used the same lawyer as his father had done,' Bliss said. 'Todd Danby, his name was. Used to have his offices on Church Street. He's dead now, of course.'

That was the trouble with this case, Rutter thought. So many people who had been involved with it were dead now.

'Yes, he was a wily old bird, was Todd,' Bliss said, the look in his eyes taking him back to an earlier age. 'Taught me a thing or two when I was starting out. Nobody could tie up a contract as tightly as Todd Danby. Once he'd worked on it, you could study it for a year, and still not find a loophole. And he certainly did a good job of keeping Fred Dodds out of gaol.'

'He did *what*?' Rutter asked.

'Kept Fred Dodds out of gaol.'

'And why should Fred have gone to gaol in the first place?'

'Because in a case of that nature, the next-of-kin is usually the most obvious suspect.'

'In a case of *what* nature?' Rutter asked exasperatedly.

Bliss looked at him oddly. 'You mean, you really don't know what I'm talking about?'

'I should have thought that was obvious!'

'I see,' Bliss said. 'Well, I must say that, since you're looking into Fred Dodds' murder, I am quite surprised

131

that you don't already know that his father was murdered as well.'

'When was this?'

'1921? 1922? Just before Freddie sold the coal yard and set himself up as Peninsula Trading.'

'And was someone eventually arrested for the murder of his father?'

'No. As I said, the police might, or might not have suspected Fred – I definitely would have in their place – but they certainly couldn't prove anything, and he inherited the whole of his father's estate. I really think someone should have told you all this before, you know – especially considering the way that Freddie's father died?'

'And how did he die?' Rutter asked – though he thought he probably already knew the answer.

'His head was smashed in,' Bliss said. 'With a coal hammer.'

Sixteen

So this was one of the places where Margaret Dodds had rested for a while on her journey from birth to the gallows, Paniatowski thought, looking up at the vicarage that stood in splendid isolation on the edge of the village of Blakebrook.

The vicarage was large, and probably extremely draughty – especially when the wind was blowing in from across the moors. It had been built at a different time, to meet a different set of needs. Thus, there were gable windows in the roof, which would allow a little light to permeate into the servants' cramped attic bedrooms. Thus, there was a driveway wide enough to permit two coaches to pass each other, and a stable block where the horses had been housed. And thus – since both the coach and the servant belonged to the past – it was now up for auction and would probably eventually be converted into rural-holiday flats.

If Rutter had been there with her, Paniatowski would probably have commented that the vicarage seemed an unlikely nursery from which to grow a full-blown nymphomaniac like Margaret Dodds. It would have been a mistake to say it, but she would have said it anyway, because scoring points off the inspector was rapidly becoming her main aim in life.

'My judgement's shot,' she murmured softly to herself. 'My bloody judgement's shot.'

'What was that you said, my dear?' asked a thin voice to her left. 'I didn't quite catch it, you see. My brain's as sharp as it's ever been, but my ears are starting to let me down.'

Paniatowski turned her head, to face the little old woman who was standing next to her.

'Sorry, Mrs Trotwood,' she said. 'I was just thinking out loud.'

The old woman smiled. 'You can afford to at your age,' she said. 'Whereas if *I* started doing it, people would just assume I'd gone batty.'

Clara Trotwood reminded her in many ways of Mrs Fortesque, Paniatowski thought, and wondered – for perhaps the hundredth time – just what the question was which she should have asked the major's wife.

'You said you started working here as a kitchen maid, didn't you?' she asked the old woman.

'That's right,' Clara Trotwood agreed. 'I was twelve years old at the time, and so, naturally, I started at the very bottom of the ladder. But I didn't stay there for long!'

Her accent was not local, and certainly not natural to the class she had been born into, Paniatowski decided. She had acquired it – perhaps deliberately, perhaps accidentally – during her long years of service at the vicarage. She had probably learned a great many other things as well, the sergeant guessed, because even now Clara looked like a woman set on self-improvement.

'By the time Mr Jeffries, Margaret's father, took over the living, I was in my mid-twenties and had already been the housekeeper for nearly two years,' Clara Trotwood continued.

'How old was Margaret when the family moved here?'

'She was seven.'

'You don't happen to know where Mr Jeffries' previous parish was, do you?'

'There hadn't *been* a previous parish. Mr Jeffries was what was called a "late entrant" into the clergy. He was considerably older than his wife, and before he'd got the call to the priesthood he worked in a big merchant bank in the centre of Manchester.'

'Were the family happy here, do you think?'

'Mr Jeffries *could* have been.'

'What do you mean by that?'

'I mean that he was very enthusiastic about his new vocation. I'm not saying it was easy for him at first, mind – folk round here were naturally suspicious of anybody who'd been contaminated by living in the big city. And it didn't help that Mr Jeffries' posh accent made him sound as if he was talking with a plum in his mouth. But it didn't take the people of Blakebrook long to realize that there was no side to him – that he really did care about his duties. And in the end, his past even started working for him, instead of against him.'

'In what way?'

'Folk became quite proud of the fact their vicar could have had a much better life – if he'd wanted to. That he'd made his sacrifice for *them*.'

'So why did you say he only *could* have been happy?'

'Because of *Mrs* Jeffries. Edith Jeffries was never any good at being a vicar's wife. She went through some of the motions – attending weekly meetings of the Women's Institute, judging cake competitions, having church workers round for afternoon tea – but her heart wasn't really in it.'

'Why do you think that was?'

'Because it wasn't what she'd been expecting out of life when she married Mr Jeffries.'

'Did she tell you that?'

Clara Trotwood laughed. 'Of course she didn't tell *me*! I was only a servant. But I used to hear her arguing with her husband. I couldn't have avoided it, even if I'd wanted to. She'd say that if he'd stayed in his old job they could have retired to a villa in the south of France after a few years. She'd complain that it wasn't fair on Margaret. "How's our daughter ever supposed to meet the right kind of young man in a place like this?" she'd say. "Margaret's still a child," the vicar would point out. "But she won't always be a child,"

Mrs Jeffries would complain. "She'll grow up in time – but we'll still be stuck in this hole." That's what she called Blakebrook – "this hole"! Never in public, of course – but everybody knew that's how she felt. She looked down on us. She wouldn't even let Margaret attend the local school, for fear that something unpleasant would rub off on her.'

'So did she send her daughter away to boarding school?'

'I expect she would have done, if she could have afforded to. But it just wasn't possible on a country clergyman's salary, so Mrs Jeffries educated her at home.'

'And yet Margaret still won a place at Oxford!'

'Not just a place at Oxford,' Clara Trotwood said. 'A *scholarship*. And that was just as well, wasn't it, because when her parents died they left her practically nothing.'

'When, exactly, *did* they die?'

'Her mother had been getting headaches even when Margaret was still living at home. She passed on in the middle of Margaret's first year at university. The doctor did an autopsy on her, and found a brain tumour the size of a duck egg. Mr Jeffries took it much worse then I'd ever have imagined that he would. Even at his wife's funeral, I could see that a part of him had already died, too. One year later, the new vicar was burying *him*.'

'Tell me about Margaret,' Paniatowski invited.

'I'm not sure there's much I can tell you,' Clara said. 'She was a very quiet child. Well, she didn't have much choice, did she, since her mother wouldn't let her play with other children.'

'She didn't ever confide in you?'

'No.'

'I'm surprised at that.'

Clara Trotwood chuckled. 'You've been reading too many romantic novels,' she said. 'You can picture it all, can't you? The cruel, indifferent mother! The beautiful, sad little girl who finds her only true friend in a kindly servant! It wasn't like that at all. Margaret was not a snob like her mother, but she didn't spend hours pouring out her heart to me. She didn't need to. Mrs Jeffries wasn't a bad mother, by her own lights. She was always prepared to listen to Margaret's worries. And to give her daughter lots of advice – even when she didn't ask for it.'

'What kind of advice?'

Clara Trotwood chuckled again. 'I knew that a smart girl like you would be able to sort the wheat from the chaff, and ask the right questions,' she said. 'It was marriage that Mrs Jeffries mostly talked about.'

'Marriage?'

'Almost from the time they moved in, until Margaret went away to university, it was Mrs Jeffries' favourite subject. "Don't marry a man already set in his ways," she'd said. "That's what I did, and look where it's got me. Find yourself a husband who you can mould – a husband you can make something out of." And as far as I can see, that's exactly what Margaret was trying to do when she went and married Rob Hartley. But, in a way, she made just as big a mistake as her mother had. Mrs Jeffries married a man already moulded, Margaret married one who was not made of strong enough clay *to* mould.'

Paniatowski shook her head in admiration. 'Did Margaret tell you all this?' she asked.

'There you go – back to the romantic novels,' Clara Trotwood said. 'Margaret no more confided in me when she came back from university than she did before she went away. But you mustn't think that because I live all of seven miles away from Whitebridge I know nothing of what goes on there. I knew the Hartley family, and if Margaret *had* asked me – which she didn't – I'd have told her that Rob was a nice enough lad, but he'd never amount to much.'

'What about his sister Helen?' Paniatowski asked.

'She was a different kettle of fish altogether. She had more than her share of the family's backbone, did Helen.'

'And Fred Dodds?'

'I can't help you there. He didn't even come to Whitebridge until he was in his twenties.'

'Do you think Margaret would have been capable of killing him?'

'I'll say this about the Jeffries women. They were all, in their own ways, very determined characters. Edith couldn't dissuade her husband from entering the Church, but she did everything she could to see that Margaret didn't suffer what she saw as the consequences of it. And just look at Jane! I was reading in the paper that she's one of the most important lawyers in England. You can't tell me that she got to that position without sheer hard work and determination.'

'You haven't answered my question,' Paniatowski said.

'That's because I don't know how to, exactly,' Clara Trotwood said.

'What do you mean?'

'If you asked me whether she had a natural inclination towards violence, then I'd have to say no. But if you asked me if she'd kill to get something that had become really important to her, well then I'd be less sure of my ground.'

Paniatowski glanced down at her watch. 'You've really been very helpful, Miss Trotwood.'

'Is that it?' the other woman asked, surprised.

'Well, yes, I think it is.'

'I wouldn't have thought a smart girl like you would leave without asking me *one* more question.'

Paniatowski smiled. 'And what question might that be?'

'Why didn't you ask me about Margaret's relationship with her father?'

A good point, Paniatowski thought uncomfortably. She certainly *should* have asked, and it wasn't like her not to. Was she starting to develop a blind spot to father-daughter relationships?

'I suppose I didn't think I needed to ask,' she said, explaining her reasons to herself as much as she was explaining it to Clara Trotwood. 'After all, you've told me about how the mother and daughter got on, and about how the mother and father got on, so I assumed—'

'And you think it's as simple as that, do you?' Clara Trotwood asked, with an amused twinkle in her eye. 'Do you really believe it's just like drawing a triangle? Do you imagine that, because you can already see two of the lines on the page, all you have to do is join up the unattached ends in order to be able to see the third side?' She shook her head. '*Human* relationships are more complicated than that, my dear. *Much* more complicated.'

'I know,' Paniatowski said humbly. 'Or at least, if I don't, I certainly should. What kind of relationship did Mr Jeffries and his daughter have, Mrs Trotwood?'

'They didn't talk much, because they knew that would only be causing trouble,' Clara Trotwood said. 'But they understood each other. He loved her – and she *worshipped* him.'

Seventeen

M ost of the early morning traffic was flowing from the suburbs into downtown Toronto, so the man in the unmarked police car travelling in the opposite direction had no excuse for clamping a siren to his roof – even though he really wanted to.

Sergeant Bill Paxton enjoyed being a member of the Royal Canadian Mounted Police. He liked the work, and he liked the power that it gave him over other people. What he *didn't* like was being introduced to new people and watching the shit-kicking grins form on their faces as they invariably said, 'A Mountie always gets his man.'

A Mountie always gets his man! What kind of half-assed motto was that, for Christ's sake?

Leaving aside the fact that it simply wasn't true – as the wanted notices pinned up on the station-house notice-board amply proved – it conjured up all the wrong kinds of images. Say 'Mountie' and people thought of policemen on horseback, men who crossed frozen wastes and hunted down guys who wore furs and had bottles of moonshine whiskey in their pockets. That wasn't how Paxton saw himself at all. He was a *Dragnet* man, a *Naked City* man – a street-smart, hard-boiled city cop who couldn't build a shelter in the snow to save his life, but who sure-as-hell knew how to get the better of any suspect who wore a suit and necktie.

The prosperous-looking house was located on a quiet, leafy street, surrounded by other prosperous-looking houses.

The front yard had the appearance of being professionally cared for, and there were two cars in the garage.

People who lived in houses like these never pulled an unwanted night shift, Paxton thought sourly. They never had to answer to their superiors for the complaints that members of the so-called 'public' had filed against them. They had it easy – real easy.

As he got out of his car, he knew he was scowling, and didn't care. After all, what the hell else was a hard-boiled cop like him supposed to do, but scowl?

He walked up to the front door of the target house and rapped imperiously on it with his knuckles. In a place like this he would not have been the least surprised if his knock had been answered by some kind of uniformed flunkey, but in fact the door was opened by a man wearing a silk dressing gown.

'Yes?' the man said, stifling a yawn.

He loved these early morning calls, Paxton thought happily as he reached into his pocket for his identification.

The other man examined the document, then handed it back. 'What's this all about, Sergeant?' he asked.

'I need to speak to Mr Cuthburtson,' Paxton said in a voice that *almost* came close to the one that Jack Webb used when he was playing Sergeant Joe Friday.

'*Need* to speak to Mr Cuthburtson?' the man in silk dressing gown asked. 'Don't you mean, *would like to*?'

He was trying to sound self-assured and in control, but he didn't quite make it. Paxton turn his steely-eyed cop gaze full on the man. Mid-forties. Limp pale hair carefully brushed over to disguise a bald patch. Weak chin. Slow twitch in right eye. Intimidation quotient? Low to non-existent! This was going to be fun!

'No, I wouldn't *like* to see him,' Paxton said. 'I *like* to see my friends. But as an officer of the law, I *need* to speak to him.'

'Concerning what?' the other man asked defeatedly.

'Official business,' Paxton snapped. 'Is he in?'

'*I'm* Mr Cuthburtson.'

'Maybe you are *a* Mr Cuthburtson, but it's the chairman of Cuthburtson Import-Export I want to see.'

'That's me.'

He didn't look like he had the personality be the chairman of *anything*, Paxton thought. Besides, he was too young to be the man that the long cable from Lancashire had inquired about. Still, there was no harm in milking a little bit more out of the game, was there?

'You're Mr Benjamin Cuthburtson?' Paxton asked sceptically.

'No. That was my father.'

'Was?'

'He's been dead for over three years now. I'm Ernest Cuthburtson.'

'Then I suppose you'll have to do,' Paxton said offhandedly. 'Mind if I come in?'

'Well—' Cuthburtson began.

'Thank you,' Paxton interrupted, barging past him.

Paxton disliked men he could dominate almost as much as he disliked men who could dominate him, and the fact that Cuthburtson's lounge was furnished so obviously expensively made him even more inclined to give the other man a rough ride.

Sitting down – uninvited – he pulled out his notebook and shot Cuthburtson a hostile gaze.

'You weren't born in this country, were you?' he asked accusingly.

'No, I—'

'Are you a Canadian citizen now?'

'Yes. Yes, I am.'

Damn, Paxton thought. Non-citizens were always more insecure, and hence easier to bully. Not that he thought he'd have much of a problem bullying this particular chinless wonder.

'What made you emigrate to this country?' he asked.

Cuthburtson gave him a weak smile, as if he still considered it possible to get on Paxton's good side. 'I didn't have much choice in the matter. I was only a child at the time.'

'All right! What made your *father* emigrate?'

'It wasn't a question I thought to ask,' Cuthburtson said, looking away.

'How old were you when you came to Canada? Twelve?'

'Yes.'

'And a twelve-year-old boy didn't "think to ask"? Who do you think you're trying to fool here?'

'If I did ask, then I've forgotten the answer.'

Leaving aside the obvious lie as something he could go back to later, Paxton consulted his notebook again.

'When you lived in England, your father was in partnership with a Fredrick Dodds in a town called Whitebridge, Lancashire,' he said. 'Are all those details correct?'

'How did you—?'

'Just answer the question, if you don't mind, sir.'

A look hardly strong enough to be called defiance came into Cuthburtson's eyes.

'Before you go any further with your questioning, I demand to know what this is all about,' he said.

'I'm afraid all that I can reveal at this point is that I'm running a joint operation with the Lancashire Constabulary,' Paxton said. 'Fredrick Dodds was your father's partner? Is that correct?'

'It's correct.'

'So you must have known him well.'

'He was a grown-up; I was a child. I couldn't swear that I ever even met him.'

It was all going even more beautifully than he could have imagined Paxton thought. He consulted his notebook again. 'Couldn't swear that you ever even met him?'

'That's what I said.'

'But according to my information, he used to come to your house *every Sunday* for lunch. And not only that, but the whole family used to go on excursions with him.'

Cuthburtson bowed his head, but said nothing.

'Well?' Paxton demanded.

'You're right, of course.'

'So why did you lie to me?'

Cuthburtson shrugged. 'Habit, I suppose. When we first arrived in Canada my father said that none of us was ever to mention Fred Dodds' name again. He said as far as the family was concerned, Dodds had never existed. We followed that rule for the last twenty-seven years of my father's life. There didn't seem to be much point in breaking it now that he's passed away.'

'Did your father go back to England often?' Paxton asked.

'Now and again. For business reasons.'

'Did he happen to go back in the summer of 1934?'

'I have no idea.'

'We can easily check up on it, you know. There'll be records of his journeys somewhere.'

'I *still* have no idea.'

'What caused the partnership to break up? How did Dodds suddenly turn from close family friend into a guy whose name should never be spoken?'

'I don't know.'

'Was it money? Did Dodds try to cheat your father?'

'If he did, my father never said so.'

'Or have I got it the wrong way round? Was it your father who tried to cheat Dodds?'

'My father would never have tried to cheat anybody. Ask any of his Canadian business associates.'

'So it *was* Dodds who was trying to cheat him?'

'I didn't say that. I couldn't be expected to know. As I've already said, I was only twelve years old at the time.'

144

'In this country, we take our kids hunting when they're twelve. We think of twelve as being almost a man.'

'I very much doubt that's true. But even if it is, I'm only Canadian by adoption.'

The bastard was getting better at defending himself, Paxton thought. Like a rat trapped in a corner, he was starting to fight back.

'So your father didn't tell you about it when you were twelve. I'll accept that,' he conceded. 'But he must have explained it to you when you were older.'

'I've told you, once we'd set foot on Canadian soil, we never discussed Fred Dodds at all!'

Paxton shook his head, disbelievingly. He recognized that psychology was not his strongest point, but a man like Cuthburtson was as easy for him to read as an open book.

Maybe Cuthburtson's father hadn't told him why he was dissolving the partnership at the time. Maybe he hadn't even explained his reasons when his son had joined him in the business. But at some time – possibly just before he died – the old man had to have come clean. So now that knowledge was locked inside the weak son's brain – and it shouldn't take too much of an effort to force that brain open and discover the truth.

'There's two ways we can do this – the easy way and the hard way,' Paxton said, his voice now more Sgt Frank Arcaro than it was Sgt Joe Friday. 'The easy way is that you tell everything I need to know here and now. The hard way is that—'

'There are eight million stories in the Naked City, and this had been one of them,' said a mocking voice from the doorway.

Paxton turned to face the new arrival. It was a woman, possibly a few years younger than Cuthburtson. The family resemblance was unmistakable, but there were clear differences, too. His chin was weak, hers determined. His eyes were watery with indecision, hers burned with the fires of anger. He might be the chairman of Cuthburtson Import-Export, but there was no doubt about who was actually running the company.

'Sergeant Paxton, my . . . my sister Louise,' Cuthburtson stuttered.

'Pleased to meet you, Sergeant – now bugger off before I call a policeman,' Louise Cuthburtson said.

Paxton stood up and stretched to his full height so that he towered over the woman. 'I *am* a policeman,' he said witheringly.

Louise Cuthburtson threw back her head and laughed contemptuously. 'You're not a policeman,' she said. 'You're nothing but an errand boy with a warrant card.'

'I'm a sergeant!' Paxton protested, outraged.

'A *senior* errand boy, then. It still doesn't give you any right to talk to the grown-ups.'

'Listen to me—' Paxton began.

'No, you listen to me,' Louise Cuthburtson said commandingly. 'My brother is of a nervous disposition. He's been that way since before we moved to Canada. He's—'

'It wasn't my fault,' Ernest Cuthburtson said in a voice that was almost a moan.

Louise Cuthburtson abandoned her attack on Paxton, and turned towards her brother. 'Of course it wasn't your fault,' she said soothingly.

'He was older than me. He should have known better,' Ernest said, as tears began to form in his eyes.

'Nobody ever blamed you,' Louise told him. 'Daddy didn't when he was alive, and I'm certainly not doing it now.'

'What's he talking about?' Paxton asked.

Louise whipped round to face the Mountie again. 'You see what you've done to him?' she demanded. 'See the state you've driven him to. It's been years since he's been anything like this. Years!'

'I only asked him—' Paxton began.

146

'Why don't you go to your room, Ernie?' Louise Cuthburtson said. 'Why don't you go to your room, and have a nice lie down.'

'Will you come and see me?' her brother asked pathetically.

'Yes, I promise I'll come and see you as soon as I've got rid of our unwanted visitor.'

'Now just a minute—' Paxton said.

'Go on, Ernie. Go to your room,' Louise Cuthburtson coaxed.

The man in the silk dressing gown headed towards the door, walking with the shuffling steps of a man twice his age. Paxton considered stopping him, but somehow couldn't quite bring himself to.

The moment her brother had left the room, Louise Cuthburtson turned on the policeman with all the ferocity of a wounded mountain cat.

'I will not have my brother bullied by an insensitive thug like you,' she spat. 'You don't know what he's been through. You have no comprehension of how much he's suffered.'

'Does this have anything to do with why you left England?' Paxton asked.

'You surely don't think I'm going to answer any more of your questions, do you?' Louise Cuthburtson said incredulously.

'I'm here on official business and—'

'And I'm a personal friend of your commissioner. If you don't get out of this house right now, I'll personally see to it that you spend the rest of your career in Inuvik, with only a dog team to keep you company. Am I making myself clear?'

'You can't talk to me like that,' Paxton protested.

But she already had – and he did not doubt for a minute that she had sufficient influence to see her threat carried through. Though he was almost exploding with frustration and humiliation – though nothing would have given him greater satisfaction than to pistol-whip the bitch

– he saw no alternative but to do as Louise Cuthburtson had instructed.

'I'm going now – but I may be back,' he said, trying to save a little face from this desperate situation.

'You know where the door is. See yourself out,' Louise told him.

Paxton walked slowly to his car, deep in thought. What had Ernest Cuthburtson done that he claimed hadn't been his fault? the policeman wondered. *Who* was older than him, and should have known better? Was what he'd done the reason that the family moved to Canada? And was he a mental wreck because of what he'd done, or had he only done it – whatever 'it' was – *because* he was a mental wreck?

The policeman sighed. There were times, he thought, when he wished he really *was* as smart as the cops on *Dragnet*.

Eighteen

Woodend and Paniatowski were already sitting at their usual table in the Drum and Monkey when Rutter entered the bar. The inspector had already dropped one bombshell that afternoon. Now, from the expression on his face, it looked as if he were about to drop another one.

Rutter pulled out a chair and sat down. 'There's nothing in Sharpe's case notes about the murder of Marcus Dodds,' he said.

'Nothing?' Woodend repeated incredulously.

'Nothing,' Rutter confirmed. I've been through *all* the documentation three times since I got back from Simcaster, and there's not a single mention.'

'Why are you so surprised?' Monika Paniatowski asked.

'Shouldn't we be?' Woodend countered.

'No. Sharpe probably left out anything on Marcus Dodds for the same reason that he made no mention of the two cars which drove down Hebden Brow on the night of Fred Dodds' murder. Because it would have been a distraction – a little annoyance which might threaten to divert attention away from his claim that Margaret Dodds killed her husband.'

'I know it doesn't seem likely, given the fact that the first murder occurred less than thirty miles from here,' Woodend said tentatively, 'but perhaps Sharpe didn't even *know* about the Marcus Dodds case.'

Rutter shook his head. 'He knew, all right.'

'How can you be so sure?'

'Because after I failed to find any mention of Marcus Dodds in Sharpe's records, I had a close look at the transcript of the trial.' Rutter reached into his briefcase and handed Woodend a folder. 'The relevant part has a blue line in the margin.'

Woodend flicked through the pages until he came to the passage Rutter had marked.

Edward Mottram QC: Were you aware, Chief Inspector Sharpe, that Fredrick Dodds' father, Marcus Dodds, was also murdered?

Sharpe: I was, sir.

Mottram: And not only murdered, but murdered in exactly the same way as his son. Were you aware of *that*?

Sharpe: Yes, sir.

Mottram: And yet it never occurred to you that there might be a connection between the two murders?

Sharpe: No, sir. As far as I can ascertain, Margaret Dodds never met her late father-in-law. And even if she had, I can think of no reason why she should have wanted to murder him.

Mottram: Are you being deliberately obtuse, Chief Inspector?

Sharpe: I'm afraid I don't understand.

Mottram: I was not suggesting that Margaret had killed both Fredrick and Marcus. Rather, I was suggesting that she killed *neither* of them – that both were murdered by a third party as yet unknown, a third party whose preferred method of murder was with a hammer.

Sharpe: Margaret Dodds had the means, the motive and the opportunity. She could provide no alibi for the time her husband was killed, there was blood on her dress and her fingerprints were on the murder weapon. She killed Fredrick Dodds. To suggest anything else is fanciful.

Mottram: Is that so?

Sharpe: Yes.

Mottram: Then can you tell me *why* she used a hammer to kill her husband? Why, of the hundreds of ways available to her, she selected exactly the same weapon as had been used on her late father-in-law?

Sharpe: *Because* it had been used on her father-in-law.

Mottram: I beg your pardon, Chief Inspector.

Sharpe: Because she hoped that by using the hammer she would create exactly the kind of confusion that you are referring to now. Because she hoped that the police would accept the absurd theory that there was a mad hammer killer on the loose, a mad killer who just happened to have a grudge against the Dodds family.

Mottram: And isn't it possible that was, in fact, the case?

Sharpe: Yes. In a 'whodunnit novel', it's perfectly possible. But I've been a policeman for a long time, and I can tell you that sort of thing doesn't happen in real life.

'An' that's it?' Woodend asked. 'That's all there is?'

Rutter shrugged. 'Not quite. Mottram mentions Fred Dodds' father's murder again in his summing up to the jury, but even just reading it cold, you can tell his heart isn't really in it.'

'That's not surprising, after the way he'd handled the cross-examination,' Woodend said. 'If they'd rehearsed it together, Mottram couldn't have done a better job at feeding Sharpe just the lines he wanted to be fed.'

'Are you suggesting that the defence lawyer made a deliberate hash of the cross-examination?' Monika Paniatowski asked.

Woodend shook his head. 'No, I don't see any conspiracy here – at least no conspiracy which involved the defence counsel. Mottram was incompetent, rather than corrupt. Sharpe had anticipated all *his* questions, but he simply wasn't prepared for Sharpe's answers.'

'You have to have a grudging admiration for the cunning way Sharpe handled it,' Rutter said. 'He never had to defend his theory that Marcus Dodds' murder was irrelevant to this case, because he never even admitted it *was* a theory. The way he talked, it was if he were stating no more than the plain, unvarnished truth. And he obviously swung the jury round to his viewpoint.'

'Maybe Marcus Dodds' murder *was* an irrelevance, just as Sharpe claimed,' Woodend said. 'Even if we rule out Margaret Dodds as the murderer, it's possible that the real killer *did* copy the method used by Marcus Dodds' murderer.'

'Why should he have done that?' Paniatowski asked.

'For the reason Sharpe gave – to confuse the issue. An' while I have nothin' but contempt for the way Sharpe did his job, it *is* still possible that he only played down the first murder because he really did believe Margaret Dodds was guilty of the second.'

'There's a "but" isn't there?' Rutter said.

'What makes you say that?'

'When you've got that look on your face, there's always a "but".'

Woodend grinned, but Paniatowski did not. Instead, she let her hand hover over Rutter's head, as if she were about to pat him for being such a clever boy. Rutter, who was looking at Woodend, did not notice the gesture. Woodend, who could see both his sergeant and inspector, did notice, but decided – for the moment at least – to ignore it.

'I'll tell you what the "but" is,' the Chief Inspector said. 'There was a dark shadow hangin' over Fred Dodds long before he was killed. His father was murdered. His best friend – his only friend, by all accounts – committed suicide. His partner sold up – for no apparent reason – an' put

A Death Left Hanging

thousands of miles between himself an' Whitebridge. Any *one* of those things could have happened to one of us. But all three of them together? I don't really think so!'

'Then there's the fact that his wife's first husband died as a result of an accident,' Rutter pointed out.

Paniatowski sighed loudly.

'Is something the matter, Sergeant?' Rutter asked.

'If it's left up to you, we'll be like a dog forever chasing round after its own tail,' Paniatowski said. 'I see no reason at all why we even need to consider Robert Hartley's death.'

'Don't you?' Rutter asked. 'Then perhaps I'd better explain it to you. We know that Margaret was having an affair with Fred Dodds before her first husband died and—'

'We know there are people who *think* they were having an affair,' Paniatowski interrupted. 'But if there were any actual proof, Sharpe would have produced it at the trial.'

'I thought you said he didn't like distractions,' Rutter responded cuttingly. 'I thought your theory was that he'd pare away everything except for the evidence which supported his own simplistic view of the case.'

'But that *would* have helped his simplistic view of the case,' Paniatowski countered, raising her voice to such a level that customers at other tables turned round to look at her. 'He'd probably have argued – and you'd probably have agreed with him all the way – that a woman who was capable of adultery was equally capable of the brutal and bloody murder of her husband.'

'I never said anything like that!' Rutter retorted. He was furious, but still enough in control of himself to keep *his* voice down. 'I never even went so far as to suggest—'

'Enough!' Woodend ordered. 'There's plenty of people already tryin' to shaft us, without us makin' things any worse by fightin' amongst ourselves.'

'Sorry, sir,' Paniatowski muttered sheepishly.

'I don't think I'm the one you should be apologizin' to, Monika,' Woodend told her.

Paniatowski glared defiantly at Woodend for a second, then slowly turned towards Rutter.

'Sorry, Inspector,' she said, dragging the words up from somewhere deep inside her, then forcing them out of her mouth.

'It's all right,' Rutter replied. 'I was probably as much to blame as you were.'

She didn't like him saying that, Woodend thought. She didn't like it at all. She'd have been so much happier if Rutter had thrown her apology back in her face, because the last thing she wanted was peace and harmony. He wondered what the hell was *happening* to his sergeant.

'Let's get back to Robert Hartley's death, shall we?' he said. 'You're right, Bob, when you say we should consider it – because we can't afford to overlook any possibilities. An' *you're* right, Monika, when you say that such considerations don't seem to be leadin' us anywhere.'

Who would ever have seen me as a diplomat? Woodend asked himself silently. An' what a diplomat! People had been awarded the Nobel Peace Prize for less than this.

'Maybe Margaret was havin' an affair with Dodds before her first husband died,' he continued. 'An' maybe it was convenient for Dodds that Hartley had his accident. But it *was* an accident. There were too many witnesses for it to have been anythin' else. Can we all agree on that?'

Paniatowski smiled triumphantly, and nodded.

Rutter said, 'Yes, I suppose so.'

'So we're left with the other things – Marcus Dodds' murder, Sidney Hill's suicide an' Cuthburtson's sudden departure for Canada. It seems to me there's a thread runnin' through them.'

'A thread?' Rutter said. 'What kind of thread?'

'Ah, now there you've got me,' Woodend conceded. 'I don't know. But I can sense that it's there! An' that once we've found one end of it, we should be able to untangle the whole bloody mess.'

'Where do you want us to start looking for the ends of this thread?' Rutter asked.

'I want *you* to start with the Marcus Dodds case,' Woodend told him. 'Did Fred kill him, an' if he did, *why* did he kill him? Were there any other serious suspects? Is it even remotely possible that whoever killed Marcus also killed his son? Got that?'

'Got it,' Rutter agreed.

'An' I want you to look into Sidney Hill's suicide, Monika,' Woodend continued. 'Did he an' Fred really have a secret shared interest, as the people they went to school with seem to think? An' does that interest – if it exists – have anythin' to do with Sidney throwin' himself in front of a train?'

'And what if we can't pick up the thread? Or we do pick it up and it leads nowhere?' Paniatowski asked.

'Well, if that *is* the case, then I'd have to say that, in my professional opinion, we're well an' truly buggered,' Woodend told her.

Nineteen

The layer of black dust covered both the floor of the yard and the storage sheds that ran around its perimeter. It clung to the windows of the office, and the chassis of the lorries. It insinuated itself into the creases on the coalmen's faces. And though he had only been in the yard for a couple of minutes, Rutter could already feel the dust beginning to tickle the back of his throat.

The office door opened, and a middle-aged man emerged. Perhaps to distinguish himself from his workers, he wore a dark-blue suit rather than an overall, but it was a suit that must already have been looking back nostalgically to a time when it could have been described as having seen 'better days'.

'Inspector Rutter?' the man in the blue suit asked. 'I'm Horace Saddleworth, the owner.'

Saddleworth held out his hand for the inspector to shake. It had been well scrubbed, but even so, the traces of coal dust were still evident.

Rutter remembered that Mr Bithwaite had commented on the fact that when they were both working in the Peninsula Trading Company, Fred Dodds had constantly been examining his own hands.

'When did you buy this coal yard?' the inspector asked.

'Coal yard?' Saddleworth repeated with mock horror. 'This isn't a *coal yard*.'

'What is it, then?'

Saddleworth grinned. 'It's a solid fuel distribution centre.'

156

Rutter returned his grin. 'Sorry! When did you buy this solid fuel distribution centre?'

'Back in 1955. It looked like a real good prospect then. How was I to know that central heating and poncy coal-glow electric fires would ever catch on? Did it ever cross my mind that the government would go all namby-pamby on me and start passing clean air acts? It did not!'

'So you never knew the Dodds family?'

'No, they were well before my time.'

'Is there anybody still working here who might have?'

'I couldn't say with any degree of certainty, but you might try talking to old Clem there,' Saddleworth said, indicated an elderly man who was slowly filling a coal sack from a huge mound of loose slack. 'I know for a fact that he's been in the business since Moses was a coalman.'

'Thanks,' Rutter said.

'My pleasure. And if you ever decide you've had enough of the clean-living bobbies' work, and want to buy yourself a real man's business, I'd be willing to let this place go at a very good price.'

Rutter grinned again. 'When I start to see my future as a solid fuel distribution merchant, you'll be the first one I'll come to,' he promised.

Clem Hodnut was only too happy to stop shovelling slack and accepted one of the cork-tipped cigarettes which Rutter offered him.

'So you were here in Mr Dodds' time?' the inspector said.

'Both Mr Dodds. The father an' the son.'

'What was Mr Marcus Dodds like to work for?'

'He was a right bad bugger. He treated his horses terrible, an' his men even worse. I'd have left, but I was livin' at home at that time, an' my dad wouldn't let me.'

'So Marcus had a few enemies?'

'No,' Clem Hodnut said. 'He had a few – a *very* few – friends. An' even they didn't *actually* like him.'

157

'How did you get on with his son?'

'I didn't really do what you might call "get on with him". Nobody in the yard did. He was neither fish nor fowl, you see.'

'I'm not sure I do.'

'His father treated him like he treated all the other men. But he *wasn't* like us, was he? He was educated. If things had turned out as they planned, he would have gone to university.'

'So what stopped him?'

'Goin' to university had been his mother's idea, an' she died durin' the great influenza epidemic of 1918. She was no sooner buried than Mr Marcus yanked Fred out of school an' put him to work on the wagons.'

'How did Fred feel about that?'

'I couldn't say for certain, but if I'd been in his place, I wouldn't have been too thrilled.'

'Can you remember anything about the day of the murder?' Rutter asked hopefully.

'Of course I can. It's not every day your gaffer gets himself killed, now is it? It kind of impresses things on your mind, does somethin' like that.'

'What do you remember specifically?'

'Come again?'

'What sticks in your mind most?'

'The bobbies swarmin' all over the place.'

'Anything before that?'

Clem Hodnut scratched his balding head. 'Are you talkin' about the row the night before?' he asked.

'What row?'

'The one that Fred had with Mr Marcus.'

'I wasn't,' Rutter admitted. 'But I'd like to hear about it anyway.'

'It was nearly knocking off time, an' I was in the yard loading up one of the wagons for the next mornin's delivery. Fred come rushin' out of the office with Mr Marcus right

158

on his heels. It was obvious that they'd been arguin' an' Fred just wanted to put it behind him, if you know what I mean.'

'Yes, I know what you mean,' Rutter assured him.

'Anyroad, Mr Marcus grabbed Fred's shoulder and twisted him around so they was facin' each other. Mr Marcus said somethin' like, "You've been a bloody fool. You could go to jail, you know."'

'Go to jail? What for?'

'I've been puzzlin' about that for over forty years, an' I still haven't got no answer,' Clem Hodnut said.

'What happened next?'

'Fred said somethin' like, "You're the one who should be in jail." Then his dad said, "That's as maybe, but I won't be goin' – because I've been clever about it." Well, Fred looked as if he was about to be sick all over the yard. "Clever!" he said, an' he was so upset that he was pretty much gaspin' his words out by this point. "Do you call what you've done *clever*?" The old man nodded, like he was really pleased with himself. "If you want to go doin' that sort of thing, why don't you get married?" he said.'

'I suppose you don't know what he meant by "that sort of thing", either.'

'I haven't got a clue. But I could see that them words had driven Fred into a rage. "Get married!" he said. "Like you! Bein' married to you was what killed my mother!" I could tell Mr Marcus didn't like that. "Your mother died of the flu," he said. "She *caught* the flu, but she *died* of a broken heart," Fred says. An' the next second he's rollin' around on the ground, clutchin' his belly – because Mr Marcus could pack a mean punch when he wanted to. Anyroad, Mr Marcus leaves Fred lyin' there an' goes back into the office. An' the next time I saw him was the followin' mornin' when I found him lyin' on the office floor, with his head stove in.'

'Did you tell the police back then what you're telling me now?'

'Well, of course I did. I told it all to the first constable who turned up. That's why he arrested Fred the moment he turned up at the yard.'

'I thought Fred was never charged.'

'He wasn't. A couple of hours later he comes back to the yard, as bold as brass, an' says that Sergeant Parker's let him go.'

'And that was that? Wasn't there any more to the investigation?'

Clem Hodnut shrugged. 'Sergeant Parker come to the yard himself, an' asked a few questions, but he didn't seem very interested in my story about the fight. If you ask me, he was just goin' through the motions. He never had no real interest in solvin' the case.'

'And why do you think that was?'

'Beats me!' Clem admitted. 'I never have been able to work out how the Law thinks.'

'So Fred inherited the coal yard.'

'He did, but I knew he wasn't goin' to stay long. He thought he was too good for this place, you see. It could only to be a matter of time before he sold up this business an' bought himself somethin' that was a bit cleaner.'

'Did you resent that?' Rutter asked.

Hodnut looked puzzled. 'Resent it. Why should I have? If you don't do what you want with the money you've been left, what's the point of killin' your dad in the first place?'

Twenty

There was an old saying, in common use during Woodend's youth, that if the mountain would not come to
Mohammed, then Mohammed had better go to the mountain.
It had always seemed to him to be one of the more sensible
adages that people tended to spout without even thinking
about them. It was, therefore, something of a shock for him
to discover that – on a morning that was just perfect for a
round of golf – the highest mountain in his particular chain
was not only in the building, but actually standing in the
doorway of his office.

'Do you think you could spare me a few minutes, Charlie?'
Henry Marlowe asked.

His choice of responses being limited to one, Woodend
rose to his feet, said that of course he could spare a few
minutes, and gestured the Chief Constable to sit down.

Marlowe did not look comfortable on the wrong side
of the desk, and for a moment Woodend found himself
wondering what had compelled the great man to leave the
security of his inner sanctum. And then he had it! If Marlowe
had summoned Woodend, it would have given the meeting
something of an official status. By dropping in as he had,
he was keeping it informal – and ensuring that there was no
record of the encounter.

The Chief Constable pulled a packet of cigars out of his
pocket, and offered it across the desk.

'No thanks, sir. I'd prefer to smoke my own kind of coffin
nail,' Woodend said, reaching for his Capstan Full Strengths.

161

Marlowe lit his cigar, puffed on it, and was instantly surrounded by a halo of blue-grey smoke.

'I had Eric Sharpe on the phone to me for half an hour last night,' he said casually.

Woodend nodded. 'I can't pretend that comes as a shock, sir.'

'He told me that he had suggested to you that if you did what he wanted, he'd see to it that you got promoted.'

'He might well have done, for all I know,' Woodend replied. 'But I can't say that I was really listenin' to him.'

Marlowe's face slipped painfully into the expression that he probably considered to be a good-natured smile. 'Oh, come on, Charlie! Pull the other one – it's got bells on!' he said.

'All right, that's what he offered me,' Woodend agreed.

'He was quite wrong to ever make such an offer, of course. And quite incorrect in his assumption that he had the power to see such an offer brought through to fruition. We, in the Mid Lancs Constabulary, are justly proud of our independence from outside influence.'

Since when? Woodend thought, remembering back to some of his previous cases.

But aloud, all he said was, 'Yes, sir. We couldn't do our job properly if we weren't independent.'

'Exactly,' Marlowe agreed. 'So what we have to consider, in any given situation, is what's good for us – the bobbies on the ground, the poor bloody infantry whose only concern is solving crimes. Now, let's examine this *current* situation. You could bring the government down, Charlie. You do know that, don't you?'

'As I explained to Lord Sharpe yesterday, that's not my intention,' Woodend said.

'And what we have to ask ourselves is, do we *want* a change of government at this precise moment? What do you know about economics and international finance, Charlie?'

'Not a lot,' Woodend admitted. 'The wife usually takes care of things like that.'

Marlowe grimaced, to show he could take a joke as well as anyone, then turned serious again. 'If the Labour Party was elected tomorrow, there would undoubtedly be a run on the pound,' he said. 'To combat it, the government would have to cut back on its domestic spending. In other words, there'd be less resources for the police.'

'That would be a pity, but as far as this investigation goes, it simply can't be my concern, sir,' Woodend said.

'Then there's our reputation to consider. It's true that Eric Sharpe hasn't been a policeman for over thirty years, but when he *was* a serving officer, he was one of our own. If he's shown to be rotten, what do you imagine people will think about the Mid Lancs force?'

Hang on a second! Woodend thought. What exactly is goin' on here?

Marlowe had rescued him from death by committee meeting not through compassion, but because the Chief Constable could recognize a hot potato when he saw one. Caught between Sharpe on one side and Jane Hartley on the other, he had quickly determined that if anyone was going to get his fingers burned, that person would be Charlie Woodend. So what had changed? Had Marlowe suddenly developed asbestos fingers – or was there some reason for him suddenly coming down on the side of the noble lord?

'Are you not the tiniest bit concerned about how Miss Hartley might react if we play it your way, sir?' he asked tentatively.

'No.'

Woodend shrugged. 'Well, I expect you have your reasons.'

'Indeed I do. A couple of days ago, Jane Hartley was a power to be reckoned with. She'd got political clout, and she had friends in high places. And then what did she do? She pissed it away! She talked to the *Daily Globe* about her mother's history – and all the influence she'd worked so hard for years to build up simply evaporated overnight.'

'You're sure about that, are you, sir?'

'Oh yes. I've spoken to her chambers. The members have absolutely no wish to see this matter go any further. Nor do any of the other people she might have been relying on. Once she starts trying to call in her debts, it won't take her long to realize that she's been cut adrift.'

'But what about the *Daily Globe*?' Woodend asked. 'To be honest with you, I can't see Elizabeth Driver givin' up a juicy story once she's got her teeth clamped round it.'

'I've spoken to Miss Driver, too. She seems quite prepared to eat a little humble pie.'

'Meanin' what?'

'Meaning that she's more than willing to write an article admitting to her mistakes.'

'What mistakes?'

'Primarily that she was completely taken in – but only for a moment – by Jane Hartley's histrionics.'

'An' what does she get in return?'

Marlowe smiled again. Woodend hated it when he did that.

'I've been thinking for some time about forming a new, elite squad – Lancashire's equivalent of Scotland Yard,' the Chief Constable said. 'And I've promised Miss Driver that if the chief superintendent in charge of it has no objections, she can work closely with it. You won't have any objections to her working with you, will you, Charlie?'

Woodend lit up another Capstan, and took a deep – disgusted – drag. 'It's a funny thing, but as independent as we are, we still seem to be doin' exactly what Lord Sharpe wants us to do,' he said.

'As I told you before, Charlie, this has nothing to do with Lord Sharpe. We'll do what's good for the Force.'

'I don't always like Jane Hartley,' Woodend said reflectively. 'She's brittle, she's untrusting – an' she can be downright rude. But for all that, I still have to admire her. An' do you know why?'

'Why?' Marlowe said suspiciously.

'For two reasons. Firstly, because while she's tried to threaten me from time to time, she's never gone so far as to insult me by offering me a bribe.'

'Careful, Charlie. You don't want to—'

'An' secondly, she seems to be the only person involved in this mess who's prepared to put her own neck on the line. Or maybe I should say she *was* the only person – because now there's two of us.'

'I can take you off this case, Chief Inspector,' Marlowe said, with a new harshness in his voice. 'I can take you off it right now.'

'You could,' Woodend agreed. 'But if you did, wouldn't you be worried that a report of my findings might be leaked to the newspapers?'

'You wouldn't dare do that!' Marlowe said.

'Of course I wouldn't,' the Chief Inspector agreed, making no effort to sound convincing. 'But if you remove me from the case, you also take away my ability to stop anybody *else* from leakin' the findings.'

'What exactly *are* these findings of yours?' Marlowe asked.

'I'd prefer not to say at the moment, sir.'

'And if I ordered you to?'

'Then I'd have to answer, hand on heart, that so far we'd come up with bugger all.'

'But you'd be lying!'

'Would I, sir? An' if I was, could you prove it?'

The veins in Marlowe's neck bulged dangerously. 'Do you know what I'm going to do, Chief Inspector?' he asked. 'I'm going to put this on an official footing. By this afternoon, I'll have formed a board of inquiry. By this evening, you'll be its star witness. Lie to it – or even hold the smallest detail back – and I'll personally see to it that you're ruined.'

'An' how will the board know if I'm holdin' anythin' back?' Woodend asked.

A smile – a genuine one, this time – came to Marlowe's face. 'Oh, it can never truly *know*,' he admitted. 'So what it will all boil down to is what the board *decides* to believe. And who do you think is best placed to sway it one way or the other?'

'You are,' Woodend said.

'*I* am,' Marlowe agreed. 'You've been walking on water for a long time now, Chief Inspector – but even the nimblest-footed self-appointed messiah eventually ends up hanging from a cross.'

It was as good an exit line as he was ever likely to be able to deliver, and recognizing it as such, the Chief Constable rose to his feet and left the office without another word.

Woodend took a further deep drag on his cigarette, and reviewed the situation he'd just talked himself into. By threatening to leak the details of the case to the press, he had effectively been buying himself time by holding a gun to his boss's head. The problem was that – though Marlowe didn't yet know it – there were no bullets in that gun.

In the previous few days, and with the help of Rutter and Paniatowski, he had learned a great deal about the lives of the people involved in the Frederick Dodds case. But in terms of actually achieving a *result*, he'd been more or less speaking the truth when he'd told the Chief Constable that he had bugger all – and as far as he could see, a *result* was the only thing that would save him now.

He stubbed out his cigarette and looked up at the clock on the wall.

'What's the time, Woodend?!' he demanded in the voice of Miss Scoggins, the harridan who had terrorized him when he'd been in Standard One of Wesley Street Elementary School.

'The little hand's on ten, an' the big hand's nearly on

twelve,' he answered, in something like the squeaky voice he had once possessed.

'And what time does that make it, Woodend?'

'Nearly ten o'clock, Miss.'

He chuckled, and lit another cigarette. Back then, life had been so much simpler – and your enemies so much more straightforward.

The big hand of the clock clicked loudly, and covered the twelve. He had eight hours before he was hauled up in front of the board, he calculated. Eight hours at the most.

He hoped to Christ that Rutter and Paniatowski could come up with some ammunition for him by then.

Twenty-One

The sign at the edge of the village of Picket Forge announced that the visitor was on the point of entering 'the Garden of Lancashire'. The boast was more than backed up by the reality. There were well-tended gardens wherever the newcomer chose to look, and most of the houses also had window boxes. Tubs of flowers stood on the streets; borders of plants ran around virtually every piece of public land. On a sunny morning – and that particular morning was *wonderfully* sunny – the whole village became one big glorious display of carefully nurtured horticulture, a treat to both the eyes and the nose.

The big, glorious display was wasted on Monika Paniatowski. She noticed neither the flowers *nor* the weather. And though her body was driving the MGA down the village's main street, her mind was alternating between roving free and turning in on itself.

She wished she knew what was happening to her. She had never got on well with Bob Rutter, but at no point in the past had their relationship ever even approached being as bad as it had become in the last couple of days.

It was almost as if, to her, Rutter had ceased being himself and become instead a symbol of everything she disliked about the opposite sex. Which meant that he could never be right – even when he so obviously was. Nor, by the same token, could he ever be given credit for being well intentioned. And yet, intellectually at least, Paniatowski was well aware of the fact that he was one of best-intentioned men she had ever met.

The real problem, she recognized, was that while she could think these things through when she was alone, in Rutter's presence she found it almost impossible to think *at all*. Increasingly, she was becoming a creature of instinct – little more than two pairs of sharp claws and a mouth full of sharp teeth – which wanted only to lash out.

She suddenly realized that she had driven straight through the village and was now more than a mile the other side of it.

'Get a grip on yourself, Monika,' she said angrily, pulling the MGA through a fast, tyre-screeching U-turn.

She did not make the mistake of driving through a second time. When she saw the village post office, she signalled and pulled into the curb. The house she was intending to visit, she had already established, was to the immediate right of the post office and belonged to Dorothy Hill, 55, spinster – and surviving sister of the long-dead Sidney Hill.

Paniatowski walked up the path. The garden on either side of it – she noted now that she had collected herself enough to becoming aware of her surroundings again – was rather neglected. So perhaps Miss Hill had no interest in growing things, nor felt any compunction to join with her neighbours and share their pride in the village.

Paniatowski rang the bell, and the door was opened by a woman who looked as if she were in her very late sixties.

'Yes?' the woman said.

'I'd like to see Miss Dorothy Hill, if she's in.'

'I'm Dorothy Hill.'

God, but the woman hadn't aged at all well, Paniatowski thought, as she forced a smile to her lips in an attempt to mask her shock.

'I'm Sergeant Monika Paniatowski, from Whitebridge Police Headquarters,' she said. 'I wonder if I might come inside.'

'Why?' Dorothy Hill demanded.

'I'd like to talk to you about your brother, Sidney.'

'He's been dead for over forty years. That's well before you were even born. What can you possibly want to know about him now?'

'It's . . . er . . . it's a bit difficult to explain here on the doorstep,' Paniatowski said, slipping effortlessly into her young-inexperienced-woman-out-of-her-depth routine. 'Do you think I could just pop inside for a few minutes?'

For a moment it looked as if the older woman had seen right through her act, then Dorothy Hill shrugged her slumped shoulders and said, 'Why not, if that's what you want.'

She led Paniatowski down the passageway, and into the living room.

'Sit down,' she said, indicating the ancient winged armchair that stood next to an equally venerable occasional table.

Paniatowski sat. It was not only the armchair and the occasional table that were close to being antiques, she realized. Everything else in the room was as old, or even older. The place could almost have been a museum.

'This all belonged to my parents,' Dorothy Hill said, reading the sergeant's mind. 'I never bought anything myself.'

'Really,' Paniatowski said, lost for any other reply.

'I was the only child in the family after Sidney's death, and my parents left me everything they had,' Dorothy Hill continued. 'On their deaths, I was suddenly quite well-off. I could have replaced everything in here if I'd wanted to – but I *didn't* want to!'

'The room certainly has . . . has charm,' Paniatowski said, knowing she was not doing a particularly good job of making a connection – yet unable to work out what approach might establish a better one.

'I don't care about *charm*,' Dorothy Hill told her scornfully. 'I don't care about *style*, either. I like this room the way it is because it reminds me of my early childhood – of a time of innocence.' She laughed with surprising bitterness. 'We never value our innocence properly, do we? We can't – because until we lose it, we don't know we've ever possessed it.'

Again, Paniatowski found the right words would not come. She was suddenly out of her depth, she realized. Here, in this room full of decaying memories, she was drowning.

'You probably know why I'm here, Miss Hill,' she said, desperate to buy herself a little time in which to pull herself together again.

'Know why you're here? Whatever makes you think that?'

'Well, it's been in all the papers that—'

'I don't read the papers.'

'And it's been on the wireless.'

'I don't listen to the wireless, either. Why should I? They hold nothing of interest for me.' Dorothy Hill paused. 'You hold nothing of interest for me, either – but at least, like a leaking tap or a sticking window, you help to break up the monotony of the day.'

She was so cold, Paniatowski thought. So cold – and yet so vulnerable.

'We're re-opening the investigation into the murder of Fredrick Dodds,' the sergeant said softly. 'We believe your brother was a friend of his. Possibly his *only* friend.'

Dorothy Hill shook her head sadly. 'Poor Sidney,' she said. 'Even in death, he's still coming second to Freddie.'

'You knew Fred Dodds, did you?'

'Yes, I knew him.'

'What was he like?'

'He was the Prince of Darkness. A fiend who, having no soul of his own, was driven to suck the souls out of others.'

'How *exactly* was Fred Dodds a fiend?' Paniatowski probed.

'I won't tell you that. I wouldn't if you were to rip out my fingernails and thrust burning brands into my eyes.'

'But surely, if you feel—'

'Sidney died to purge himself of evil. It is not for me to resurrect it now. I will take his secret with me to the grave. Even before the Judgement Seat itself, I will maintain my silence.'

She meant it, Paniatowski thought. If any more information were to be extracted from this woman who was old before her time, it would have to be done through extreme stealth.

'Your brother was killed in a railway accident, wasn't he?' she said.

'His death was no accident. And I should know. I saw him die with my own eyes.'

'You saw it!'

'Isn't that what I said?'

'How did it happen?'

'He was killed by a train.'

'I know. But how did you come to see it?'

'I caught a severe chill shortly after my ninth birthday,' Dorothy Hill said, her voice now as flat and toneless as if she were reading aloud from a telephone directory. 'I was in bed for over a week, and even when the doctor allowed me to get up, it was only for a few hours a day. Then, one bright sunny morning, my father announced that it was time that I started going out in the fresh air again. He would have taken me himself, he said, but he had church matters to attend to.' She paused. 'He *always* had church matters to attend to. Being a bishop meant something important in those days – much more than it does now – and my father so desperately wanted to become one himself. But you weren't going to be elevated to a bishop's throne if you were merely a part-time priest. You were expected to sacrifice everything to your work – and "everything" included your *family*.'

Her questions were opening old wounds, Paniatowski thought, but she wasn't sure they were the wounds she *needed* to open.

'Your father was too busy,' she prompted. 'Did he suggest that Sidney should take you for your walk?'

'Suggest!' Dorothy Hill echoed. 'Did *your* father ever suggest things to you?'

'I never knew my father,' Paniatowski said. 'I was brought up by my mother.'

'By your mother *only*?'

'At first,' Paniatowski said. 'Later on, I had a stepfather.'

And if I knew where he was buried, I'd go to his grave and spit on it, she added mentally.

'*My* father spoke with the voice of God,' Dorothy Hill said. 'And he had the *wrath* of God to back up those words of his. Sidney didn't *want* to take me for a walk. He didn't *want* to be in my company at all. He would gladly have done almost anything else instead. But he was given no choice.'

'How old was Sidney at this time?'

'He was sixteen.'

'And still at school?'

'Yes. It was planned that he should take his school certificate, then go to university. He'd read religion once he was up, of course, and after he graduated he'd join the Anglican priesthood.'

'You said, "it was planned" rather than "*he* planned". Why?'

'Do I really need to tell you that?' Dorothy Hill asked disdainfully. 'If you truly are so dull and insensitive that you can't keep track of the story even at this point, then I don't think I will waste my time by telling you any more of it.'

I'm losing her! Paniatowski thought. I'm bloody losing her!

'I'm sorry,' she said aloud. 'I *do* know. I *do* see what you mean.'

'Then why did you ask?'

'It's my police training,' Paniatowski confessed, because though opting for the truth was a dangerous tactic, there were even more pitfalls in risking an unconvincing lie.

'Your police training?' Miss Hill repeated.

'We make inferences if we're forced to, but it's always better to get a direct statement if we possibly can.'

From the expression on the other woman's face, she saw that she had chosen the right course – understood that if she had tried to lie, she would now be being shown the door. But she was still not out of the woods.

'I will not be interrogated,' Dorothy Hill said. 'Do you understand? You may listen to what I have to say, and draw from it whatever conclusions you choose – but I will *not* be interrogated!'

'I understand,' Paniatowski said contritely.

'The vicarage was half a mile from the nearest village. To get to the village, we had to cross a bridge over the railway line. That was the direction we set out in. I said it was a lovely day, didn't I?'

'Yes, you did.'

The birds are singing prettily, and Dorothy can hear tiny insects buzzing busily in the grass. Sidney is quiet and moody, but Dorothy has got used to that over the previous few months. When they are halfway across the bridge, Sidney stops. And so, a moment later, does Dorothy.

Sidney squats down so that his eyes are on a level with his sister's. His mouth starts to move as if there is something he desperately wants to say. But no words come out.

Somewhere in the distance, they hear a sound. It is only the commonplace whistle of a train, but from the expression on Sidney's face, it is almost as if he's heard heavenly trumpets. He has been avoiding touching his sister – even accidentally – for quite some time, but now he reaches out and takes hold of her hand. He squeezes it – very hard. Dorothy wants to cry out in pain, but she doesn't, because she knows that he hasn't meant to hurt her.

'*I want you to stay here, Dorothy,*' *he says.* '*Whatever happens, I want you to promise me you'll stay here.*'

'*All right.*'

He releases her hand. 'I'm so sorry, Dorothy,' he says. 'I'm so very, very sorry.'

He walks to the end of the bridge, and disappears down the steep embankment. Dorothy goes over to the parapet. It is not a high wall, but she is very small, and when she stands on tiptoes to look over the top, she can feel her nose rubbing against the rough brickwork.

Behind her, she can hear the sound of the approaching train. Ahead of her, she can see Sidney standing by the track.

'Come away, come away!' she shouts, because she knows it is dangerous to be so close to speeding locomotives.

Sidney cannot hear her over the roar of the train, but even if he could, she senses that he wouldn't take any notice. He knows what it is he wants to do. He has made up his mind, and nothing will change it now.

He waits until the engine is under the bridge, then steps out into the middle of the track. Even if the engine driver spots him, there is nothing he can do to stop the inevitable carnage.

Sidney has been staring straight ahead of him, but now – moments before the train will strike him and pulverize every bone in his body – he raises his head. Raises it and – for the first time in an age – looks his little sister squarely in the eyes.

'I thought he'd look frightened,' Dorothy Hill told Paniatowski. 'But he didn't. Not at all. In some ways, I wish he had, because the expression that filled his face was far more terrible and terrifying than simple fear could ever be. It burned itself into my brain. And it will stay with me until the day I die.'

'How *did* he look?' Paniatowski asked.

'Relieved,' Dorothy Hill replied simply. 'He looked relieved.'

Twenty-Two

'You did a good job with that old coalman, Clem Hodnut,' Woodend said.

'Thank you, sir,' Bob Rutter replied.

Woodend glanced up at the clock. It was nearly noon. He wondered how close Marlowe was to getting his board of inquiry together.

'The problem is, I'm not sure how much further down the line it takes us,' the Chief Inspector continued. 'In this bloody case, we never seem to be able to find an answer without it leadin' on to half a dozen new questions.'

'*At least* half a dozen,' Rutter agreed gloomily.

'We now know *when* Marcus Dodds was killed,' Woodend said. 'What we *don't* know is what he was arguin' with his son about. Why did Marcus say Fred could go to prison? Why did Fred say his father should be the one in jail? What was it that Marcus had done which he thought made him safe? That's three questions so far, an' I've only *begun* to scratch the soddin' surface.'

'So what?' Paniatowski said. 'I don't see why we're even wasting our time considering it at all.'

What was coming next? Woodend wondered, alarmed. Had Monika cranked up her instability to the point at which it was not enough for her just to attack Rutter? Did she now feel the need to have a go at her boss as well?

'Why do you think it's a waste of our time?' he asked, preparing himself for the worst.

'If Fred did kill Marcus, then it's of no interest what they

176

said to each other, because they're both dead,' Paniatowski said, keeping her voice level and her tone more reasonable than Woodend had feared might be the case. 'And if Fred *didn't* kill Marcus – and I, for one, don't think he did – then the only conversations we need to be interested in are ones between Marcus and whoever murdered him. Unfortunately, we don't know who this other person is.'

'What makes you think Fred didn't kill his father?' Woodend asked.

'There are two reasons. The first is that it only took Sergeant Parker a couple of hours to decide that Fred wasn't guilty.'

'An' the second?'

'The second is exactly the same as the one we used for arguing that Margaret wasn't guilty of killing Fred.'

'You mean, if he was going to kill his father, why do it in a way that was bound to draw attention to him?'

'Exactly. The two cases are identical – except for the fact that Margaret was hanged and he wasn't.'

'So, correct me if I'm wrong, you're puttin' forward the theory that there was only one killer, an' that he *tried* to frame Fred for one of his murders an' *succeeded* in framin' Margaret for the other.'

'It's a possibility, isn't it?'

Woodend lit up a Capstan Full Strength. '*Anythin's* a possibility,' he conceded. 'But not only do we not have a suspect who fits in with that particular theory, we don't even have a motive. Unless, of course, you're suggestin' that Bithwaite killed Marcus Dodds – in the hope that Fred Dodds would sell up, buy an import-export business and then take him on as the chief clerk.'

'Cuthburtson could have committed both crimes,' Paniatowski argued.

'What makes you think that, lass?'

'Cuthburtson wants to go into business with Fred Dodds, but Fred hasn't got any money for his half of the investment.

So Cuthburtson kills Marcus Dodds, and Fred inherits. Later on, after Fred and Cuthburtson have their big row – which is probably about money again – Cuthburtson kills Fred, too.'

'Very neat,' Woodend said. 'Except that if Cuthburtson wanted Fred to inherit, he wouldn't have committed the murder in a way which was bound to throw suspicion on his future partner.'

'Shit!' Paniatowski said. 'I hadn't thought of that!'

'Even so, the Cuthburtson connection is not one that we should ignore,' Woodend said. 'You didn't find the cable we got from Canada very helpful, did you, Bob?'

'Not helpful at all,' Rutter replied. 'As far as I can tell, the Mounties went to the Cuthburtson house, the Cuthburtsons told them they had nothing to say, and the Mounties left it at that.'

'I'll ring the family myself an' see if I can get a bit more information out of them,' Woodend said.

He looked from Rutter to Paniatowski, then back to Rutter again, hoping to see a look of sudden inspiration light up on one of their faces. Nothing! Still, there was no harm in asking.

'Any more theories?' he said. 'Any suggestions? Any possible connections?'

'I've got one possible connection, but it's pretty weak,' Rutter said.

'Let's hear it anyway.'

'Margaret Dodds' father was a vicar, and so was the father of Fred Dodds' friend Sidney Hill.'

'Oh, for God's sake!' Paniatowski exploded.

Rutter shot her an angry look. 'Your helpful comments are always appreciated,' he said.

'Well, really! Talk about tenuous! What's your theory? That there's a curse on the children of Church of England clergymen? That the whole thing's the work of a group of Satanists?'

'Monika . . .' Woodend said.

Paniatowski ignored him. She knew she was losing control of herself again – and she didn't give a damn!

'Maybe that's how all the young women fit into this case!' she continued. 'Maybe Margaret Dodds, Dorothy Hill and Louise Cuthburtson were all sacrificial virgins. Yes, and maybe Fred Dodds is really Satan, and all his friends are fallen angels. That would make sense – or at least it would make *more* sense than Rutter's grubby little idea that Margaret was some kind of nymphomaniac and—'

'That's enough, Sergeant,' Woodend said, more sharply this time.

'But, sir . . . !'

'Don't make me have to send you out of the room, Monika,' Woodend threatened.

The words hit Paniatowski like a bucketful of iced water. Sent out of the room! Exiled from the case! She couldn't bear that.

'I'm sorry, sir,' she said. 'I'm sorry, Inspector Rutter. I know it's no excuse, but this case has got right under my skin.'

'I don't think it's makin' any of us exactly happy,' Woodend conceded. 'Do you want to go back to what you were saying, Bob?'

Rutter cleared his throat. 'All I was attempting to suggest was that the two people Fred Dodds got closest to – his best friend and his wife – both had fathers in the Church. I was wondering if it was this connection that made them both appeal to Dodds.'

Woodend nodded thoughtfully. 'Monika?'

'I'm sure Inspector Rutter has a point,' Paniatowski said.

Woodend sighed. 'You're of no more use to me when you're sayin' nowt than you are when you're flyin' off the handle,' he told his sergeant. 'What do you *really* think, Monika?'

'I can understand why Inspector Rutter brought the point up,' Paniatowski forced herself to say. 'Superficially it's an attractive connection, but ultimately I think it's a red herring.'

'Would you care to expand on that?'

'No.'

'Then I will. Both fathers were clergymen, but they had very little else in common. All Margaret's father wanted was the life of a country priest. Sidney's, on the other hand, was determined to rise to the top of the ladder. Margaret was an only child; Sidney had a sister. Margaret grew up and went off to university; Sidney killed himself before he'd even left school. If there's a common factor between the two households, then I've no idea what it might be. Is that what you wanted to say, Monika?'

'Yes.'

'Then why didn't you?'

She shouldn't speak – she knew she shouldn't – but the goblin that seemed to have taken control of her would not let her be silent.

'I let you say it rather than me because, if you say it, it's good detective work,' Paniatowski told Woodend.

'An' if you say it?'

'If I say it, it's nothing but an irrational, hysterical, vindictive attack on Inspector Rutter's latest theory.'

Woodend turned to Rutter. 'Could you give us a few minutes, Bob?'

'Of course,' Rutter replied.

'I'm all right,' Paniatowski said, when Rutter had closed the door behind him.

'No, you're not,' Woodend contradicted her. 'You're strung tighter than I've ever seen you, and if you're not careful, you'll snap.'

'It's Inspector Rutter's fault. He—'

'You get up his nose just as much as he gets up yours. It's been that way ever since fate an' the Mid Lancs Constabulary threw you together. You both used to be able to control it. He still can.'

'One slip!' Paniatowski said angrily. 'One slip and I have to listen to all this crap.'

'It's more than one slip, Monika. It's been building up since this case started. That's why I want you to take some time off.'

'You mean I'm being suspended?' Paniatowski asked disbelievingly.

Woodend shook his head. 'The very fact that you could even think I'd suspend you proves your judgement's been shot to hell. Of course you're not suspended. You won't even be on leave – officially.'

'But I will *be* on leave?'

'The rest will do you good, Monika.'

'And just how long is this "rest" of mine supposed to go on for?'

'I don't know,' Woodend admitted. 'I was rather hopin' that you'd be able to gauge that for yourself. But since you can't even seem to understand that if you don't take a break you'll—'

'You need me here,' Paniatowski said desperately.

'No, I don't,' Woodend said, shaking his head and looking up at the wall clock again. 'What I need right at this moment is a trusty bagman. That's what you used to be – an' what I hope you'll be in the future. But we're not talking about the future – we're talkin' about the here an' now. An' here an' now, you're nothin' but a liability.'

Paniatowski felt her eyes begin to moisten. 'I never thought that you – of all people – would ever stab me in the back,' she said bitterly.

'Go home, Monika,' Woodend said. 'Get your head down an' have a good night's sleep. Who knows, by tomorrow mornin' you might be feelin' fit enough to come back.'

'Charlie, please . . .'

'Go home now!'

Paniatowski sprang to her feet, and saluted. 'Yes, sir,' she said crisply.

Then, before he could see her tears, she opened the door and stepped out into the corridor.

181

Twenty-Three

'Follow the main corridor to the end, then turn left. The matron's door is the first on your right,' said the young woman who was mopping the tiled entrance hall of the Councilman Stephenson Old People's Home.

As Rutter walked down the corridor, he was aware that his progress was being followed by several pairs of eyes. He supposed he should not have been surprised. Visitors at that time of day were probably a novelty, especially relatively young visitors with a full head of hair and their own teeth.

The home had once been the town workhouse, which, while turning away the poor it had judged to be undeserving, had served as a refuge for any of the *deserving* poor who were willing to leave their personal dignity in a wicker basket by the entrance. Some attempt had been made to soften the atmosphere of the place since those austere days – the bare brick walls had been plastered and painted, pictures of seaside towns had been hung – but to Rutter the atmosphere seemed still to be thick with the odour of carbolic soap and the clogging sickliness of the workhouse attendants' self-satisfied piety.

The matron's office was located in the heart of the building, and the matron herself was a stocky woman with blue-rinsed hair captured in a tight perm.

'So you'd like to see Mr Parker, would you?' she said, when Rutter had introduced himself. 'Not on official business, I trust.'

'Well, in a way it is,' the inspector admitted.

'But Mr Parker can't have done anything wrong! He hasn't put a foot outside the home for years.'

'I'm probably not making myself clear,' Rutter said. 'It's more in the nature of a professional visit. I want to consult him about a case he worked on when he was a sergeant in the Mid Lancs Police.'

'But he's been retired for years.'

'Since 1945,' Rutter agreed. 'Mr Parker retired from the Force as soon as the war was over, and they had the fresh manpower available to be able to release him from his duties.'

The matron laughed. The sound of her amusement had an unexpected tinkling bell quality about it. 'I'd have thought all the cases Mr Parker worked on would have been closed long ago,' she said.

'You don't know just how much I wish that was true,' Rutter told her.

Mr Parker turned out to be a very old man who was confined to a very old chair. When Rutter offered him one of his cigarettes, the ex-sergeant shook his head.

'Can't be doing with them modern cork-tipped things,' he said. 'They make me cough.'

Rutter reached into his pocket, and pulled out a packet of Players' Navy Cut. 'How about one of these?' he suggested.

A twinkle came into the old man's eyes. 'Now you're talking,' he said. 'Smoke them as well, do you?'

'No,' Rutter replied. 'I brought them for you. It was my boss, DCI Woodend, who suggested you might prefer them.'

'Sounds like the right kind of boss to work for.' Mr Parker lit his Players' with trembling hands and inhaled greedily. 'A real fag,' he said happily. 'I've not been able to afford anything more than roll-ups since the Coronation.'

'The reason I've come is because I'd like to ask you about the Marcus Dodds case,' Rutter said.

A look of caution instantly flooded into the old man's eyes. 'Oh aye?' he said.

'You were the detective in charge of the investigation, weren't you?'

'You know I was.'

'And at first you arrested Fred Dodds.'

'No, I didn't. It was a uniformed constable who arrested Fred. I was the one that let him go.'

'Yes – why *did* you do that?' Rutter asked casually.

'How do you mean?'

'He was the obvious suspect, yet you released him less than two hours after he'd been taken into custody. I wouldn't have thought that was anything like enough time for you to have examined all the evidence and decided you could rule him out.'

'What if he'd had a cast-iron alibi?' Parker asked.

'Did he?'

'He might have done.'

'What about other suspects? Were there any?'

'Aye, every other bugger on two legs in the whole of Simcaster. Marcus Dodds was a brute and a bully. Nobody liked him, and when his wife died of the flu, there were them as said it came a blessed relief to her. I never actually heard anybody say they were sorry Marcus was dead, but if I had've done I'd have wondered why – and probably put him right at the top of my list of suspects. Even if we'd put some poor sod on trial, we'd never have found a jury in this town that didn't want to give him a medal.' The old detective smiled. 'I'm exaggerating, of course, but you get the general picture.'

Rutter returned his smile. 'That was a very nice little speech,' he said.

'Thank you.'

'Very smooth. Very polished. I wonder how many times you've delivered it, over the years.'

'I don't know what you're talking about.'

'Of course you do. Every time anybody's asked you why you didn't get a result on the Marcus Dodds case, you'll have given them that little speech. But what's the real reason you came up empty-handed, Sergeant Parker?'

'It's like I said—'

'No, it isn't. It's not like that at all. Listen, Sergeant, Marcus is dead, Fred is dead. And if you think I'm the sort of chap to persecute an old bobby for something he did over forty years ago, you're not as good a judge of character as I took you for.' Rutter paused for a moment. 'Come on, Sergeant Parker! All I want from you is the truth.'

'Could I have another fag?' Parker asked.

'You can keep the packet,' Rutter said. 'And if you tell me what I want to know, I'll see to it personally that you get a fresh packet delivered every week.'

Parker was silent for perhaps half a minute, then he said, 'I'd not been back from the War that long when Marcus Dodds was killed. And it's the Great War I'm talking about, you must understand – not that fussy little thing your dad probably fought in.'

'Understood,' Rutter said.

'It was a real bugger of a war. We lost a million men in less than four years. Most of them were killed by the Hun, but I had two pals who committed suicide – shot themselves in the mouth with their own rifles. Now why do you think they did that?'

'I don't know,' Rutter confessed.

'They did it because, as terrible as dying is, there are some things that are worse. And most of the things that are worse are done to you by other people. I think there must have been times when Fred Dodds thought about committing suicide. Are you following what I'm saying?'

'I think so,' Rutter said.

'The reason I didn't look too hard for Marcus Dodds' murderer was that I already knew who it was. Fred confessed to me in the first ten minutes. But he also told me *why* he'd done it. He thought he had good reason for killing his father. And so did I. That's why I let him go.'

Twenty-Four

M audsley Tower had been built to celebrate Queen Victoria's Diamond Jubilee. It stood fifty feet high, and the fact that it tapered as it rose meant that it could almost have been mistaken for a primitive attempt to build a spaceship out of dressed stone. It was located at the crown of a hill which overlooked the Whitebridge valley, and though it was possible to drive almost the whole way there on crumbling tarmac road, the last fifty yards – up the dog-legged path – had to be covered on foot.

Monika Paniatowski, standing at the base of the monument, was not there to pay her respects to the memory of Queen Victoria. She had climbed the hill solely for the view it would afford her. She did that sometimes – climbed the hill, and looked down on the town that Arthur Jones, her stepfather, had brought her to at the end of the war.

She had been eleven, and after years as a refugee in war-torn Europe, the town of Whitebridge – for all its industrial ugliness – had seemed like her own personal Jerusalem.

Her mother had shared her hopes. 'We're going to be happy here, Monika,' Blanca Paniatowski (now Blanche Jones) had promised.

And perhaps they could have been. If Arthur Jones had not turned out to be such a swine. If his frustrations at his own inability to get on in the world had not led to his drinking – and then to what inevitably seemed to follow it.

Yet despite the obstacles in her way – Jones' desertion of

the family, her mother's premature death brought by years of hardship – Monika had managed to build a life for herself. She had her own flat, she had a career. She could pull a man – *most* men – whenever she felt like it. She had not found love, but that was all to the good, because she didn't trust love. Yes, she had every reason to feel pleased – perhaps even every reason to be *proud*.

'I've built a life for myself!' she shouted down the hill towards the smoky town in the valley.

'I've built a life for myself!' she repeated, turning around to face the wild moorland.

And now she was in danger of losing that life, she thought. Because though she had told Woodend he was wrong, she had known in her heart that he was right. He *couldn't* trust her any more. He could no longer rely on her judgement. Somehow, in the short period between the interview with Jane Hartley and that present moment, she had lost control. She didn't know – she could no longer tell – whether it had been a gradual process or whether it had happened in a flash. That was how bad a state she was in!

She was drowning in a morass of emotion and illogicality, and though she was doing her best to claw her way back to firm ground again, she had no idea whether she would ever make it – whether she'd ever be stable enough to serve as Cloggin'-it Charlie's bagman again.

Her hands were trembling; her heart was galloping. On unsteady legs, she made her way back down the dog-legged track towards her car. She didn't ask herself where she was going next. She didn't have to. There was only one place she knew of where she might find the life belt that could save her.

There were senior police officers who thought they could conduct their interviews almost as well over the phone as they could do in person, but Charlie Woodend was not one of them. He felt the need to see the man or woman he was talking to – wanted to look into their eyes and sense the rhythms of their being. But this time there was no choice. Louise Cuthburtson was in Canada, and if he wanted to speak to her at all, then it would have to be done down a wire.

She kept him waiting for at least two minutes before she came to the phone. Even then, she merely acknowledged she had arrived, rather than apologizing for the delay.

'I've already spoken to the RCMP,' she said.

'I know you have,' Woodend conceded. 'But you don't seem to have told them much.'

'Perhaps that's because there was not much to tell.'

'I don't believe that,' Woodend said – knowing he was running the risk of her hanging up on him, fully appreciating the fact that if she *did* hang up, there was absolutely nothing he could do about it.

'Are you calling me a liar?' the woman demanded.

Woodend sighed. 'No, Miss Cuthburtson. All I'm sayin' is that you must have been nine or ten when your father packed up an' moved the family to Canada. An' at that age, you're no longer a baby.'

'So?'

'So I've got a daughter of my own, an' you should have seen what emotional gymnastics she put me through when I told her we were leavin' London to come back to Lancashire. Now I don't know you, but you sound to me like a woman of spirit. An' that's why I can't believe you accepted the move any more easily than my Annie did. You'd have wanted to know why you were movin' away from your friends an' the places you loved. You'd have *demanded* to know.'

'Perhaps I did,' Louise Cuthburtson said. 'And perhaps, once my father had told me his reasons for moving, I found them too compelling to kick up a fuss about what I was being made to leave behind.'

'An' what might those reasons be?'

'I don't want to talk about it.'

'Come on, lass, give me a break,' Woodend said. 'This ain't just me shoe-leather I'm wearin' out, it's taxpayers' money. An' when me boss sees t' bill for this call he'll have me guts for garters!'

Louise Cuthburtson laughed – just as he'd hoped she would.

'It's been a long time since I've heard a proper Lancashire accent,' she said. 'I like it. Did you miss the place while you were in London?'

'Aye, I did. What about you? Do you *still* miss it?'

'Canada's really a wonderful country.'

'But . . . ?'

'I didn't say there was a "but".'

'You didn't put it into words, maybe, but I could still sense it.'

'You're right,' she confessed. 'I still do think of Lancashire as home.'

'You could come back,' Woodend suggested.

'No, I couldn't,' Louise Cuthburtson said. 'Because I'd never be able to find *my* Lancashire again. My Lancashire ceased to exist when Fred Dodds . . . when Fred Dodds . . .'

'Go on,' Woodend encouraged.

'I can't. There are other people to consider, apart from myself.'

'Who?'

'My brother. My poor dead father. I tell myself the family's got nothing to be ashamed of, and I *know* that's true, but I still think that there are some secrets which are better kept buried.' She paused. 'It's been a pleasure talking to you, Chief Inspector – it really has – but I'm afraid I'm going to have to hang up now.'

Once she put the receiver back on its cradle, he'd lost her. Woodend felt the beads of sweat forming on his forehead, and wondered what he should say next.

'Well, goodbye,' Louise Cuthburtson said.

'Wait!' Woodend urged her. 'You say there are other

189

people to consider, and you're right. How about considerin'
Jane Hartley?'

'Who?'

'You knew that Fred Dodds got married, didn't you?'

'Not until he was already dead. Some friends in England
mistakenly thought it would be a kindness to send us a
newspaper report of the murder. In the very first paragraph
of the article it said that the police had arrested his wife.
We didn't read any further than that. We'd wished Dodds
dead often enough, and now that he was, we hoped we could
finally lay his memory to rest.' Louise Cuthburtson paused
again, as if she'd suddenly realized that she'd been going
off at a tangent. 'What does any of this have to do with this
Jane Hartley woman?'

'She was Dodds' stepdaughter,' Woodend said. 'She's
convinced her mother didn't kill him. She half-believes
she'll go insane if I don't find out who the real murderer was.'

'Oh, my God!' Louise Cuthburtson gasped. 'Fred had a
stepdaughter!'

'That's right.'

'How . . . how old was she when he was murdered?'

'Nine.'

'And was she living with her mother and Fred?'

'Aye, she was.'

'Sweet Jesus!' Louise Cuthburtson said, and it sounded
to Woodend as if she was starting to cry. 'We didn't know.
Nobody told us.' She was sobbing in earnest now. 'If only
we'd realized . . . if . . . only . . . we'd . . . realized . . .'

'Better not try to say any more just for the moment,'
Woodend said, concerned.

'I . . . I . . .'

'Take a couple of deep breaths. Look out of window. Do
anythin' to take your mind off it for a second.'

The sobs on the other end of the line grew shallower,
then stopped altogether. Woodend noticed that he was

gripping the receiver so tightly he was in danger of breaking it.

'Are you still there?' Louise Cuthburtson asked in a small, broken voice.

'Yes, I am.'

'And do you still want to know why we emigrated to Canada?'

'Yes. Very much so.'

Louise Cuthburtson took a deep gulp of air. 'Then I'll tell you,' she said.

Monika Paniatowski stood in the Catholic churchyard, reading – though she already knew it by heart – the inscription on her mother's grave.

BLANCA PANIATOWSKI
1916–1953
Death Brought Her the Peace
She Was Denied in Life

It was the inscription Monika herself had wanted, but she had had to fight like a lion to get it.

'Everyone round here knew her as Blanche Jones,' Harold Jones, Monika's stepuncle, pointed out. 'Surely that's how she'd like to be remembered. Don't you think that's what we should put on her grave?'

'No!' the eighteen-year-old Monika replied firmly. 'No, I don't.'

She wanted to bury her mother with the name she had been happy with – the name she'd had before the war, when she'd married her handsome cavalry officer and conceived her only child.

'And that line about death bringing her peace, Monika?' Harold said. 'It's not very nice, is it?'

'No, it's not very nice. But it's the truth.'

'You see, Monika, what with you being not much more

than a kid, you've probably not considered all the implica-
tions. But we – the family – have to. We have to take into
account what other people will think when they read that
headstone. I mean, they might get the wrong idea.'

'The wrong idea!' Monika repeated. 'Are you telling me
you think my mother had a happy life with your brother?'

Harold Jones looked uncomfortable. 'Well, it may not
have exactly been blissful,' he admitted. 'I mean, like most
married couples, they had their ups and downs.'

'And most of my mother's downs were because that
bastard brother of yours had knocked her down!'

'There's no call to go blackening people's names at this
stage in the proceedings, Monika,' Harold Jones told her.

'And then that bastard brother of yours left!' Monika continued, unrelenting. 'Not just left my mother – but actually
left Whitebridge. And we all know why that was, don't we?'

'Now then, now then,' Harold Jones said in a tone that
was midway between rebuke and panic. 'You don't want
to go around making accusations you can't substantiate,
Monika. That could land you in serious trouble.'

'And it could do your family's reputation far more harm
than my inscription ever could,' Monika countered. 'So
that's the deal. You agree to inscription, and I'll agree to
keep quiet about why he ran away. All right?'

'All right,' Harold Jones had agreed, defeated.

'He never hit me anything like as hard as he used to
hit you, but you did know that he *was* hitting me, didn't
you, Mum?' Monika Paniatowski asked, looking down at
the grave.

Of course her mother had known. She had seen the bruises
for herself. But she had said nothing about them. She had not
wanted to admit the problem existed, because however badly
Arthur Jones treated them both, he had at least given them
some kind of security. And after all those years as refugees
in war-torn Europe, security was not a prize to be lightly
cast aside.

But what if she had known about the rest? Monika wondered.

What if she'd known about what went on those nights when she was out of the house? What if she'd found out that her husband stalked her terrified daughter? That he took her into the bedroom he shared with his wife, and locked the door? That he touched Monika where he should not have, and then made *her* touch *him*?

What would Blanca Paniatowski have done about *that*?

She would have killed him, Monika thought.

And suddenly she understood why it was that she felt she had so much in common with Jane Hartley.

Twenty-Five

From Woodend's office the sound seemed, at first, to be no more imposing than the tapping of a death-watch beetle. Then, as the woman drew closer – as her high heels pounded the floor with even greater urgency – the clicking assumed the deadly earnestness of lethal machine-gun fire.

'Monika!' Woodend said.

Rutter nodded. Of course it was her. It *could* only be Paniatowski.

The clicking stopped, the office door was flung unceremoniously open – and Paniatowski was standing there. She was gasping for breath. Her blonde hair was dishevelled, her cheeks flushed and there was a puffiness around her eyes that showed that she'd been crying. But she still looked more like the bagman Woodend had come to trust – more like that Monika he'd grown so fond of – than she'd been at any point since the bloody Margaret Dodds case had started.

'You know, don't you?' the Chief Inspector said to his sergeant. 'You've worked it out.'

Paniatowski was astounded. 'You too?' she asked, looking first at Woodend and then at Rutter for confirmation. 'But how *could* you?'

'We got a couple of lucky breaks,' Woodend said, almost apologetically.

'I . . . I need to sit down,' Paniatowski told him.

'Aye, I'll bet you do, lass,' Woodend agreed. He turned to Rutter. 'An' I think that you, Inspector, need to leave.'

'Of course,' Rutter agreed, beginning to rise to his feet.

'The inspector should stay,' Paniatowski said firmly.

The comment troubled Woodend.

'It's a bit difficult, is this,' he said. 'You see, Monika, in order to get a clearer picture of what's been goin' on in this case, I'm goin' to need to ask you some questions about your own life, an'—'

'You know about what happened to me in my childhood?' Paniatowski demanded.

'Not the details, no.'

'But how could you know anything at all? How did I give myself away? Was it something I said? Something I did?'

'It's my belief her stepfather didn't just hurt Monika – I think he interfered with her!' DCI Turner had counselled Woodend, that day in Blackpool.

'How *could* you know?' Monika demanded with urgency.

'Your old boss told me,' Woodend said. 'When you an' me were workin' on our first case together. He didn't mean any harm. He really did think it was for the best.'

'So you've known about what happened right from the start?'

'More or less,' Woodend agreed.

'Yet you never said anything! You never let it show that you knew!'

Woodend shrugged to hide his discomfort. 'Why should I have? There's a lot about my past that you don't know either. It's got nothin' to do with the way we work together or the way we treat each other as people.'

'Thank you!' Paniatowski said. 'Thanks for being so different to almost any other boss I *could* have worked for.'

Woodend coughed – though, strictly speaking, he felt no need to. 'Let's get back to the Fred Dodds' case, shall we?' he suggested.

'Yes,' Paniatowski agreed. 'Let's do that.'

'Would you like to think about whether Inspector Rutter stays or goes?'

'He's no fool,' Paniatowski said. 'Even if he goes, he'll probably have a pretty good idea of what we're talking about.'

'True,' Woodend conceded, 'but there's no need for him to hear all the details. It's your choice, lass. Nobody'll think the worse of you if you say he should go.'

Paniatowski hesitated, but only for a second.

'The inspector's a part of the team investigating this case,' she said. 'It's only right that he stays.'

'You're sure?'

'I'm sure.'

'All right,' Woodend said. 'Now all we have to decide is what order we deal with things in. Anybody have any objection if I kick off – with my phone call to Canada?'

Rutter and Paniatowski shook their heads.

'When Cuthburtson an' Dodds were partners, Fred was still a single man, and Cuthburtson treated him like one of the family,' Woodend continued. 'That was a big mistake from Cuthburtson's side, because his daughter, Louise, eventually reached the age at which Fred started to find her irresistible. An' that's when the sexual abuse began.'

'What I don't see is why the family ran away to Canada, instead of simply informing the police,' Rutter said. 'Unless, of course, Cuthburtson was worried by the fact that Fred had made Louise's brother, Ernest, his accomplice in his dirty little game. Do you think that could have been the reason?'

Woodend was almost on the point of answering himself. Then he changed his mind and turned to Paniatowski. 'What do you think, Monika?'

'Despite Ernest being a minor, Cuthburtson may still have been worried that his son would get into trouble for taking part in the abuse,' Paniatowski said. 'But even if the boy hadn't been involved, my guess is that the father probably wouldn't have reported it.'

'Why not?'

'Because of what other people would say.'

'Do you want to expand on that?'

'When a criminal breaks into your house and steals something, it's no reflection on the family. Even if he kills somebody during the course of the robbery, nobody blames the victim. But if that same criminal rapes the woman of the house, or sexually assaults one of the children, then that's a different matter entirely. Some of the shame attached to the act sticks to the family. There are even people who'll say that they must have been asking for it – that it would never happen in a *really* decent family.'

'That's surely an exaggeration,' Rutter said.

'No, it isn't,' Paniatowski contradicted him. 'And it's not just outsiders who can make that assumption, either. Arthur Jones' family at least partly-blamed *me* for what he did to me. And worse than that, I blamed myself. Because if it wasn't my fault, why didn't it happen to other girls?'

'It *did* happen to other girls,' Woodend said.

'I know that now, but it didn't know it then. And most people *still* don't know it. Do you think that all cases of child molestation are reported? Of course not! And one of the main reasons is that people are *ashamed* to report them. That's why Cuthburtson never said anything. That's why he took his family to Canada. So they could put it all behind them. But you can *never, ever* put it all behind you.'

'We know now why Dodds made friends with Sidney Hill – and why Hill eventually killed himself,' Rutter said.

'Yes,' Woodend agreed. 'Ernest Cuthburtson's mental health was wrecked by what he and Dodds did to Louise, but Sidney Hill took what they'd done to his sister, Dorothy, even worse. That's why he killed himself – because he couldn't bear to live with the memory of it.'

Paniatowski saw Dorothy Hill's aged face in her mind's eye – and shuddered. 'Marcus Dodds?' she said, to change the subject. 'What do we know about him?'

'That Fred killed him,' Rutter said.

'But why?'

'It was probably done in the heat of the moment,' Woodend said. 'They'd been arguing the night before. Possibly they were continuing that argument at the moment Fred picked up the coal hammer and hit his father with it. Marcus was worried that the police would find out what Fred had been doing, you see. And the *reason* he was worried was because he thought that once Fred was in police custody, he might talk about what his own father had done to him! And he was right about that – after a fashion. Because when he was arrested for killing Marcus, Fred *did* tell Sergeant Parker that his father had been abusing him – and that's what made Parker decide to look the other way.'

'That's the part I just can't understand,' Rutter admitted. 'Fred knew from first-hand experience how terrible it was to be abused. How could he then inflict the same suffering on others?'

'There are alcoholics' sons who despise their fathers, yet can't stay off the drink themselves,' Woodend said. 'There are compulsive gamblers' kids who've seen what it can do to a family, but still can't resist placing a bet. Children don't necessarily *have to* follow in their parents' footsteps – but we shouldn't be surprised when they do.'

'What about Jane Hartley?' Rutter asked.

'What about her, Monika?' Woodend said. 'Why didn't she tell us that Fred Dodds had abused her?'

'Because she may not even know about it.'

'How's that possible?'

'She could simply have blanked it out of her mind. A lot of us do suppress the memory.'

'Are you sure that's true? *You* didn't suppress the memory, did you?'

Monika smiled awkwardly. 'What makes you think that?'

'Because you *do* know about it.'

198

'But I didn't always. When Arthur Jones suddenly left home, I'd no idea it was because he was afraid he'd be in trouble for what he'd done to me. Because some part of my brain – perhaps the part that cares about survival – had already locked all my memories of those terrible evenings safely away. It was years before an upheaval in my personal life brought them back to the surface again.'

'Is that what it takes?' Woodend asked. 'Some kind of upheaval in your personal life?'

'Not always. But from the women I've spoken to, that's usually the cause of it.'

'Jane Hartley's life hasn't exactly been without its ups and downs, now has it?' Woodend asked. 'So why hasn't she got her memories back, Monika?'

Paniatowski shrugged. 'You're asking me something that I'm not sure I'm qualified to answer,' she said. 'I'm a detective sergeant, not a psychiatrist.'

'That's as maybe,' Woodend agreed. 'But modesty aside, you do *think* you know, don't you?'

'Perhaps.'

'Then for heaven's sake tell us, lass!'

'Most women only have one trauma to lock away in their subconscious,' Paniatowski said. 'Jane Hartley had two – the things that Fred Dodds did to her, and the knowledge that her mother had been hanged for his murder. And she was never forced to confront the first one, because she'd always got the second to fall back on. If she drank more than she knew was good for her, it was because her mother was hanged. If she had trouble in her relationships with men, that was because her mother was hanged, too. If she was unhappy with her life in general – well, she knew the reason for that. And if she could just prove that her mother was innocent, then all her problems would melt away. Now we're going to have to tell her that her mother wasn't innocent after all – that though she might have had good reasons for killing Fred Dodds, she was still the one who kept swinging the hammer until his skull was little more than dust.'

'I'm sorry to have to contradict you, Monika,' Rutter said – and he sounded as if he genuinely was, 'but we still don't know that Margaret *did* kill Fred.'

'Don't we?' Paniatowski asked.

'No, we don't. We have a different motive now – but motive's never been the problem. Whether we assume that she killed him to protect her daughter or that she did it to get her hands on his money, we're still left with the one important question that has been bugging us this whole investigation.'

'An' what's that?' Woodend asked.

'Why should she have killed her husband in a way which was bound to draw suspicion to her? She was an intelligent woman. Surely she could have come up with a better plan than that.'

'So you're sayin' that we're no further on than we were before?' Woodend said. 'That it's still a distinct possibility that Fred Dodds was killed by person or persons unknown?'

'That's exactly what I'm saying.'

'If she'd found out what Dodds was doing to her daughter, she'd have wanted to kill him!' Monika Paniatowski protested, with a hint of her previous loss of control creeping back into her voice. 'Any mother would!'

Yet even as she spoke, she was considering the possibility that her own mother *had* known – that Blanca Jones had decided that letting the assaults continue was the lesser of two evils.

No, that wasn't true!

It *couldn't* be true, because, if it was, then everything she believed about her mother and their life together was nothing but a lie!

'I don't care how stupidly Margaret went about killing

Fred,' Paniatowski continued fiercely. 'She still did it! She was so outraged by what her husband had done to her daughter that she just couldn't stop herself.'

Woodend was starting to look at her worriedly again. 'It's the timing that's got me bothered,' he admitted.

'To hell with the timing!' Paniatowski said.

'We can't just ignore it – not if we're to do our job properly,' Woodend told her gently. 'Let's trace things backwards. Let's assume that Margaret went out for a walk, just as she claimed she did, on the night of the murder. All right?'

'All right,' Paniatowski agreed, with some show of reluctance.

'She gets back to the house. Fred is in the lounge, probably watching television. Now, we know from his previous history that he's a seasoned offender who's never shown any qualms of conscience. So he's not likely to confess to what he's been doing with Jane. Agreed?'

'Agreed.'

'Which means that she already *knows* about it. So for her to kill him at that particular time – and in such a violent manner – there has to have been something specific which sparked her off. An' I just can't think of anythin' that would have done.'

'Can't you?' Paniatowski said. 'Then it's a good job for the sake of this investigation that I *can*, isn't it?'

Woodend shook his head dolefully, and if Bob Rutter had not been in the room he would probably have reached across the desk and put his hand on Paniatowski's shoulder.

'I know there's a certain way that you'd *like* things to have been, Monika,' he said softly. 'An' I can understand *why* you'd feel like that. Honestly I can. But we're bobbies. We have to look at the facts coldly. We have to deduce what we can solely from the evidence.'

'That's just what I'm doing,' Monika insisted. 'I think I know what caused the spark which made Margaret kill her husband at that moment – and I also think I know how I can prove it.'

She seemed sincere, Woodend thought. She seemed convinced. There was no longer any sign of the irrationality that had threatened to take her over only a couple of minutes earlier.

'Somethin's happened, hasn't it, Monika?' he asked.

'Yes, it has.'

'An' are you goin' to tell us what it is?'

Paniatowski smiled. 'I've just remembered what question I *should* have asked the Fortesques,' she said.

Twenty-Six

'Back again, are you, Sergeant?' Mrs Fortesque asked pleasantly. 'What's the reason for your visit this time? More questions?'

'That's right,' Paniatowski agreed.

Mrs Fortesque looked beyond the sergeant to where the big man in the hairy sports coat was standing.

'I see you've brought one of the big guns with you this time,' she said.

Paniatowski nodded. 'My chief inspector,' she said.

'It's not necessary, you know,' Mrs Fortesque said to Woodend.

'What isn't necessary, madam?'

'Your being here at all. Probably have some doubts about this young woman's ability to do her job properly, simply because she *is* a young woman. Had the same doubts myself at first, I'm ashamed to admit. But you and I will just have to learn to change with the times, you know. Monika is a fine young officer. She'll go far.'

Paniatowski smiled, though that was the last thing she felt like doing. 'Thanks for the vote of confidence, Mrs Fortesque,' she said, 'but I'm afraid you're not going to like it when I tell you the reason we've come back.'

'Won't I?' Mrs Fortesque asked, her voice remaining friendly but her body tensing – as if she'd already guessed what the sergeant was going to say next.

'We need to talk to the Major,' Paniatowski said gently.

'Can't allow that,' the other woman replied instantly.

'He's not been well. Simply isn't up to being interrogated by the police.'

'It *is* important.'

'Can't accept that. He doesn't know anything that I don't know.'

'We think he does. We think he – and *only* he – knows something which is of vital importance to our investigation.'

'Maybe you're right. Still don't care. You can't see him.'

'I was a soldier myself,' Woodend said.

Mrs Fortesque looked at him with new interest. 'What rank?'

'Sergeant.'

'And did you see service in India, Sergeant?'

'No, I didn't.'

'But you weren't some office wallah pushing chitties around in Aldershot, were you? Don't look like the type of man who'd be happy with that sort of soldiering.'

'You're right,' Woodend agreed. 'I've never been much good at filin' papers.'

'So where did you serve?'

'North Africa an' Europe.'

'During the war itself?'

'Yes.'

'Right in the thick of the action,' Mrs Fortesque said approvingly. 'Did you win any medals?'

'I don't really think that matters one way or the other, now the whole thing's over.'

'Spoken like a man who doesn't need medals because he's been awarded plenty,' Mrs Fortesque said. She smiled, still not quite relaxed but certainly less tense than she had been a few moments earlier. 'I'm well aware of what you're trying to do, you know.'

'Are you?'

'Of course. You're doing what we used to call "Playing the Old Comrade". You're trying to soften me up, so I'll let you see the Major.'

'You're half-right,' Woodend admitted. 'But what I was also tryin' to show you is that I've had quite a lot of experience dealin' with officers, an' I think I can say that I understand them.'

'We all know what that means,' Mrs Fortesque said. 'Means you think that all officers are jackasses!'

'No, it doesn't,' Woodend promised. 'There's all kinds of officers. Good an' bad, cautious an' foolhardy, clever an' stupid – but do you know the one thing most of 'em had in common?'

Mrs Fortesque thought for only the briefest of moments. 'A sense of duty,' she said.

'Exactly,' Woodend agreed. 'Your husband knows that his duty is to give us the answers we need. You're not goin' to prevent him doin' that duty, are you, madam?'

Mrs Fortesque looked at him with an expression that showed both defeat and admiration.

'You'd have made a damned good Political Officer out on the North West Frontier,' she said. 'You'd better follow me into the lounge.'

The Major was sitting in his armchair as he had been the last time Paniatowski had seen him, but now he looked as if he wished it would swallow him up even further than it already had.

'These two officers want to ask you a few questions, Major dear,' Mrs Fortesque said gently. 'I promise you it won't take long.'

The Major's eyes filled with panic. 'Send them away!' he gasped. 'Send them away.'

'I can't do that, Major dear,' his wife told him. 'If I could, I'd spare you this by helping them myself. But they say it has to be you. And I believe them.'

'Don't want . . . don't want . . .'

The old woman knelt down and took one of her husband's gnarled hands in both of hers.

'You've always been my hero, Major dear,' she cooed

softly. 'You know that. Please don't let me down now, so close to the end. I know it will take a lot of courage, but I know my man, too, and I'm sure he'll find it from somewhere. Help them, my dear!'

'I'll . . . try,' the Major promised feebly.

The old woman released her husband's hand and rose arthritically to her feet. 'I'll leave you to get on with it in peace,' she said, her eyes rapidly filling with tears. 'Call me if you need anything.'

Woodend and Paniatowski waited until Mrs Fortesque had left the room, then sat down on the sofa opposite the Major.

'Do you remember the last time I was here?' Paniatowski asked.

'Yes, I remember.'

'Your wife was talking about the cars which pulled up in front of the Doddses' house on the night of the murder, and you said, "They took Jane away." At the time I thought you were saying that, after the murder, they took Jane away to live with her aunt. But that wasn't what you meant at all, was it?'

'No.'

'What you really meant was that they took Jane away on *the night of the murder*. In one of the two cars that your wife heard. Isn't that right?'

'She . . . she had been staying with her Aunt Helen,' the old man said weakly. 'I thought she was *still* with her aunt. But . . . but when I heard the second car pull up, I was curious. I went over to the window.'

'An' what did you see?' Woodend asked.

'I saw Jane's mother helping her into the car.'

'Why didn't you volunteer this information during the course of the investigation?'

'I . . . I didn't see the point. It had nothing to do with the murder. They'd already arrested Margaret. What good would it have done to have them bothering Jane?'

The old man hesitated. 'Besides, I was afraid,' he confessed.

'Afraid?'

'I . . . I'd lost my nerve by then. I'd stayed in India too long, you see. It's a country that can destroy a man. Or . . . or at least, it destroyed me.' A tear rolled down his cheek. 'I'm s-so sorry.'

'Don't upset yourself, Major. It probably wouldn't have made any difference if you had come forward,' Woodend lied. 'But there is one more way you can help us.'

'What . . . what do you want to know?'

'When you went to the window an' saw the car which took Jane away, you didn't happen to notice what make it was, did you?'

'I had a car in India,' the Major said nostalgically. 'And a driver. I would have liked to have one when we came back to England, but we couldn't afford it. Still, I took an interest in the latest developments, and this car was a beauty.'

'Do you mean that you *did* notice the make?'

'Of course,' the Major said, as if surprised that he even needed to ask. 'It was a Morris Isis.'

'Well, that's it then,' Paniatowski said, looking at Woodend across the table in the Drum and Monkey.

'Is it?' Woodend asked.

'Of course. Margaret Dodds comes home and finds her husband sexually assaulting her daughter. She flies into a rage – as any mother would – and kills him with the hammer. We don't need to know any more.'

'What about the two cars – the one which stopped there earlier and the Morris Isis which took Jane away?'

'*What* about them?'

'Who was driving them?'

'That's a detail. It doesn't really matter.'

Woodend placed his hands on top of Paniatowski's. 'You want it to be the mother who killed him, don't you?' he said.

207

'It *is* the mother.'

'You can't bear the thought that she might have known that Fred was assaulting Jane, and still did nothing about it.'

'She *did* do something about it. She crushed his skull to a pulp.'

'An' because you're so set on believin' what you want to believe, you won't admit there's even the slightest possibility that whoever was in the first car which stopped outside the house could be the murderer. That by the time Margaret got home, Fred was already dead.'

'It didn't happen like that.'

'It might have, Monika.'

'We have to work with probabilities. Margaret Dodds had the means, the motive and the opportunity. What possible grounds can you have for doubting that she was the killer?'

'She said she didn't do it.'

'What?'

'You've forgotten that, Monika. You've forgotten it because you wanted to. When Margaret Dodds was being interviewed by DCI Sharpe, she said, "I didn't kill my husband."'

'She was lying!'

'Why should she have lied?'

'To protect Jane from gossip! To prevent what Dodds had done to her daughter from becoming public knowledge. I know that's what my moth— . . . what I would have done in the same circumstances.'

'She could have come up with another reason for killing Dodds. She could have said she'd done it for the money.'

'You don't understand!' Paniatowski said exasperatedly.

'An' you don't *want* to understand,' Woodend said softly. 'Look, Monika, you may well be right. Perhaps Margaret Dodds did kill her husband. But until we've tied up all the loose ends that are hangin' over this case, we won't know for sure.'

Paniatowski took a slug of her vodka. 'That's the second time in this investigation I've stopped thinking like a bobby, isn't it?' she asked ruefully.

'I haven't been countin',' Woodend said. 'An' even if I had, I've got a terrible memory for cases once they're over an' done with.'

Paniatowski gave him a weak smile. 'I don't deserve a boss like you,' she said.

'Bollocks!' Woodend said. 'Everybody's got to take the rough with the smooth, an' you've just been landed with the rough for a while.'

'These loose ends?' Paniatowski said. 'Which one do you think we should start with?'

'Well, we could do worse than find out who in Whitebridge owned a Morris Isis in 1934,' Woodend told her.

Twenty-Seven

The big house had an elevated position that overlooked the Corporation Park. It had once stood in splendid isolation, but the grounds had long since been sold off to speculative builders. Now it was surrounded by other detached houses that would have looked impressive in their own right, had they been elsewhere, but in this location seemed no more than dwarfish intruders hunkering down in the mansion's shadow.

There had once been any number of houses like this in Whitebridge, Woodend thought as he walked up to the front door. But now that cotton was no longer king, this was the last one remaining.

He rang the bell. The door was answered by a round little woman in her early sixties. She looked up at him suspiciously.

'Yes?' she said.

'I'd like to see Mr Earnshaw, please.'

'Mr Earnshaw doesn't see people himself, these days. I'm his housekeeper. Anything you have to say, you can say to me.'

'It's in the nature of a personal matter,' Woodend explained.

'A personal matter?' the guardian to the gate repeated sceptically.

'I'm an old friend.'

'All Mr Earnshaw's old friends are dead. And even if they weren't, you're too young to have been one of them.'

It would have been easy enough to produce his warrant card but, if possible, Woodend wished to avoid putting the whole matter on an official footing.

'Will you ask Mr Earnshaw if he'll see Charlie Woodend?' he said.

The housekeeper sniffed. 'I'll ask. But it won't do you any good. Like I said, he never sees anybody.'

The housekeeper returned two minutes later. If he would follow her, Mr Earnshaw would be delighted to see him, she informed Woodend, with a touch of annoyance in her voice.

She led him into a hallway that would have swallowed the entire ground floor of his cottage, and from there up a wide staircase that could easily have been the setting for one of the Douglas Fairbanks' swashbuckler films that Woodend had revelled in as a child.

The housekeeper knocked on a door just to the left of the head of the staircase, opened it without waiting for an answer, and gestured to the Chief Inspector that he should go inside.

The room he entered was a large one, but then all the rooms in this house – with the exception of the servants' quarters – were probably large. Against one of the walls was a double bed, and lying propped up in the bed was Seth Earnshaw. He had been a big man in his time, but his time had gone, and now he looked so frail and wispy that Woodend was almost surprised his trunk made even the slightest dent in the pillows that were supporting him.

'You've given Mrs Green the hump, in no uncertain manner,' the old man said. 'She doesn't like visitors. They make too much work for her. We used to have eight servants running this house. People who took a pride in their jobs – and a pride in the place they were looking after. Now it's all down to Mrs Green and a weekly contract cleaning firm.' Earnshaw sniffed. 'The contract cleaning firm!' he repeated. 'It has such a large staff turnover that we rarely see the same face in this house twice.'

'That's the way of the world,' Woodend said philosophically.

'Pride in their work?' the old man said. 'These young lads don't know the meaning of the words. And the only reason Dolly Green stays with me is because she expects me to leave her something in my will.' He paused for a second. 'It's been a long time, Charlie.'

'Must be twenty-five years,' Woodend agreed. 'My dad's funeral.'

'Now there was a man who took pride in what he did,' Earnshaw said with enthusiasm. 'And he'd have been proud if he could have seen you now. Chief Inspector Woodend! Who would have thought it?'

'You shouldn't be so surprised,' Woodend said. 'You always told me I had more imagination an' drive than most of the folk round here.'

'So I did.'

'That's why I was the one you sent to stand outside Strangeways Prison while Margaret Dodds was hung.'

'Yes, I thought you were the best man for the job, and I was right. Listening to you describe it, it was almost like being there myself.'

'What kind of car did you drive in those days?' Woodend asked.

A flash of anger appeared in the old man's watery eyes. 'Don't insult me, Charlie. I'm not quite a basket case yet – and I still read the papers. I know why you're here.'

'So what kind of car *were* you drivin'?'

'It was a 1931 Morris Isis.'

'An' on the night of Fredrick Dodds murder, you made a visit to the Doddses' house.'

'Wrong!' the old man said, perhaps just a little triumphantly. 'I made *two* visits to the house.'

'Two?'

Earnshaw smiled. 'You're a clever lad, Charlie, and no doubt you'd eventually get the truth out of me with all your questions. But wouldn't it be quicker if I just *told* you what you wanted to know, in my own words?'

'All right,' Woodend agreed.

'Margaret started working for me about a year after Jane was born. I was attracted to her from the start, but I never planned it that we should become lovers. Nor would we have been, if that first husband of hers had been anything of a man. But he wasn't. He was weak, and he was useless. I wanted to give him that promotion he'd put in for, Charlie. I wanted to do it for Margaret's sake – but I just couldn't.'

'Why not?'

'One of my responsibilities to my employees was to run the mill as well as I could – because that way they all stayed in work. And that meant putting the right people in the right jobs. Rob Hartley could never have handled that promotion. I knew it. He knew it. I don't think he even wanted the job, if the truth be told. It was much easier to stay where he was – and he'd always been a man for following the easiest course.'

'Don't marry a man already set in his ways,' Margaret's mother had told her, all those years ago. *'Find yourself a husband you can mould – a husband you can make something out of.'* And hadn't that just worked out a treat? Woodend thought.

'Anyway, he didn't get the promotion, his wife was almost crushed with disappointment, Rob started drinking – and Margaret and I became lovers,' Earnshaw said.

'Both before *an'* after her first husband's death?'

'She broke it off for a while when Robert died. Guilt, I expect. But a few months later we were back in each other's arms again.'

'Did you promise to marry her?'

Earnshaw gave the frailest shake of his head. 'No, that was never on – and she knew it. I'd made it plain right from the start. I loved her more than I'd ever loved my wife, but I could never have divorced Edith. She needed me, you see, whereas Margaret only *wanted* me. Edith would have gone completely to pieces without me, but Margaret had this amazing inner strength.'

Why were men always such fools? Woodend wondered. How could Earnshaw say that Margaret had wanted him but never *needed* him? Had it not, at some point, occurred to him to ask himself why a very pretty young woman should wish to start an affair with a not-particularly attractive older man? Couldn't he see that perhaps his main appeal to her had been more to do with him being a substitute for the father she'd adored?

'Did you continue seein' Margaret until her second husband was killed?' the Chief Inspector asked.

'It wasn't anything like as simple as that,' Earnshaw told him. 'When Margaret began getting serious about Fred Dodds, she broke our affair off for a second time.'

But why did she ever even *begin* to get serious about Fred Dodds? Woodend asked himself.

Because, he thought, answering his own question, she had made the wrong choice with her first marriage and wanted to ensure that it did not happen again. Fred Dodds would not disappoint her as Rob Hartley had done. Dodds had already proved that he could be successful.

And so it was that, in order not to make the same mistake twice, Margaret had made the biggest mistake of all – by not asking herself what it was that Dodds wanted from her.

'If you want to keep on doin' that sort of thing, why don't you get married?' Marcus Dodds, another child abuser, had advised his son. And for once the son had followed the father's advice.

'Are you still with me, Charlie?' Seth Earnshaw asked. 'You look miles away.'

Years away would be closer to the mark, Woodend

thought. But aloud he said, 'Yes, I'm still with you. You were tellin' me about your on-off affair with Margaret.'

'That's just what it was,' Earnshaw said. 'An on-off affair. Because when her marriage to Dodds turned sour, she came back to me for a third time.'

'Did you ever ask her what it was that made her marriage to Fred Dodds turn so sour?'

'No, I didn't.'

'Weren't you even curious?'

'I was just so grateful that she'd come back to me. She was the love of my life.'

Love without responsibility, Woodend thought. It was probably most men's dream – but he knew it would never have suited him.

'Shall we get on to the night of the murder?' he suggested.

'Why not? We were out together that night.'

'Somewhere in Whitebridge?'

'No. We were always very careful about where we were seen together. We used to drive to country pubs, where we wouldn't be recognized. And when we got back to town, I'd always drop her off on the outskirts and she'd get a bus home. Anyway, we were in a pub that night and she said, "I'll just ring my sister-in-law, to make sure that Jane's all right." Jane was staying with her father's sister, you understand.'

'Aye, I know about that.'

'When she came back from using the phone, she was as white as a sheet and her hands were trembling. "Helen's taken Jane home!" she said. I asked her what she meant. "Jane was supposed to be staying with Helen all week, but Helen's had a last-minute invitation to a dinner-dance, and she's taken Jane home." I know it doesn't sound very dramatic when I say it like that, Charlie, but believe me, it was. Margaret was on the verge of hysterics.'

'Understood,' Woodend said. 'What happened next?'

'Margaret insisted that I drive her home immediately. Not to the edge of town as usual, you understand, but straight up to her front door. I pointed out that her husband might see us through the window, and she said that she didn't care. In fact, she said that she didn't *bloody* care. And Margaret was never one for swearing.'

'You did as she'd asked you to?'

'Yes. I didn't want to – I had my marriage, and reputation in the community to consider – but given the state she was in, I didn't see I had any choice.'

'Still, you didn't drive her *straight* home, did you? You stopped once on the way.'

'How in God's name did you know?'

'That doesn't matter. Just tell me *where* you stopped. An' why.'

'We were crossing town. The Isis started to misfire, then stalled. I told Margaret I'd have to look under the bonnet. She'd been upset before. Now she became even worse. Still, there was nothing for it but to take a look at the engine. It was a minor problem – dirty points – but by the time I'd fixed it Margaret had disappeared. Then she came running back. "I've just phoned Fred!" she said. "He won't answer! The swine won't even pick up the phone!" I told her that really didn't matter, since I'd have her home in a few minutes.'

'Where did this breakdown of yours happen?' Woodend asked. 'Near St Mary's Church?'

'Yes, I . . . I can't imagine how you've found all this out.'

'That particular piece of information came from a reformed burglar named Harold Brunskill,' Woodend explained. 'He told the police he'd seen Margaret near the church. But that wasn't something that the man in charge of the investigation particularly wanted to hear, so he decided to ignore it. But that's neither here nor there at the moment. What happened after you'd got the car started again?'

'I drove Margaret to Hebden Brow. The second I'd

stopped the car, she was out of the door and running up the path to her front door. She didn't even say goodnight.'

'So what did you do then?'

'I came back here.'

'Weren't you worried that your wife would be suspicious if you got home earlier than you'd said you would?'

'Edith was away. She was staying with her mother.'

'How long had you been back at home when you got the phone call from Margaret?'

Earnshaw shook his head in wonder. 'Talking to you is like talking to a mind reader, Charlie,' he said. 'How do you do it?'

'No trick,' Woodend assured him. 'You've already told me you went back to the Doddses' house. The only thing that could have made you do that was a phone call. When did that call come?'

'The phone was ringing as I walked through the front door.'

'How did Margaret sound?'

'Calmer than she'd sounded earlier. Too calm, now I think about it. Almost as if she was holding her real feelings in – but only by a tremendous effort of will.'

'When you got back to Margaret's house, she brought her daughter out and handed her over to you. What state was Jane in?'

'Very quiet. Docile. Almost as if she'd been drugged.'

'Do you think she *had* been?'

'No. Drugged was a bad choice of word. She seemed dazed. Perhaps even shocked. But then so would any child who'd just seen her mother batter her stepfather to death with a hammer.'

'You think that's what happened, do you?'

'Of course that's what happened! What other explanation could there possibly be?'

'What did Margaret ask you to do with Jane?'

'She asked me to keep her with me until eleven o'clock.

217

By then, the dinner-dance would be over, and I was to take Jane to her Aunt Helen's house. And that's just what I did. I brought Jane here, put her on the sofa and covered her with a blanket. I asked her if she wanted a glass of warm milk or some biscuits, but she didn't seem to hear me.'

'Did any of the servants see her?'

Earnshaw gave a dry laugh. 'We're not talking about the days before the First World War, Charlie. This was the thirties, and while you still could *get* servants, it was rare to find one willing to live in. By the time I got back here with Jane, all my servants had gone home.'

'So you waited until the dinner-dance was over, then you took Jane to her aunt's. What did you tell Helen?'

'I told her exactly what Margaret had instructed me to tell her. That whatever she heard about the events of that night, it was vital she never reveal the fact that she'd taken Jane to Hebden Brow – or that I'd brought her back.'

It wouldn't have taken any bobby worth his salt long to uncover the truth, Woodend thought. Even a simple check on alibis would have revealed that Helen couldn't have been taking care of Jane and also been at a dinner-dance. But Eric Sharpe had not bothered to follow even such rudimentary procedure. He had someone who he could make a case against – and that was good enough for him.

'I felt so helpless,' Earnshaw said. 'If Margaret had ever told me anything about what had happened between her and Fred Dodds before that fatal night – if she'd said that he'd beaten her up or something of that nature – then I'd have gone to the police. And I'd have testified at her trial, even if that had meant ruining both my marriage and my career. But she'd told me *nothing* – and I'd been so worried about holding on to the happiness she brought me that I'd never bothered to ask. So all I could do was let justice follow its natural course.'

But *had* justice taken its natural course? Woodend wondered.

Suppose Margaret really *had* killed Fred. Why should she have denied it? Why not tell the court the *reason* she'd committed the murder? And if she didn't want to do that – if she wished to keep Jane's name out of it – why not agree with the prosecution that she'd done it for the money? Yet despite the other options open to her, she'd steadfastly maintained throughout the investigation and trial that she was not guilty.

There had to be some logic behind the way this highly intelligent woman had acted, Woodend told himself. All he had to do was find it.

'Is there anythin' else you can tell me about that night?' he asked Earnshaw. 'Anythin' that Margaret said – or Jane did.'

'Jane was very restless while she was lying on my sofa. She kept mumbling something like, "Bad man! Very bad man!" I expect that's what her mother had told her – that Fred Dodds was a very bad man.'

'Anythin' else? Any little detail? It doesn't matter how insignificant it seems to you.'

'I don't think so,' Earnshaw said. 'No! Wait! There *is* something. I'd forgotten all about it until this very moment, and I still don't see how it could help you. But since you did say *anything* I could remember . . .'

'Go on,' Woodend encouraged.

'Margaret gave me something she'd brought with her from the lounge, and asked me to destroy it. It seemed a strange request to me, but everything about that night was strange, so I did as she'd asked.'

An image of the inventory which one of Sharpe's men had so painstakingly constructed flashed through Woodend's mind.

Packet of Embassy Cigarettes (three smoked, stubs in
the ashtray – see below)
Box of England's Glory matches

Ashtray (souvenir of Fleetwood)
Ball of wool (light blue)
Knitting needle
Magazine (*Woman*, 16th June)
Daily Herald (15th June), corner of page containing crossword ripped out
Pair of pinking scissors
One shilling and threepence (1/3d) recovered from back of sofa (sixpenny piece, threepenny piece, four pennies, four ha'pennies) . . .

'What *was* this thing that Margaret asked you to get rid of?' he asked. 'Something valuable? Something personal?'

'No, it was neither of those things. That was what made the request seem so strange. Why on earth did Margaret want me to destroy a common-or-garden knitting needle?'

A knitting needle! Woodend thought. A simple bloody knitting needle, which you could buy from any wool shop and couldn't have cost more than fourpence or fivepence at the most. Yet as simple as it was, it provided an answer to those aspects of the case that had been giving him the biggest headaches.

He knew now why Fred Dodds had died that night. He knew now how Margaret Dodds could first pulverize his head with a hammer – until nothing was left but powder and bone splinters – and then stand up in court and say that she had not killed her husband!

He had all the answers – and there was at least a part of him that wished that he hadn't!

Twenty-Eight

Woodend sat behind his desk. Gazing at the wall. Gazing at the *clock* on that wall. Listening to the ticking of the clock. Believing – though his mind told him it could not possibly be true – that the ticking was growing louder every time that the big hand jumped.

He would have to go back as far as the war in order to remember a time in which he felt so unsure of himself, he thought. No, even that wasn't true. In the war, he'd not liked what he'd had to do, but he'd known that it was right that he do it. To come anywhere close to his present state of uncertainty, he would probably have to travel as far back in time as Miss Scoggins' Standard One class.

'It's five past four,' Monika Paniatowski said impatiently. 'The board of inquiry is due to meet in less than two hours.'

'I know,' Woodend said, and it was all he could do to prevent himself from adding 'Miss' to the end of his sentence.

'But it doesn't *have* to meet at all, does it?' Bob Rutter asked, his voice more angry than impatient. 'You could stop it, if you wanted to.'

Why had this reversion to childhood happened? Woodend wondered. By what psychological mechanism had he ceased to be the head of the family and instead become the recalcitrant child to Rutter and Paniatowski's firm parents? Had he lost his power because he was merely being stubborn? Or was it because the other two had grown so jaded and cynical that they could no longer understand the innocent simplicity of his argument?

'You *have* to ring Lord Sharpe, sir,' Bob Rutter said.

'An' what do I do when I've got him on the phone?' Woodend demanded, aware that, to the others, he might well be sounding petulant. 'Do you want me to lie to him?'

'No!' Paniatowski said. 'Not lie to him. There's no need for you to go that far.'

Who would ever have imagined that Rutter and Paniatowski could have found it in themselves to put aside their differences and form a united front? Woodend thought. And did the fact that they'd been able to achieve the almost impossible automatically make them right?

'So there isn't any need to go that far, isn't there, Monika?' he said. 'Then would you mind tellin' me just *how* far you do want me to go?'

'Tell him the truth – but not all of it,' Paniatowski said.

Woodend ran his hand across his forehead, and was not surprised to discover that it was damp.

'I've been a bobby for a long time,' he said. 'Durin' the course of my career, I've been offered all kinds of bribes. Money, cellars full of booze, holidays, holiday *homes*, every variety of sex you could imagine – an' some you probably couldn't. An' do you know what? I've turned them all down without a second's hesitation.'

'This is different,' Rutter argued.

'I've met plenty of bobbies who thought what *they* were doin' was different,' Woodend countered. 'It was different because the only reason they took a bribe was to get their children's teeth fixed. It was different when they accepted a free night with a high-class prostitute, because if they didn't sleep with the girl, then somebody else would.'

'We're not asking you to take any money or—' Rutter began.

'It's *always* different,' Woodend interrupted. 'Each an' every time you can find a reason which makes it different.

An' that's why you have to steer clear of it – because it always leads down the slippery path to hell.'

'If you don't make the call, then what happens to us?' Rutter asked. 'Who'll protect us when you're gone? Or are you going to try and pretend that we won't need any protection?'

Woodend shook his head. No, he couldn't pretend that.

Maybe they did have a right to demand that he compromise himself, he thought. They had followed him willingly into shark-filled waters often enough. Could he now leave them to the mercy of those sharks while he was airlifted out into the rescuing arms of retirement or another meaningless committee?

He would do it! He would make the phone call for *them*. Yet he still wished that one of them could say something that would make him despise himself a little less – that would tip the balance just far enough for him to believe that he still had a little integrity left. But there was nothing either of them *could* say, was there?

And then Monika Paniatowski said it.

'Don't do it for yourself,' she told him. 'Don't even do it for us. Do it for Jane Hartley.'

Twenty-Nine

Until around an hour earlier, there had been at least a dozen other drinkers in the hotel bar. Though Jane Hartley had made no attempt to talk to any of them, they had provided a pleasant background noise to accompany her drinking. They had been – somehow – reassuring. Then the barman had rung the bell to announce that the bar was now closed except to residents of the hotel, and the other drinkers had all drifted away. Suddenly, she was surrounded by emptiness. But she did not really mind that, she told herself. She was perfectly capable of drinking alone.

Jane placed her glass as far along the bar as her arm could stretch, then focussed her eyes on it. The rim of the glass did not undulate. The surface of the double whisky inside it appeared not to have been struck by any sudden, unexpected tempest.

Good, she was still relatively sober. She did not need to wrestle with the question of whether or not she should walk away from the bar – a battle she already knew the sensible side of her would lose – until she'd at least drained this dose of anaesthetic.

'I'm sorry, sir,' the barman said, looking at someone behind her. 'We're closed.'

'That's all right,' answered the man. 'I don't want a drink. I'm here to talk to the lady.'

Jane Hartley turned cautiously on her bar stool, and found herself looking at a rather attractive younger man in a smart suit. She was almost sure that she'd seen him before, though the alcohol was making it slightly difficult for her to recall quite when.

'DI Rutter,' the man said.

'I know,' Jane replied, remembering now. 'You're Mr Woodend's little friend.'

If he registered the insult, he certainly didn't let it show. 'Mr Woodend was wondering if you could spare the time to come to police headquarters,' he said.

'What's it about?' she asked, being careful not to slur her words.

'I imagine it's about the matter you wished him to investigate.'

'I see. And has he come up with any startling new relav— . . . revelations?'

'I'm afraid I couldn't say.'

He was a liar, she thought. But then all men were liars.

Liars *and* cheats!

Insects!

Scum!

Vermin who must be continually slapped down – because if they were not kept in their place there was no telling what they might do.

'You didn't say *when* your chief inspector would like me to come down to your headquarters,' Jane Hartley said.

'I mustn't have made myself clear,' Rutter said pleasantly. 'He'd like you to come now.'

'Now?'

'Now. With me.'

'I'll just go upstairs to my room and change,' Jane Hartley said.

'That won't be necessary, madam,' Rutter assured her. 'You're fine as you are.'

'It won't take a minute,' Jane Hartley insisted. 'You can wait here.'

She made her way to the foyer, concentrating her efforts on walking in a straight line. Woodend wanted to see her.

That was good, because it must mean that he had uncovered some new evidence. For years she had been hoping for this moment. *Praying* for it. And now it had finally arrived. She would get changed and return to the bar, just as she'd promised she would – but what she really wanted to do was run away!

Woodend had told the switchboard operator at the Houses of Parliament who he was. She had promised to ring the appropriate extension. Now it was up to Lord Sharpe to decide whether or not the conversation took place.

'Woodend? Is that you?' asked a growling voice from the other end of the line.

'It's me,' the Chief Inspector confirmed.

'Why are you calling me? To make threats?'

'From what I can remember of our one an' only meetin', it's you, not me, that's a dab hand at makin' threats,' Woodend said.

'You've got a bloody nerve!' Sharpe exploded.

'Maybe I have,' Woodend agreed. 'But I've also got somethin' very interestin' to say. If you want to hear it, you're goin' to have to climb down off your high horse and listen without interruptin'. If you don't want to hear it, you can hang up now. Which is it to be?'

A pause.

'Is it good news or bad news?' Sharpe asked suspiciously.

'Who for?'

'For *me*, of course.'

'Of course for you,' Woodend said. 'I really can't think why I even bothered to ask. Because as far as you're concerned, it's not really news at all unless it affects you.'

'Well, which is it?' Sharpe asked impatiently. 'Good news or bad?'

'It's a bit of both. An' since I'm the one who's callin' the shots here, you'll have the bad news first. Agreed?'

'Agreed,' Sharpe said reluctantly.

'The bad news is that even after spendin' only three days on it, I've seen enough of the way you handled the Dodds case to know that you made a bloody lousy job of it. You failed to check on alibis; you didn't follow up on leads. You probably suppressed some evidence as well, if—'

'Now just a minute!' Sharpe said, outraged.

'Shut up an' listen!' Woodend ordered him angrily. 'As I was sayin', you've probably suppressed evidence as well. I haven't found it yet, but if I keep lookin' I've no doubt I will. The result is that the case you put together was so full of holes that a decent defence counsel could have got it kicked out of court. The problem was that Margaret Dodds' counsel wasn't even *halfway* decent. Where did she find him? In the Home for Incompetent Barristers?'

'I've no idea. I didn't choose him.'

'No, *she* did. But you still must have thought that all your birthdays had come at once when you realized he wasn't doin' his job properly. His cross-examination of you, for example, was a perfect model of what a defence should *never* do. Did you ever stop to think *why* she'd chosen such a complete deadbeat to defend her?'

'No, I—'

'An' you didn't really care, did you – not as long as you got a conviction? You didn't even care if the verdict was overturned on appeal. Because the wheels of justice grind exceedin' slow, an' by the time the appeal was heard in the high court, you'd already have won your parliamentary seat. But there *was* no appeal, because Margaret Dodds didn't choose to lodge one for much the same reason as she didn't select a strong counsel for the defence. She didn't want any *doubts* raised, any *questions* asked – because she was terrified that the police would start lookin' elsewhere, for a different answer to the one they'd got already.'

'She was guilty!' Sharpe protested.

'No, she wasn't,' Woodend told him. 'She was innocent

227

– an' I can prove it, if I have to. I can completely discredit you, Lord Sharpe. I can bring you down, an' you'll drag the whole government down with you. An' I'm very tempted to do just that, but . . .'

He paused. He could hear the other man's irregular breathing. He could picture the sweat spreading under the armpits of Sharpe's shirt.

The silence continued.

'But *what*?' Sharpe said, when he could stand the suspense no longer.

'But Margaret Dodds has been dead these thirty years, an' there's nothin' I can do to bring her back to life now, is there? Which means that I just might be open to a deal.'

'What kind of deal?'

'For the last few months, I've been wearin' out the seat of my pants by sittin' on various committees. An' why? Because our esteemed Chief Constable, Mr Marlowe, would just love it if I got so pissed off that I handed in my resignation. Failin' that, he's happy to keep on movin' me from committee to committee to committee – because as long as I'm wastin' my time doin' that, I can't go creatin' havoc anywhere else.'

'What are you complaining about?' Sharpe asked, sounding genuinely mystified. 'You're getting your full pay, aren't you, whatever job you do?'

'You have no idea what goes on inside my head, do you?' Woodend asked. 'My job's neither just a meal ticket to me nor a steppin' stone to somethin' better. I like bein' a workin' bobby. I like puttin' in all the hours that God sends on a case. I enjoy livin' off a diet of bacon butties, nerves, frustrations, headaches, an' strong cigarettes.'

'Do you want to spell out to me *exactly* what it is you want?' Eric Sharpe asked.

'I should have thought that was obvious enough. As a result of your phone call last night, Marlowe's set up a board of inquiry to meet this afternoon, so now I want you make another phone call to persuade him to call it off. An' by tomorrow mornin', I want to be back in the field, where I belong. You do those two things for me, an' in return, I'll give you a clean bill of health on the Dodds investigation. Fair enough?'

'You don't want me to get you a promotion?' Sharpe asked suspiciously.

'No.'

'You're quite sure about that?'

'It wouldn't be a promotion – not what I mean by one, anyway – if you got it for me.'

'You're a fool!' Sharpe said scornfully.

'You've told me that before, an' even then you weren't the first – not by a long way. Do we have a deal or don't we?'

'We have a deal.'

'Good,' Woodend said. 'Listen, Lord Sharpe, we're both havin' such fun that I'd love to stay chattin' to you all day. The thing is, though, I've got this sudden urge to take a very hot shower and then wash my mouth out with soap an' water.'

'You self-righteous bastard!' Sharpe said.

'It's been nice doin' business with you, an' all,' Woodend said, replacing the receiver on its cradle.

He lit another cigarette – his forty-first of the day – and thought back to that early morning thirty years earlier. The two groups of people facing each other outside Strangeways Prison (the hangers and the anti-hangers) had both been absolutely certain that they knew what was right, even though – by logic – at least one of them must have been wrong. And young Charlie Woodend, sent to the prison on a mission he was not to understand for another three decades, had made a decision then and there not only to become a policeman but to become a *certain kind* of policeman.

Was he still that kind of policeman? he wondered. Could the kind of policeman he'd planned to be back then ever have made the call to Eric Sharpe? Had he, at some point, lost his way? Or was it merely that the path he'd chosen to follow was far more complex and intricate than the younger Woodend could ever have imagined?

He lit his forty-second Full Strength from the butt of his forty-first. In a way, he was in the same situation that Margaret Dodds had found herself in all those years ago, he thought. Like her, he was a prisoner of the circumstances he'd found himself trapped in.

'An' then there was Jane Hartley to consider,' he said softly to himself.

Yes, when everything else had been weighed and balanced, when all the plusses and negatives had been held up for comparison, there had still been Jane Hartley to consider.

Thirty

Jane Hartley glared at Monika Paniatowski across Wood-end's desk.

'Why isn't your chief inspector here?' she demanded. 'Can't he be *bothered* to see me? Or is it just that he asked you to do it because you've attended some kind of special course on how to fob people off?'

'Nobody's trying to fob you off, Miss Hartley,' Paniatowski said. 'And if you still want to see Mr Woodend later, he's more than willing to make himself available.'

'If I *still* want to see him? Why *shouldn't* I still want to see him?'

'Perhaps you will,' Paniatowski said evenly. 'But then again, after we've had our little chat, perhaps you won't.'

'Maybe *you* can afford to sit around having "little chats" – when where you should really be is out on the streets, catching criminals – but don't ask me to do the same. I'm far too busy for "little chats".'

'You've petitioned for your mother's case to be re-opened on two separate occasions, with a gap of over twenty years between them,' Paniatowski said. 'What, do you think, prompted you to make your requests at those specific times?'

'"Specific times"!' Jane Hartley mocked. 'My, but aren't we using big words for a mere detective sergeant. I would have thought you'd have to be at least a superintendent before you were allowed to say "specific times".'

She'd always known that this interview was going to be

a difficult one, Paniatowski reminded herself. She'd always understood that there was a part of Jane Hartley that would fight her tooth and claw – that would do or say anything – in order to avoid having to face the truth.

'The first time you petitioned for a review was when you were just about to get married,' the sergeant said. 'The second time was shortly after your Aunt Helen died. That's often the way it goes. Something dramatic happens – and it forces to the surface the very thing we've been trying so hard to hide from ourselves.'

'You're talking gibberish,' Jane Hartley said. 'You've got two minutes to start making sense.' She made an ostentatious show of glancing down at her watch. 'Two minutes – or I'm leaving. And you can be certain of one thing, Sergeant – you don't waste my valuable time and get away with it. I'll make complaints about you at the highest level.'

'I was eighteen when my mother died,' Paniatowski said in a strange, almost dreamlike voice. 'Until then, I'd always thought that the reason *my* stepfather ran away when I was eleven was because he couldn't face the responsibilities of family life any longer. But standing there, looking down at my mother's body, I saw the truth at last. I couldn't help it. It was as if her death had broken a dam somewhere in my mind, and the truth just came flooding out, whether I wanted it to or not.'

'You've already wasted one of the two minutes I gave you,' Jane Hartley said sharply.

'He came back for my mother's funeral,' Paniatowski continued. 'He knew he was running the risk of being arrested – his brother had told him that I finally knew the truth – but he still came. So he must have cared about my mother in some way, mustn't he? That's the trouble with monsters – they're never quite monstrous enough.'

'It's so smoky in here,' Jane Hartley said. 'Haven't you people ever heard of ventilation?'

'I can open the door to the corridor, if that will make it any better,' Paniatowski suggested.

'No, no! That would waste even more time.'

'We stood opposite each other – my stepfather and I – across my mother's open grave. He wouldn't look at me. In my memory, I'd pictured him as a giant. Now I saw him for what he really was – a shabby little man, grown old before his time. I was a fit young woman by then. I could probably have snapped him in half if I'd wanted to. Yet despite all that, he still managed to terrify me.'

'I don't have to listen to any more of this, you know,' Jane Hartley said uneasily.

But she made no move to leave.

'He sexually assaulted me – continually and unmercilessly – during the years we lived in the same house,' Paniatowski said. 'And being by that grave was like getting in a time machine and travelling back to my childhood. It wasn't just that I could remember what he'd done – I was actually reliving the way I'd felt at the time. And do you know – can you guess, Jane – what my strongest feeling had been?'

Jane Hartley put her hands over her ears. 'I'm not here to listen to your sick ramblings,' she gasped. 'I'm . . . it's . . .'

Paniatowski reached across the desk, grabbed the other woman's wrists, and pulled her hands clear of her head.

'I'd thought that it was all my fault, Jane,' she said. 'I thought that somehow I was the one who was doing wrong. You can understand that feeling, can't you?'

'No!' Jane Hartley croaked. 'No, I can't!'

But she could!

She could!

'Do you like it when I do that, Jane? It's nice, isn't it?'

'No, it's . . .'

'You know you want it. You know I wouldn't be doing it if you didn't want it. It's all your idea – not mine. You're leading me on.'

233

How long had it gone on for? A week? A month? A year? She didn't know. But it seemed as if it had been that way for ever – had always gone on and *would* always go on.

Her mother had found out, as she was bound to do inevitably, and then the arguments had begun.

'*You need help, Fred. Medical help.*'

'*I don't know what you're talking about.*'

'*You're a sick man.*'

'*Sick! You're the one who's sick. Here I am, doing my best to win your daughter's affection – trying as hard as I can to replace her dead father – and you go and accuse me of being some kind of pervert.*'

'*I can't take any more of this.* Jane *can't take any more of this. I'm leaving you. I'm getting a divorce.*'

'*Please don't do that. It's not like you think, I promise. I was just giving Jane a cuddle, and if I've given the wrong impression, then I'm very sorry.*'

'*Stay away from her. Stay away from my daughter.*'

'*If that's what you want, of course I will. But like I said, you're making a mistake.*'

'*If you touch her again, I'll kill you.*'

'Your Aunt Helen thought the only reason you were staying with her was to give your mother a break,' Paniatowski said. 'She didn't know about your stepfather, did she?'

'No, she didn't. She couldn't have, because if my mother had told her . . . if she'd been told . . .'

'If she'd been told she would never even have considered leaving you alone with Fred, that night she got the unexpected invitation to the dinner-dance.'

Aunt Helen helps Jane on with her coat. 'I'll pick you up again in the morning and take you to school,' she says as she fastens the buttons with her swift, sure fingers. 'And tomorrow afternoon we'll have a special tea to make up for the fact that I've messed you around tonight. All right?'

'*All right,*' *Jane says.*

She knows what she really wants to say – that her mother

will be out, as she always is on a Thursday, which means that she will be left alone with him. *But she doesn't know how to express it in a way which Aunt Jane will approve of – a way in which it won't all seem like* her *fault!*

It is less than a mile from this house to the one on Hebden Brow, and Aunt Helen decides they will walk it.

'It'll do you good,' she says. 'Tire you out so you'll have no trouble sleeping.'

Jane doesn't normally hold other people's hands now she's a big girl, but this time she does, gripping Helen's hand so tightly that the aunt has to tell her to relax a little.

Jane keeps hoping that something will happen to prevent them reaching home – an earthquake, an elephant stampede – but the streets are almost deserted at this hour of the evening. She thinks about falling over and grazing her knee, but she knows that Aunt Helen will merely dust her down and tell her to be more careful in future.

Aunt Helen really wants to go to this dinner-dance. She will be annoyed if Jane tries to stop her. And Jane doesn't want to annoy her. Jane doesn't want to annoy anybody.

They reach the front door, and Aunt Jane knocks.

Oh, let him be out! Jane prays silently. Please let him be out.

But she knows that Aunt Helen would not have come to the house on spec – that before they ever set out she will have rung to make sure that Fred Dodds is in.

Dodds opens the front door. He is excited – Jane can see it in his eyes – but he is doing his best to give Aunt Helen the impression he is slightly cross that the peaceful evening he had planned to spend alone has been disrupted by the arrival of this child.

'Make sure she's in bed by nine,' Aunt Helen says.

'Don't worry,' Fred Dodds assures her. 'Nobody knows better than me how to look after Jane.'

He rolls the words around his mouth in anticipation. Why doesn't Aunt Helen see what she can see and hear what

she *can hear? Jane wonders. Why can't Aunt Helen seem
to understand what will happen once Jane is on the other
side of that door?*

*It is just after half past seven when Fred Dodds closes
the door and imprisons her in his torture chamber. But he
doesn't assault her immediately. Oh no! He takes her into
the living room, lifts her on to the sofa, and switches on the
television.*

*'I'll be back in a few minutes,' he says, going into
the hall.*

But it will be nearly an hour before he returns.

*Why does he wait so long? Because he wishes to mentally
savour the pleasure to come? Because he knows that the
longer she is kept waiting, the more nervous – and perhaps
the more appealing – she will become. She doesn't know.
She will never know.*

Perhaps he doesn't even know himself.

*She looks around the room. At the pictures on the wall. At
the coffee table, on which lie his cigarettes and her mother's
knitting.*

*Her mother is knitting her a blue cardigan. She doesn't
need to do it – now that she is married to Fred Dodds
she can afford to buy all Jane's clothes in a shop –
but it gives her pleasure. She* always *enjoys doing things
for her daughter, however big or small each of those
things might be. She loves Jane. She would give her life
for her.*

*The hands on the wall clock say it is nearly half past
eight. The phone rings, but Jane daren't answer it, and her
stepfather chooses not to.*

*Another minute or two tick away. Jane can hear the sound
of a car at the far end of the street. And she can hear her
stepfather's heavy footfalls as he comes down the stairs. She
bites her bottom lip as hard as she can. It hurts, but she
wants it to hurt. She needs to punish herself for what has
happened before and is about to happen again. She didn't*

*think it was possible to despise anyone as much as she now
despises herself.*

*He opens the door and enters the lounge. His whole face
is filled with a wide, obscene leer.*

*'Did you find it hard, having to wait so long?' he asks. 'I
bet you did. I'll bet you were so impatient that you wet your
little knickers. I certainly* hope *that's what happened.'*

*He kneels down in front of the coffee table, so that his
head is on the same level as hers. The car which she has
heard earlier is getting closer.*

*'Now how shall we begin?' he asks. 'Where would you
like us to start?'*

'I . . . I don't want . . .' she stutters.

*'Of course you want! All this is your idea. I'd never have
done it if you hadn't encouraged me.'*

'I . . . I didn't . . .'

*'Oh, you may not have put it into words, exactly, but the
message was clear enough.'*

*His hands start to reach for her. She doesn't want it to
happen! Whatever he* says, *she knows* she *doesn't want it.
She picks up one of the knitting needles that are lying on
the table.*

*Her only wish is to stop him going any further. She's not
aiming the needle at anywhere in particular. It is just chance
that the needle goes up his left nostril.*

*His eyes bulge and he slumps over to the side. In the road,
the car comes to a stop.*

'She battered his head into a bloody pulp not because that
was the way in which his father had died, and not because
she hoped to dangle the possibility of another killer before
the police and the jury,' Paniatowski said. 'She did it in
order obliterate any evidence of the real cause of death.'

Jane Hartley, tears streaming down her face, nodded.

'Why did she do it?' she sobbed. 'Why didn't she just
tell the police the truth? What I did was in self-defence.
No court in the land would ever have punished me for it.'

'She probably guessed that herself,' Paniatowski said. 'But she didn't have your legal training and experience, so she couldn't know for sure. And even if there was only a very slight chance you'd be locked up, that wasn't a chance she was prepared to take.'

Jane Hartley dabbed her eyes with her handkerchief. 'So what happens now?' she asked, a little more in control of herself.

'Nothing happens now,' Paniatowski replied.

'But there'll have to be a trial. Or if not a trial, then at least some kind of hearing.'

'My boss doesn't think that will be necessary.'

'If there isn't a hearing, how will my mother's name ever be cleared?'

'Your mother took the blame for killing Fred Dodds because she didn't want you to take it,' Paniatowski said. 'But I think there was another reason she kept quiet. She didn't want what had gone on between you and your stepfather to become common knowledge. She didn't want you to go through life with everybody pointing you out as some kind of freak.'

'But . . .'

'She died in order to keep what had happened to you a secret,' Paniatowski told Jane Hartley, 'and the best way you can honour her memory is to keep it secret yourself.'

Thirty-One

They sat at their usual table in the Drum and Monkey, drinking their usual drinks. It would've been stretching things to call this end-of-case booze-up a celebration, but at least they could all agree it was a relief.

'How do you think Jane Hartley will be feelin' right now, Monika?' Woodend asked.

'I couldn't say for certain,' Paniatowski replied. 'But if she's anything like I was when I learned the truth, she's probably wishing she could have stayed screwed up and ignorant.'

'I can't understand that,' Rutter said. 'Surely, it's always better to know *why* you're acting like you are, isn't it?'

Paniatowski shook her head. 'If you don't mind me saying so, that's a typical outsider's view. When you're on the inside, things look very different. How can I explain it to you?' She frowned as she turned the problem over in her head. 'You don't mind if I get a bit fanciful, do you?' she said finally.

'Not if it'll help you to say what you want to say,' Woodend told her.

'Say you have a gammy leg,' Paniatowski began. 'You'd know it's dragging you down and stopping you from achieving your full potential, but you think there's nothing you can do about that. Then, one day, a doctor tells you that gangrene's set in, and the leg has to come off. Once it's been amputated you discover that, for the first time in your life, you have a real choice to make. If you want to, you can

239

spend the rest of your days in a wheelchair, wishing that the leg had never gone bad in the first place. Alternatively, you can take the artificial limb the doctor's offering you, and learn to walk again – perhaps even better than you ever have before. That's the situation Jane Hartley's in right now – she can sit there wishing she'd never been assaulted, or she can learn to walk. The second option's the one she should take. But it's not an easy choice to make.'

'You managed it,' Rutter said, with an unexpected hint of admiration in his voice.

'I kept away from men for a long time,' Paniatowski said. 'Even when I did start going out with them, I kept feeling this urge to hurt or humiliate them. It was years before I could finally convince myself that they weren't all just Arthur Jones in disguise.'

The door swung open. The Chief Constable's secretary entered the bar, and made a beeline for Woodend.

'Sorry to disturb you like this, Chief Inspector,' he said, 'but Mr Marlowe wanted me to remind you that you have a six o'clock meeting with him.'

Paniatowski and Rutter looked at each other, their eyes filled with a sudden panic. Was that *still* on? the eyes asked. Wasn't the Inquisition Circus supposed to have left town by now?

'This meetin'?' Woodend said to the secretary. 'Who'll be there? Just him an' me? Or is he plannin' a big party?'

'Mr Marlowe has been in consultation with some of his senior staff,' the secretary said, 'but I think they've all gone off duty now.'

Woodend smiled. 'That's all right then,' he said. He turned to Paniatowski and Rutter. 'Are you two comin' back to headquarters with me?'

'Yes, we'll—' Rutter began.

'We won't be long, but there's no point in rushing down our drinks, is there?' Paniatowski interrupted.

'None at all,' Woodend agreed, looking down at his sergeant's empty vodka glass.

Though Marlowe never appeared best pleased to see Woodend, it seemed to be causing him particular pain that late afternoon.

'Surprised to find me alone, Charlie?' the Chief Constable asked.

'Not really, sir,' Woodend admitted.

'Not really,' Marlowe repeated, rolling the words around in his mouth as if he were sucking on a sour plum. 'How do you do it, Charlie?'

'How do I do what, sir?'

'How do you always manage to wriggle your way out of almost impossible situations?' Marlowe said.

'I'm afraid I'm not quite followin' you, sir.'

Marlowe sighed heavily. 'On that *Maddox Row* case, it seemed as if whoever was in charge of the investigation wouldn't be able to do right for doing wrong, yet you managed to emerge as some kind of hero. You investigate the death of a school teacher, and end up making some of Scotland Yard's finest officers look about as competent as a drunken tinker. You actually get suspended *and* investigated for corruption while investigating that shooting on the moors – but it's other people who end up going to prison. What's your secret?'

'Clean livin' an' a clear conscience?' Woodend suggested.

'And then there's this latest case of yours. Lord Sharpe and Jane Hartley wanted two completely different results. You couldn't possibly satisfy them both. Yet Hartley has written me a note to say she doesn't want us to pursue the matter of her mother's execution any further, and Sharpe has rung me up to say – ' he reached for the pad on his desk – 'and I bloody-well quote, "It would be a great pity if the Mid Lancs Police were to continue using an officer with the experience and talent of DCI Woodend on purely administrative matters." What do you make of that, Charlie?'

'I must say, I'm surprised, sir.'

'You can't even be bothered to lie properly, can you?' Marlowe growled. 'But just remember this – the papers might say you have the devil's own luck, but that luck can't last forever. You'll put a foot wrong eventually, and when you do I'll be waiting to fall on you like a ton of bricks.'

'I've absolutely no doubt about that, sir,' Woodend said. 'Will there be anything else?'

'No, nothing else,' Marlowe made a sudden furious sweeping gesture with his hand. 'Get out, Charlie. Leave me in peace.'

'Certainly, sir,' Woodend agreed.

'What's this all about?' Rutter asked, as Paniatowski signalled the waiter for another round of drinks.

'What's *what* all about?' Paniatowski countered.

'The only time we're normally alone together is when the job demands it. But the job's over. So why are we still sitting here?''

'We're still here because, before you go, there's something I wanted to talk to you about. Do you remember what I said earlier? About how I used to feel the urge to hurt and humiliate men?'

'Yes?'

'I think meeting Jane Hartley for the first time brought it all back to me. I think I started seeing men as the enemy again. All men – but you especially. And I'm so sorry.'

'Forget it,' Rutter said. 'We've all got our blind spots. Look at me. As soon as I learned that Margaret Dodds had had an affair, I refused to see *any* good at all in the woman.'

'But you don't still feel like that, do you?'

'Jesus, no! After all that Margaret Dodds went through,

I don't blame her for finding what relief she could in Seth Earnshaw's arms.'

Paniatowski looked sceptical. 'You *really* don't blame her?'

'I *really* don't,' Rutter insisted. 'If I've learned one thing from this case, it's that there are a hundred worse things you can do to a person than be unfaithful to them.'

'What about us?' Paniatowski asked.

'Us!' Rutter repeated, sounding slightly alarmed.

'Us,' Paniatowski reiterated. 'Our relationship. The way we work together.'

'Oh, that,' Rutter said. 'What about it?'

'As convenient as it would be to blame all our problems with each other on this particular investigation, we both know it goes deeper than that,' Paniatowski said. 'We've been at each other's throats from the moment we met. Do you think we'll *ever* learn to get on?'

'Yes, if we both try hard, we might eventually end up with some sort of decent working partnership,' Rutter said. 'Especially now I know *why* I've kept dipping your pigtails in the ink well.'

'Pigtails?' Paniatowski said, puzzled. 'Ink wells? What the hell does that mean?'

He hadn't realized he'd said that last bit out loud. 'I think it means I'm losing my mind,' he said evasively.

'Oh, don't worry about that,' Paniatowski told him. 'We all lose our minds in the end. It's an occupational hazard.'

'Well, that's reassuring – I *think*,' Rutter said, smiling gratefully.

They lapsed into silence, but it was not the kind of silence they had known in the past. There was none of the old antagonism bubbling below the surface now. Instead it was a calming silence. A relaxing silence. An almost *companionable* silence.

Rutter found himself wondering if Monika liked nature as much as he did. If it thrilled her to watch a kestrel swoop down from the skies. If she saw fantastic images in the clouds, and beauty in the swaying grasses. If looking at a tree could make her think that whatever else happened, life was worthwhile.

'It's funny the way everyone's different,' Paniatowski said, as if she had been following her thoughts as the kestrel follows the air currents.

'How do you mean?' Rutter asked.

'Take marriage. It really suits some people. You, for example. You love Maria with all your heart, don't you?'

Rutter nodded. 'And I admire her more than anyone else I ever met. I don't think I'd ever be able to summon up the courage – even once – that she has to summon up every day of her life.'

'And, of course, you'd never even imagine leaving her.'

'Never. Losing her would be like losing the biggest part of myself. I wouldn't know who I was or *where* I was without Maria.'

Paniatowski nodded, as if he had merely confirmed her suspicions. 'I've thought seriously about marriage myself,' she said, 'but now I'm sure that it's not for me. I like being with other people some of the time, but at others I feel like being alone – and when I get that feeling, I don't see why I should have to justify it to anyone else. Can you understand that?'

'Yes,' Rutter said, 'I think I can.'

'So what I look for is nice, uncomplicated relationships. No promises and no commitments on either side. No one getting hurt – especially those people on the fringes of the relationship. I don't drag my private life into anyone else's, and I don't want anyone else's dragged into mine.'

Rutter found himself thinking of birds again – and of rabbits scurrying to their holes, and squirrels scampering along tree branches.

'You've gone very quiet,' Paniatowski said. 'I've not been too profound for you, have I?'

'No,' Rutter replied, a little startled. 'No, not at all. I was just wondering if we really have to go back to the station.'

'Doesn't seem much point in it, does there? We'd only be sitting around, twiddling our thumbs.'

'Of course, if Cloggin'-it Charlie was still with us, we'd stay here until we were all rolling drunk, and then piss off home.'

'True, but I don't really feel like getting rolling drunk today,' Paniatowski admitted.

'Neither do I,' Rutter agreed. 'So why don't we do something else instead?'

'Like what?'

'It's a lovely day, and there are still a few hours of light left. We could go for a drive in the country. We might even wait around to watch the sun set. What do you think?'

'That would be nice,' Paniatowski said.

Epilogue

Jane Hartley stood on the platform at Whitebridge Station, waiting for the train that would whisk her back to London. She would never return to her home town again, she decided. There would be no point in doing so now.

The mental film of that last, fateful night in the life of Fred Dodds was still playing in her head. But it was more than just a repetition of her previous viewings of it. Much, much more!

When she'd seen the film for the first time, under Paniatowski's guidance, it had been running at high speed, so while she had gained a general impression of what had gone on, the details had all been a bit of a blur. Now the film had slowed down, and she could linger on some of the parts which she had missed the first few times through.

Fred Dodds has just entered the room. Jane calls him 'Daddy' – because she has been told to, and because she can't think of what else to call him – but she knows he is not her real father.

He is bending over her now, his face a contorted mask of unnatural lust. Jane's small hand gropes around on the coffee table, and then she feels the knitting needle between her fingers. She jabs – and sees it disappear up her stepfather's nostril.

He barely has time to topple backwards before the door is flung open and her mother rushes into the room.

'Oh my God, you've killed him,' Margaret Dodds gasps.

246

Jane feels hot tears forming in her eyes. 'I didn't mean to, Mummy. I didn't mean—'

'It wasn't your fault, darling. Don't ever think that it was your fault.'

Margaret picks her up, carries her across the room and deposits her in the armchair furthest away from the supine Fred Dodds.

'I want you to stay right here until I say you can move,' Jane's mother tells her. 'Have you got that?'

'Yes, Mummy.'

'There's my big brave girl.'

Margaret goes into the hallway, and Jane can hear her talking urgently into the telephone. When Margaret returns to the living room she looks down at Fred – as if wondering what to do next – then starts to walk towards the back door.

'Don't leave me, Mummy,' Jane says in a panic.

'I'm not. I'm just going out to the shed. I won't be a minute.'

She is true to her word. She has returned in no time at all, and in her hand she is carrying a heavy hammer. Jane knows instinctively what her mother is intending to do with it, though she is not exactly sure why.

Still with the hammer in her hand, Margaret cuddles up against her daughter in the armchair. When they hear the sound of the car stopping outside, Margaret drops the hammer on to the floor – what a loud bang it makes! – and leads Jane out through the front door.

Margaret opens the car door. 'Climb in, Jane. You can sit next to Mr Earnshaw. Won't that be exciting?'

'Mummy, do you know what Daddy did?' Jane asks.

'Yes, I do know. And I'm so sorry I let it happen. But there's no time to talk about it now.'

'I don't mean what Daddy did before. I mean what he did when—'

'Get in the car, darling.'

'But Mummy—'
'Get in the bloody car.'
Jane climbs into the car. The seat smells of leather, and is so high that her feet don't touch the floor. Her mother closes the door behind her and rushes back into the house. Mr Earnshaw pulls away from the curb and Jane wishes her mother had let her say what she wanted to say.

The train came to a halt, and Jane Hartley was shocked to realize that as it had been slowing down she had not scanned the carriages in the hope of finding one which did not contain a man.

As she climbed on to the train, the film was still replaying in her head. But now, she was trying to insert new dialogue into it – trying, even after thirty years, to make things clear to her dead mother.

'You don't understand what I'm saying, Mummy. I'm not talking about what Daddy did before you got home. I mean after. While you were out in the shed. He woke up, Mummy! He woke up and said he had an awful headache. Then, just before you came back with the hammer, he fell asleep again.'

1 800 970 6077